The Grovers

Vol 1: Who's Afraid of the Boogeyman?

Jay Jesse Edwards

Barnstormer Publishing

The Grovers Vol 1: Who's Afraid of the Boogeyman?

Paperback ISBN 978-1-967232-23-9

www.**BARNSTORMERPUBLISHING**.com

Content Advisory

This story contains mild language, references to past trauma, abusive relationships, and the emotional aftermath of violence. It also explores themes of class divides, body image, and self-worth. While the narrative treats these subjects with care and emphasizes resilience, friendship, and healing, readers who have experienced similar challenges may find some sections triggering.

The Grovers

Vol 1: Who's Afraid of the Boogeyman?

Jay Jesse Edwards

Barnstormer Publishing

Contents

Prologue

20 years ago...

It's a chilly autumn afternoon in the woods of Hillstone Park. There's a black nineteen-year-old man with braided cornrows and baggy clothes with his back pressed against a tree. His name is Brian, and he is *not* having a good day. He's fighting for his life, and losing. *ZAP!* With a grunt, Brian shoots a bolt of lightning from his hands. It's a bolt powerful enough to injure his target severely. *CRACK*! He misses by a hair, hitting a boulder rather than his attacker. Brian curses. Sweat is pouring from every part of his body. He's tired and severely outmatched, but he can't give up. Not with his life at stake. *WOOSH*! A rather large branch is launched straight at his head from several feet away. Brian reacts just in time and drops to the ground. The branch falls harmlessly into a bush, giving him the chance to retaliate. Brian's hands spark with crackling electricity, charging up for another blast. He's just about to let it loose when suddenly, *SHWACK*! With one mighty swing from his opponent, Brian is sent flying twenty feet from where he was standing. He screams in terror as he realizes he can't stop what's coming on impact. *THUNK*! His back slams into the trunk of an elm tree. Only, it's not just the trunk he hit. There's an unimaginable wave of pain that wracks through Brian's body as he involuntarily coughs up a glob of blood. His head shakes violently as he looks down at his chest. He's pinned against the tree, suspended two feet above the ground with a branch deeply embedded in his back. There's a severely uncomfortable wetting of his pants as warm blood waterfalls down his legs, decorating the twigs and leaves of the forest floor—his blood.

No! He begins thinking. *No! No! Not now! I'm not supposed to die!*

The moment he takes a breath, another wave of unbearable pain ripples through Brian's body. He can't form words. He can't even scream. All that escapes his mouth is a nausea-inducing gurgle. His lungs are filling with blood. He's choking on his own bodily fluids. Brian wants to stay angry at his attacker. Anger is an emotion. A feeling. An indication that you are alive. But he can't. His brain is already rapidly going fuzzy. He tries summoning his electricity to at *least* retaliate, but it rapidly fizzles from his fingers with a loud buzz. Brian was hoping for the cliché of having his own life flash before his eyes. But it isn't. Consciousness is already slipping from him. As if he's involuntarily being put to sleep. A sleep he will never awaken from. No anger comes. Not even sadness. Only the heavy burden of acceptance. Acceptance that not only was he dying, but at the hands of one of the only people he'd ever loved, now nothing more than a monster. Said monster approaches him. It was in the shape of a man, but not of flesh and blood. Rather, a shroud of shadow and darkness. Ever shifting and moving. Like a misty, black and gray Rorschach in human form. The monster slowly advances on Brian, its featureless face encroaching his own. And even as he's dying, Brian knows the true eyes behind the creature. Part of Brian wishes he could see his friend's true face. Just one more time. As the last of Brian's strength leaves his body and his eyelids descend, the monster speaks in a scratchy, distorted voice, the last thing he'll ever hear.

"*This is your own fault*!"

A pained chuckle escapes Brian as he thinks, *Have fun with your kid, Corty.* The monster shifts into a formless cloud, enveloping his victim in pure darkness.

Chapter 1

Tasha

Present day...

It wasn't supposed to be like this. The weather in Olligrove, Illinois was ideal. No clouds. Light breeze. Temperature in the high sixties. Perfect springtime conditions for a Friday in late March. Unfortunately for Tasha Monét Simone, she wasn't going to be able to enjoy it. The early morning sun cutting through the blinds in her window only serves to annoy her. Not because she wasn't a morning person. In fact, quite the opposite. The sunlight was just a harsh reminder that today, she was going to suffer through the pure, dreary boredom of detention after school. Tasha rolls her eyes. It wasn't even her fault. It wasn't fair. Tasha kicks off her blanket to get dressed. She picks out a pair of black jeans, an oversized army green jumper with matching shoes, then goes to the bathroom to freshen up. Tasha looks at herself in the mirror as she washes her face. She's a young, black woman with coffee brown skin and matching eyes. Tasha sighs as she removes her bedtime bonnet, letting her long, ginger-red locs fall free around her shoulders. She'd gotten them professionally washed and colored as an early birthday gift a few days ago.

Right. My birthday. Tasha thinks to herself as she applies moisturizer to her skin. She has her mom's round nose and her father's thick eyebrows. Though neither of them is around, there are plenty of photos of them all around the house. Photos that do little more than remind her of their absence. She'll be turning eighteen this weekend. Sunday, in fact. And her parents won't be around to celebrate this milestone with her. Tasha starts to tear up a little, but then stops herself. *Not now, girl. Don't focus on that.* She shifts her brain to focus on the positive. She still has her older sister, Bree. Though she works almost nonstop to support them both, Bree promised to be there for Tasha's birthday. Tasha sniffles and wipes her eyes. *She'd damn well better.* Deciding to keep it simple, she applies minimal eyeliner and uses Chapstick instead of gloss. No reason to glam up just to be in detention. After getting dressed, brushing her teeth, and gathering her school supplies, Tasha leaves the bedroom she'd much rather be spending the day in. Bree isn't in the kitchen once she comes downstairs. Typical. Bree works as a CNA at Pleasant Brooks, a retirement home on the other side of town. Due to low staff and hectic hours, Bree constantly covers shifts and is sparsely seen. Since her sister wasn't there to give her a ride, Tasha grabbed her bike out of the garage instead. Not that she minds. It keeps her in shape.

Tasha stops at Caffeine Commute, the local coffee shop, to grab herself an iced caramel shaken espresso. Her favorite. Olligrove High School is bustling with activity when Tasha arrives. Her drink was already finished well before she parked her bike. She's going to need the extra caffeine to get through this day. As Tasha slowly enters the school and walks down the hallways, she briefly sees the bane of her existence. The wannabe influencer known as Catherine-Bethany Charles. Tasha quickly runs around a corner before the other girl can see her. Anger starts burning all throughout Tasha's body. It was Catherine's fault that she was going to be stuck in detention later. And on a Friday no less. Tasha turns her back as she hears Catherine-Bethany and her air-headed friends laugh about something stupid. Luckily, they don't notice her as they walk past. Good. Tasha knows she'd probably do something to worsen her punishment. She curses to herself as she continues her way to first period. It just wasn't *fair*!

School goes pretty normally for Tasha during the course of the day. Her essays for history are turned in. Her notes are taken for the trigonometry quiz coming the following Monday. English literature goes by without her being called on, thank goodness. It's boring as usual. Lunch brings her some much-needed brevity with her friends from AP Bio. After lunch came the computer lab, the study hall, and finally, economics. After school is typically when she'd grab her friend Jasmine Watson to hang out. Usually at the plaza or Jasmine's house. Sadly, plans had to be changed for the day. As Tasha exits Economics when the final bell rings, a light-skinned black girl with bleached blond hair in a buzz cut and a face adorned with freckles is there to greet her. Good old Jasmine.

"Hey, T. On your way to diet juvie?" she asks jokingly. Tasha rolls her eyes but smiles. "Always with the jokes, Jaz. Tell me again why you aren't doing stand-up?" "Cus we both know you'd be the only one who'd show up. What does that say about me?" "That I'm supportive and you're corny."

Jasmine mock gasps and dramatically throws her hand to her chest.

"Right there. You stabbed me right in the heart, girl."

Tasha laughs as she smacks Jasmine's back.

"If someone stabbed you in the heart, I don't think you'd still be talking," she jokes. The two young women continue laughing and talking as Tasha slowly makes her way to the lower levels of school, where the detention hall is. The lights on the lower levels were purposefully darker and occasionally flickered. It had to be some sort of cruel joke. Tasha could already feel the caffeine from her morning espresso wearing off, which was a shame. Once they reach the main office, Jasmine turns to Tasha asking,

"This is my stop. Do you want me to get you after?" Tasha shakes her head. "Nah. I rode my bike today, so I'll probably just go right home."

Jasmine gives Tasha a quick hug.

"Alright girl, good luck. I'll make sure to slash Catherine-Bethany's tires on my way out."

Tasha snickers. They both know that Jasmine would never do *anything* to get her hands dirty. Still, the sentiment is appreciated.

"You do that, Jaz. I'll text you the minute I'm free." "Alright. See ya." "See ya."

Tasha sighs as she watches Jasmine leave. Part of her wants to just say 'screw it' and go with her. Unfortunately, Isaac Charles was on his way. Not only was he the principal, he was Catherine-Bethany's father. Tasha feels herself get angry all over again. The man lets his daughter get away with *everything*. Textbook nepotism was the only reason Catherine-Bethany got to roam free. Of course, Tasha can't exactly say that to Mr. Charles. He'd probably give her long-term suspension for daring to say anything bad about his precious little jellybean. Tasha bites down on her lip to keep from swearing. Mr. Charles was a hook-nosed, thick-browed, middle-aged man with a *painfully* obvious toupee. He approaches Tasha with a cocky smirk on his crinkly, weathered face.

"Ah. Right on time, Ms. Simone. Wonderful to have you here," he says.

Every word out of his mouth was *dripping* with insincere pleasantry. Tasha knows he's enjoying this. He's the definition of a "Not my child" kind of parent. The kind of parent who would do anything and everything to avoid having their spawn take *any* kind of accountability. Tasha considers herself a pretty laid-back girl, but this kind of thing just irks her to the core. Instead of responding the way she wanted to, she simply grunts. Principal Charles gives her a facetious smile as he holds up a small wooden box.

"Phone, please. Standard rule for all students in detention. You'll get it back before you leave."

Tasha begrudgingly places her cellphone in the box. She wasn't aware of this rule. God forbid she has anything to help the time go by.

"Thank you, Ms. Simone. Have a seat in the office with the others. A faculty member will be arriving shortly." "Whatever," Tasha mumbles as she enters.

It's just as dreary as she thought. Beige walls. No windows. Overhead fluorescent light with a low but noticeable buzz. No decorations or personalization of any kind like a normal classroom. To Tasha's surprise, there were only three other students in the room. The first is a tall, olive-toned boy with blue eyes and curly brown hair. The second, a short young woman with light brown skin, long black hair, and lime green eyes. Tasha was definitely surprised to see her here. She didn't know her name, but she's seen her with the honor roll society. The final individual was a broad, husky boy with fluffy blond hair, brown eyes, and scruffy stubble. From his demeanor, Tasha guessed this one was probably a regular. They were all sitting as far from each other as their desks would allow. Tasha is not sure why she expected more people, but it's totally fine. The less to deal with, the better. At least they'd also be bored with no phones. Misery loves company as they say.

After a quick second to consider her position, Tasha decides to find a seat closer to the boy with the dark hair. She figured Ms. Pretty and Blondie were possibly more hostile. Not that she meant to be presumptuous, but hey, they were in detention.

The four teenagers all sit in uncomfortable silence. Nothing but the sound of a ticking clock and the buzzing of the overhead lights permeate the room. Tasha looks around. Dark Hair looks down at his shoes while playing with a loose string on his shirt. Ms. Pretty twirls a pen between her fingers. Blondie stares at the ceiling, probably daydreaming. It's only been forty-five seconds and already Tasha is feeling antsy. How was she supposed to deal with this for three and a half more hours? Remembering she has her sketchbook, Tasha fishes it out of her backpack. It had been a while since she drew anything. Now was as good a time as any. Sure, there was some homework she could probably get a head start on, but come on.

"Just a heads up, you might get that book taken," Blondie says out of nowhere. Ms. Pretty and Dark Hair both look at Tasha, whom Blondie was obviously acknowledging.

"That's ridiculous. Why?" she asks.

"According to Mr. Charles, detention is a place where 'we're supposed to quietly reflect on the behavior that led us here," Blondie replies,

"Most supervisors don't mind, but a few think that even reading a book is a distraction from our 'purpose' here. It depends on who they assign."

Tasha guessed right. Blondie was definitely a regular. As if reading her mind, Ms. Pretty says,

"I guess *you'd* know. I heard detention is basically your second home." Blondie just chuckles at her. "*Ooh*. Princess has a spicy side to her." Ms. Pretty rolls her eyes. "Yeah, well, I'm here too, aren't I?" she asks rhetorically.

"Indeed you are, your highness," Blondie retorts with a smirk. Tasha snickers a little. "Well, I've also got snacks if anybody wants something before our warden arrives," she offers.

There were some cracker rolls, a bag of pretzels, and some sour gummy straws in her backpack. She tended to have emergency snacks on standby in case symptoms of her cycle decided to show up early. Plus, she's always down to share if she has enough. Dark Hair looks up.

"Did I hear you say 'snacks'? Hell yeah. I haven't eaten all freakin' day." "Better make it quick," says Blondie.

Ms. Pretty smiles softly but politely declines. Shrugging, Tasha hands out her backpack to the two boys. Dark hair takes some sour straws while Blondie grabs a roll of crackers. They both give Tasha a nod as thanks and start munching. As the four go back to sitting in silence, they all hear Principal Charles talking to someone outside the door.

"Ah, Ms. Castillo! Glad I caught you. I need you to do something for me."

Tasha in particular leans forward. Ms. Castillo was her teacher for World History class. Nice lady.

"Um, I suppose. What is it, Mr. Charles?" Ms. Castillo asks cautiously. The principal clears his throat.

"You see, Mr. Ollum was originally supposed to be in charge of detention today, but it seems he canceled at the last minute. I need *you* to do it."

Letting her nosiness get the better of her, Tasha leans forward at her desk to try to hear better. The others follow her lead. Ms. Castillo huffs,

"With all due respect, Mr. Charles, I can't take on that responsibility today," she tells him. "May I ask why?" Mr. Charles asks. Tasha scoffs.

"Maybe because she has better things to do and you're a total prick," she says quietly. Blondie and Dark Hair both snicker at the comment. Ms. Pretty bites on her finger to keep quiet.

"If you must know, *Isaac*, I volunteered to help chaperon my son and his class to Hillstone Park for a nature scavenger hunt they're doing." Ms. Castillo replies.

Tasha feels her respect for this woman grow. Mr. Charles was someone most students and faculty felt the need to be meek and watch themselves around. Meanwhile, here is Ms. Castillo calling him by his first name and standing her ground. She's always been a fair but no-nonsense kind of teacher. One of Tasha's favorites. Mr. Charles smacks his lips.

"Your son. Right. Fifth grade, isn't he?" "*Seventh*, actually." "Perfect. You can bring the delinquents along with you."

Tasha's eyebrows go up.

"What the-? Surely, you can't be serious." Ms. Castillo tries. Mr. Charles snorts, "Oh, but I *am.* A boring nature hike surrounded by a bunch of little kids sounds like a *perfect* punishment for them." "Listen, I really don't think this is appropriate." "Well, good thing I'm the one in charge, right?" "Look, I can't just-!" "Make sure they're back by five-thirty."

With that last snide remark, Tasha hears Mr. Charles' steps recede and Ms. Castillo sigh in annoyance.

"Wow. Dick move," says Dark Hair. Ms. Pretty shakes her head and whispers, "Typical." Tasha shrugs. "Could be worse. Ms. Castillo is pretty cool," she says. "True, but apparently we're gonna be playing babysitter." Blondie retorts.

The four go quiet as the door finally opens and their escort walks in. Ms. Castillo was a short, curvy woman of Hispanic descent with her thick, light brown hair in a bob. No older than her early thirties, tops. Beautiful woman. Tasha has heard comments from boys calling Ms. Castillo one of, if not the hottest teacher in school. Not that she looks at her that way, but she can see why. Ms. Castillo smiles awkwardly at the four, putting her hands on her hips.

"I suppose you all heard what just happened outside this door, huh?" she asks, getting right to the point.

The four teens all slowly nod. No use denying it. The woman exhales through her nose and shrugs.

"Well then, who's up for a field trip?"

Chapter 2

Sky

Of all the things Sky Xavier Harris expected for his millionth day in detention, going to help watch a bunch of seventh-graders against his will was not in the cards. He looks around at his other three "cellmates" for the day. The good-looking curly-haired guy, the princess, and the cute red-haired girl. Most days in detention, Sky was either by himself or with some wannabe bad boys who thought back-talking teachers was the height of comedy. Despite being a regular, Sky actually *hates* "bad boys". They're all the same. Obnoxious tools in serious need of therapy. These three, however, Sky has a good feeling. It could be because they all shared a few laughs and some snacks. Or perhaps he was just overthinking since he stopped partaking in the green stuff a few months ago. After getting in trouble one too many times, he decided it was time for a change. As the four gather their belongings, Ms. Castillo addresses them.

"Listen, I know this is supposed to be punishment or whatever, but all I'll ask is that none of you act like a-holes while we're with my son and his class. Is that okay with you?"

Sky and the others nod. He likes Ms. Castillo's vibe. The woman sighs.

"Good. Since we're going to be outside of school, feel free to call me Andrea if you want. What're your names?"

Ginger girl speaks first.

"Tasha." Then the princess. "Mileena." Cute guy. "Giovanni, but you can just call me Gio." Then Sky. "Some call me for a good time. Everyone else just calls me Sky."

Tasha and Mileena both giggle. Gio noticeably blushes. Sky raises an eyebrow at the reaction. *Is he-? Nah,* he thinks to himself. Unimpressed with his joke, Andrea turns around and exits the room. The teens follow.

The drive from Olligrove High to Hillstone Park is rather nice. Andrea drives a Volvo station wagon, so the five of them are able to comfortably fit. Being the oldest, Sky got to ride shotgun. Tasha and Gio sat in the back with Mileena in the middle. Andrea has classic hip-hop from the 90s playing on the Bluetooth. No one talks, but at least none of them seems to be unhappy with another. Sky wonders what each of them did to earn detention. He wants to ask, but he'd rather not be the one to break the silence. Sky was more social than people gave him credit for. At the same time, he doesn't want to seem annoying, especially to Gio. This might be the only time he's ever in this guy's presence. He wants to make a decent impression.

Hillstone Park was an extensive walking trail surrounded by deep forests that go on for miles. It's a popular place for bird watchers and fitness fans getting their steps in. It used to be a go-to location for camping as well. Rumors of the woods far off the designated trails being haunted for the last twenty years or so have halted that particular activity. Sky is almost glad to be out here and away from the craziness that is his household. Away from his grumpy uncle, four rowdy cousins, and the occasional roach. Sky shivers. He hates bugs. Unfortunately, he's also the only one who cares about cleaning the house once in a while. A house with *six* people. Once they arrive and park next to a school bus. Andrea says,

"Once again, *all* I'm asking is that you behave yourselves. Get through this with no BS and I'll buy you guys lunch on the way back. Deal?"

Sky smiles, giving her a mock salute. "Hell yeah."

Tasha gives Sky an eyebrow. He clears his throat, "I mean, yes. You can count on us." Tasha smiles at Sky, then turns to Andrea.

"I believe you have a deal," she says. Andrea beckons for them to follow. The seventh-graders are getting off the bus and forming a single-file line. There's only about eleven or twelve of them, so that's good at least. A middle-aged redheaded man and a blond woman, at least six months pregnant, are the last to step off. The woman notices Andrea and walks over to greet her.

"You're Andrea Castillo, right? I just want to say thank you again for volunteering to help me. Your son is one of my best students," she says. Andrea shakes her hand.

"It's really no trouble, Ms. Davis. I know you're not having the greatest time with your pregnancy, so I'm happy to help you and Mr. Murphy. In fact, I've got some helpers of my own today."

Andrea replies, gesturing to Sky and the others. Sky smiles and waves at the other teachers. He appreciates them being referred to as "helpers" rather than some random kids from detention. As Andrea and Ms. Davis talk about what the plan was for the day, Sky turns back to his "cellmates" and notices Tasha smiling up at the treeline.

"What's got you in a good mood all of a sudden?" he asks. Tasha shrugs. "I was kind of upset this morning when I thought being in detention would mean missing out on this weather. At least we're outside now," she answers. Mileena brushes a finger through her hair. "Fair point, I guess. Too bad it's with a bunch of toddlers."

Gio scoffs.

"I live in a house with an *actual* toddler. Middle-schoolers aren't so bad in comparison." Sky chuckles. "Amen to that, bro. I have four cousins, all under the age of ten. I live with the person who drives me *crazy*." Tasha purses her lips.

"Could be worse, y'know? I'd rather be doing this than picking up litter off the side of a highway," she adds. Sky turns to her and clicks his tongue. He's definitely had to do that before. As if reading his mind, Tasha covers her mouth.

"Oh crap, I'm sorry. That came off judgey," she apologizes. Sky waves her off. "Nah, you're cool. I mean, it's probably pretty obvious I've been to juvie once or twice. On the bright side, I look great in a neon-orange vest." Mileena shakes her head. "Oh, please. *Nobody* looks good in neon-orange."

The four all share a soft laugh. Afterward, Gio looks over and smirks.

"I think you've got an admirer, Tasha," he says. "Who?" asks the girl in question. Sky smirks as well.

"I think it's pretty obvious," he says.

While Andrea and Ms. Davis continue discussing whatever, there's one boy in particular in the line of kids failing at being inconspicuous. He's short, about twelve or thirteen, with glasses and spiked up black hair, and unsuccessfully pretending to read the notebook in his hands. Every ten seconds, he peeks directly at Tasha. Sky snickers loudly, giving her a small nudge in the shoulder.

"How much do you wanna bet he's gonna find a lame excuse to come talk to you?" he asks. Tasha nudges him back. "Oh, grow up." Sky gives her an eyebrow. She sighs and relents, "Five bucks." "Ten," says Mileena. Gio looks at Sky. "I don't have any cash on me, but I'm betting on you," he says. Sky winks at him. Gio blushes again. *Hm. My odds are looking more and more favorable.* Finally, Andrea waves them all over. Leading the charge, Tasha sighs.

"C'mon. Let's do this." "Whatever," Gio says behind her.

"I am *so* not wearing the right shoes for this." Mileena grumbles to herself. Sky goes last, bringing up the rear.

"Don't worry, your highness. I'll protect you from the vicious dirt."

Seeing how Andrea acquired some extra "helpers", Mr. Murphy and Ms. Davis decided to extend the trip a bit. First, they explored the lower part of Hillstone Park near the creek that leads to a pond. Afterwards, they headed to the upper wooded area, which was about a mile and a half walk uphill. Once everything was complete, they were to hike back down to the entrance and compare their findings between the two areas. The kids all had a list of different bushes, flowers, leaves, and trees to find and categorize for the scavenger hunt. Sky wasn't exactly a fan of trekking like this, especially on a rather steep incline. At least he and his "cellmates" had the easy job. All they had to do was stay in the back of the group and make sure none of the little rugrats wandered off. Sky's not really concerned about that at the moment, however. He's just doing his best to make sure he's not wheezing too hard in front of Gio. He's a big boy, yes, but he'd still like to maintain some pride.

"You good?" Tasha asks quietly. She was kind enough to keep pace with him while Gio and Mileena were slightly ahead. Sky huffs a sarcastic laugh.

"Yup. It's just, usually I don't spend my time outdoors," he admits. Tasha shrugs. "I usually go for walks or a bike ride," she says. Sky laughs again. "Yeah, I don't really do that either.

After the twenty-minute walk to the level of the park, the next half an hour or so goes by rather uneventfully. Once the group finally makes a stop in a clearing near a patch of trees, Sky and his group lean up against the trunk of a big oak tree and mostly just observe. The seventh-graders walk about looking for the plants they're supposed to catalog or whatever. Being pregnant, Ms. Davis finds a rock to rest her feet on. Andrea and Mr. Murphy go around here and there checking on the students. It's easy work for the teens to simply make sure none of them go where the teachers can't see. However, the weather is also getting hotter by the minute. The sunlight began cutting through the branches Sky was using for shade. Not wanting to become a sweaty mess, he takes off his sweater. Luckily, he's wearing a t-shirt underneath. It's a little oversized, but he likes it that way. It helps hide his gut and side rolls.

"Any chance you brought a water bottle or two?" he asks Tasha. She shakes her head. "Nope. Wasn't expecting to go on a field trip today." Sky shrugs. "Fair enough." "Anyone else already bored?" asks Gio. "Absolutely," Mileena replies.

"Let's just enjoy the fresh air. I think we lucked out, honestly," says Tasha. Mileena chuckles sarcastically as she swats away a moth.

"Yeah. Real lucky."

The sound of someone clearing their throat draws Sky and the other four's attention. They all turn around and see the short, spikey-haired boy with glasses from earlier. *Bingo*! Sky thinks to himself. He can already feel Tasha giving him side-eye.

"What's up, little man?" he asks. The boy clears his throat again and then holds up a twig with thin, serrated leaves.

"I um, I was just wondering if any of you knew whether this was a rowan leaf or an ash tree leaf. Since you're older and everything."

Tasha puts her hands on her hips. The boy starts to stammer.

"N-not that I'm calling you old, of course. I-I-I just mean you're all older than *me.* So I thought maybe-" "Maybe what?" asks Tasha. The boy's face goes red as a tomato. "Never mind. I'll just ask my mom."

He quickly scuttles away and rejoins the other kids.

"That must be Ms. Castillo's kid," says Tasha. Sky immediately has a devilish grin spread across his face as he holds out his hand.

"A bet's a bet. Pay up."

Chapter 3

Gio

It's been an eventful year for Giovanni Dante Carano. First, he and his mother, Ava, move from Indianapolis, Indiana, to Olligrove, Illinois, thanks to a job transfer. It was a bit of a shell shock, to say the least. Not long after, as Gio is barely settled in this new town, his mom decides she's tired of being single. Within six months, she remarried to a man named Kevin McFadden. Gio's had maybe three interactions with him before the wedding and no strong feelings whatsoever for the man. With the marriage, however, came Kevin's four-year-old daughter, Phoebe. Gio's new stepsister. Yet another big change. *Then*, because Olligrove High doesn't have a gymnastics team, Gio decides to break out of his comfort zone and attend an audition for a local band. The process of which landed him detention for the day.Now here he is in Hillstone Park with three different schoolmates. One of them was not so subtly hitting on him.Admittedly, Gio had only recently discovered he was bi. He's had relationships with girls since middle school, but nothing long-lasting. This is his first time having another guy blatantly show interest in him (as far as he knows). It's making him a little nervous. But also kind of giddy at the same time. He's not quite sure what to do about it. So for now, he decides on nothing. It isn't likely they'd see each other again after today anyway. *I do like the attention, though.*

Gio sighs as he wipes a few drops of sweat from his forehead. His hair's gotten longer recently. Though he likes the look, he's starting to wonder if it's worth keeping. A moment later, he sees Sky turn around and start laughing.

"No freaking way, dude," he says. Gio faces the same direction to see what he's talking about and says,

"Well, well, well."

Tasha puts her hand on her forehead. Once again, the short boy with glasses is approaching them. This time, holding several water bottles.

"Hey! Mr. Murphy was passing out water for everyone. I figured you guys were thirsty, too," he tells them. Though his eyes are only on Tasha, it's still a nice gesture. Tasha leans down and smiles at him as she takes a bottle.

"Thank you. That's very kind of you," she compliments.

The boy blushes deeply. Not that Gio could blame him. Tasha was a very beautiful girl. The boy snaps out of his stare as Gio reaches down and grabs water for himself.

"Yeah. Thanks, kid." Sky and Mileena each take one as well. The boy frowns, which makes Tasha raise her eyebrows.

"Something wrong?" she asks gently. The boy crosses his arms. "I'm almost thirteen. I'm *not* a kid."

Gio tries his hardest not to snicker. He was seventeen himself, so seeing a twelve-year-old trying to say they're not a child was pretty funny. Then again, he remembers being twelve and having that exact same attitude. So instead of laughing, Gio puts up his hands in mock surrender.

"My bad, bro. Is your mom our teacher, Ms. Castillo?" he asks. The boy nods. Gio grins. "Cool." "What's your name anyway?" asks Tasha. The boy goes back to smiling and replies, "Rocky."

Gio is slightly taken aback. *Kid sure doesn't look like a boxer to me.*

"That's your real name?" he asks. Rocky nods. "Yeah. Why?"

The second Gio opens his mouth, Tasha gives him a stern side-eye, so he shuts it. The joke probably would've been too obvious. The poor boy probably gets a million references to that movie already. Tasha then looks back at her admirer.

"Well, Rocky, I'll be sure to tell your mom how nice her son is when we leave."

At a loss for words, Rocky turns red and practically runs away. As soon as he does, Gio, Sky, and Mileena all begin snickering loudly. Tasha shakes her head.

"Oh, *shut up*."*

Ten minutes later, boredom begins to take over once more. It had been at least an hour and a half since they arrived at Hillstone Park. The kids continue marking down each plant they find. Gio and his detention mates don't talk much or ask each other any more questions. Instead, they all sit on the ground against a tree and try their hardest to deal with the heat and lack of entertainment. Gio thinks to himself, *At least I don't have to deal with Phoebe for a while. Little twerp.* To his left, Mileena is staring off into the distance. Tasha and Sky are to his right. Tasha takes out her sketchbook from earlier and begins drawing some of the trees around them. Gio gets a peek at her drawings. They're quite well done. Sky has his head down while drumming his fingers on his knees. A moment later, Andrea approaches them with Rocky not too far behind. Mileena's head perks up at the sight of their teacher.

"Any chance this is almost over?" she asks, exasperated. Andrea chuckles. "Yes, actually. I have to get you all back to the school by five-thirty anyway." "We're still getting lunch, right?" asks Sky. Andrea chuckles some more. "I think you've all earned it." Sky does a fist pump.

Rocky looks as though he's about to say something when a male voice nearby screams and follows with a resounding,

"*Dammit!*"

Immediately, all of their heads turn toward the source. About thirty feet away, Gio and company see Mr. Murphy on the ground writhing in pain. Ms. Davis and several middle-schoolers begin crowding around him. Andrea ushers Rocky away as she rushes over to see what's wrong. Burning with curiosity and having nothing better to do, Gio stands up, brushes some dirt off his shorts, and follows. Tasha, Mileena, and Sky do the same.Mr. Murphy is grabbing at his lower right leg, wincing and on the verge of tears.

The kids are all a mix of concerned, shocked, and grossed out. Once Gio sees why, he immediately cringes into himself. Mr. Murphy's right foot is twisted at an unnatural angle. Gio also notices the ankle bone is on the verge of jutting out of the skin. Sky gags and backs away from the crowd. Andrea gently pushes several kids back as she leans down.

"Oh my god! Craig, what on earth happened?!" she asks the man in question. Mr. Murphy only lets out another shout of distress as he tries to move his leg.

"He tripped over a rock and landed on his foot wrong," one of the kids explains. "Yeah, no kidding," Rocky mutters. "*Rocky*! Not helpful!" his mother scolds. "I don't think we can carry him all the way downhill like this. What can we do?" asks Ms. Davis.

"Oh god! Somebody do *something*!" Mr. Murphy practically growls.

Andrea snaps her fingers, suddenly getting an idea.

"Okay, okay, here's what we're gonna do. You kids look for some thick enough branches so we can make a splint for his foot. Ms. Davis, collect as many bands as you can to hold it together and keep Craig's leg elevated. I'm gonna call 911 and find the nearest park staff to come help. Go! *Go*!"

As soon as she barks those orders, all the kids immediately scatter off to see what they can find.

"Should I go with you, Mom?" Rocky asks. Andrea shakes her head. "No. Stay here with your class."

Andrea then faces the teens.

"Ms. Davis is obviously pregnant, so help her if need be. It's a bit of a walk down to the main entrance, but I'll be back as soon as possible."

Before they can even respond, she's already jogging on the dirt path back downhill. Gio wipes some sweat droplets off his brow. This day was far more eventful than he thought it would be. As he turns around, he notices that only Tasha and Mileena are behind him.

"Uhhh, where's Sky?" he asks.

He and the girls look around for their talkative new acquaintance. There are kids running in every direction, looking for suitable branches. Mr. Murphy continues hissing through his teeth, swearing and shaking in agony. Poor Ms. Davis is waddling around trying to contain the chaos. Gio shakes his head. Teachers really don't get paid enough. Eventually, he catches a flash of blond hair going down a steep hill far off the trail from the clearing they were all in. Gio beckons for the girls to follow him as he heads in that direction. All the noise and commotion quickly fade to the background as the three descend the hill. Being off trail, it was a bit harder for Gio to keep his footing as they half walked, half hopped. They all catch up with Sky a minute later once the ground finally evens out.

"Hey yo!" Gio calls out. Sky keeps walking but turns his head to acknowledge him.

"'Sup, bro?" he greets back. "You okay?" asks Tasha. "Yeah, sorry. I may be a big guy, but I've got a weak constitution when it comes to seeing injuries. Don't judge me," he answers.

Gio finds this all too relatable.

"Are you kidding me? I don't watch horror movies for that same reason," he tells him.

Sky gives him a thankful smile, which does something weird to Gio's chest. He feels himself blushing again. Only this time, instead of looking away, Gio smiles back.

"I get all that. Still, though, why are we going so far? Don't you think they're gonna wonder where we are?" Mileena asks. Sky laughs a little, turning around and walking backwards as he acknowledges Mileena.

"Number one, I'm pretty sure they're all too occupied with Mr. Crooked Foot to worry about us. And number two, I needed a break from that whole crowd anyway."

Mileena starts rubbing her arms nervously.

"Still, these parts of the woods are supposed to be haunted or something," she says. Sky puffs out his chest like a superhero.

"Your highness, I already vowed to protect you from the dirt. I shall also protect you from any ghosties."

The four trek on for some time. The trees here are thicker and much closer together. The ground is rife with leaves, twigs, and bushes to step over. The teens take care of navigating their way through. Gio can't tell which direction they came from anymore. Or exactly which hill leads back to the class. His nerves are starting to intensify, but he doesn't voice his concerns just yet. He's enjoying his time with the other three, even though they might be potentially lost. Sky is back to his normal jokey self. Tasha, Gio and Mileena are content to just walk along and make small talk. Eventually, they come across a gorge about sixty feet across and at least one hundred feet deep. At the bottom of the gorge is a coursing river. It's flowing, churning waves crashing over massive, jagged rocks. There's a wooden bridge connecting the space to the other side, but Gio's stomach still turns. He *hates* heights. And the bridge looks ancient.

"If we're this far off the designated path, why is there a bridge in the middle of the woods? What's on the other side of the river?" asks Mileena. Sky shrugs. "Maybe it's here for anybody who gets lost," he says.

He then turns to Tasha and asks,

"Do you think we've gone far enough, or do we wanna go to the other side?" Tasha raises her eyebrow.

"You're asking *me*? It was *your* idea to come all the way out here," she points out. Sky simply smiles. "I know."

Tasha shakes her head, then looks at Gio and Mileena.

"We've already been out here a while. What do *you* all want to do?" she asks.

Gio scratches the top of his head in thought. Tasha had a point. If somehow Ms. Davis and Mr. Murphy hadn't noticed their absence, Andrea surely would whenever she returned. She's been very kind to them. How much trouble would they get in if they weren't back on time? Gio doesn't really want to add to his punishment. Then again, if they were out this far, maybe they were *already* in more trouble upon return. The path they came from wasn't clear. Which means it would take them extra time to get back, regardless. With a cheeky grin, Gio says,

"Screw it."

Mileena looks down at her shoes. They've gone from pristine white to stained green and brown. The girl slumps her shoulders.

"My dad's gonna kill me for ruining these brand new shoes. Might as well delay it as much as I can." Tasha softly laughs. "Alright then. Across we go."

She takes the lead and walks across the bridge first. Mileena follows suit. Before Sky takes a step, Gio reaches out and gently grabs hold of his arm. The blond looks at him in confusion.

"Uh, you okay, dude?" he asks. Gio takes a deep, shaky breath. "I don't like heights and uh, this bridge looks kinda sketchy." Sky laughs. "What, you need me to protect you, too?" Gio laughs back, "Maybe."

Arm in arm, the two slowly edge their way across. The girls are already halfway there. Gio tries his best to put on a brave face, but then he makes the mistake of looking down. It's a *long* way to the bottom. The sound from the river is surprisingly loud. If the impact of hitting the water doesn't take him out, the jagged rocks along the way would surely tear him apart. Gio shudders at the thought. He tries pushing the intrusive thoughts away, but every step is loud, creaky, and untrustworthy. Sky gives Gio's arm a reassuring squeeze.

"It's alright. If anyone's in trouble, it's *my* fat self." Gio immediately feels a lot less nervous. "If it makes you feel any better, I used to be in gymnastics. I feel dumb being able to walk a balance beam but afraid to cross a high bridge." "Don't sweat it, bro. Plenty of people are scared of heights. Ever been on a plane?" "Nope, and I don't plan to anytime soon."

After what feels like an eternity, Gio practically deflates once they all finally reach the other side. He makes sure to give Sky a pat on the shoulder as thanks once their arms unlink. This time, Sky is the one who blushes and looks away. It gives Gio a bit of a confidence boost knowing he has an effect on another guy. *Maybe I'll do something about it after all when we get back.* He thinks. Tasha suddenly turns around and puts her hands on her hips.

"Are you *kidding* me?!" she exclaims.

Gio, Sky, and Mileena look to see what she's talking about. Wouldn't you know it? There's a short, latin boy with glasses at the other side of the gorge they just crossed.

"Rocky?! What the *hell* are you doing here?!" Tasha yells.

Rocky fearlessly runs across the bridge to them. Gio feels embarrassed that he had to be escorted, while this little pipsqueak just does it like it's nothing. Once he reaches them, Rocky tirelessly greets them with a simple,

"Hi." "Have you been following us this entire time?" Tasha asks with the tone of an exasperated mother. Rocky smiles.

"Yeah. I saw you guys sneak off while everyone else was helping Mr. Murphy. Betcha didn't notice me, huh?" "Rocky, you can't leave like that! Your mom told you to stay with the class."

Tasha says sternly. Sky shrugs.

"It *is* impressive how little man tailed us," he says. Tasha scowls at him. "*Not* helping!"

Then she turns back to the boy in question.

"Explain yourself, *right now*!"

Gio can't help but be impressed. This whole time, they've really only seen Tasha's mostly upbeat attitude. It was interesting seeing her a little peeved. Rocky nervously gulps.

"Well, at first, I was only following you to see if you guys were looking for stuff to help. Then I heard you talking and I, I-I-I was bored with the whole nature project and I-I-I-,..."

Tasha puts a hand up, stopping him.

"Look, we're already in enough trouble. We can't have our teacher's son with us in the middle of nowhere. You gotta go back."

Rocky's eyes widen.

"*Alone*?!" he asks. Gio crosses his arms. Their situation just got weirder.

"He's already here," he points out.

Tasha frowns at Gio which makes him hunch his shoulders apologetically. She then looks back at Rocky, who's awkwardly smiling.

"I'm cool, I promise. Just let me stay. *Please*?"

Tasha grabs Rocky by the back of his collar and shoves him in front of her.

"Fine. But you *better* tell your mom we were model chaperones. And stay *exactly* where I can see you," she orders.

Gio catches the sly smirk that spreads across Rocky's face. Of *course,* he was going to stay where she could see him. The kid didn't have him fooled. He was most definitely into the nature project. He just wanted an excuse to be with his new crush. As the five begin to walk once more, Gio makes sure to stay by Sky's side. *I guess I'm doing the same.*

Chapter 4

Mileena

If it wasn't already obvious, Mileena Kimiko Jane-Yoshida was *not* an outdoors kind of girl. This whole experience should be one of the worst days of her life. Dirt. Sweat. Leaves. Being outside at all. On top of that, detention. Mileena had never even been in a timeout before. Now here she is. And for the *stupidest* reason. It was bad enough that things weren't so chipper outside of school, either. What, with the messy divorce her parents just finalized after two awkward years of separation. Dealing with that fallout was unpleasant to say the least.The Janes, her father's side of the family, are black. The Yoshidas, her mother's side, were Japanese-American. Both families never quite got along. There was racial tension on either side and strained tolerance at best during get-togethers. And there, in the middle of it all, was Mileena. When it was announced that Terrance Jane and Valerie Yoshida were no longer going to be married, there wasn't much sympathy. One of the only extended relatives who'd ever shown Mileena any kind of love and acceptance was her maternal grandfather. Her *Sofu*. Unfortunately, he passed away about a week ago. All of this was why Mileena seemed prickly at first. Hillstone Park was a *big* place, and they were far from the designated path. This should be awful for her. But it isn't.

After crossing the crappy bridge, the now five-strong group went down another series of steep hills. They soon found a small clearing covered in clover. With thick pine trees surrounding the area, it was hard to make out what lay beyond. Sky takes a seat on a rather large boulder next to a fallen log and sighs.

"I think we've gone far enough," he says. Gio sits on the boulder next to him. Mileena can't help but scoff.

"Yeah, ya think?" she asks rhetorically. She and Tasha rest on the log with Rocky between them. He's swinging his little legs, doing his best not to stare at Tasha. Mileena brushes her hair behind her ears and asks,

"Nobody else finds this a little weird?" All eyes turn to her. "What do you mean?" asks Gio. Mileena sighs, not quite sure what she's asking herself.

"I don't know. I mean, if you just wanted some space from the kids, we could've done that a *long* time ago. Now we're God knows how far away in some secret section of Hillstone Park doing *what* exactly?" Tasha looks over to her. "Are you complaining?" she asks pointedly. Mileena shakes her head.

"No. Obviously, I *chose* to come with. I'm just venting."

Rocky looks around the group and chuckles softly.

"You guys obviously aren't volunteers. Let me guess: detention," he says.

Sky claps his hands.

"Bingo, little man. Your mom wasn't even supposed to be our 'warden' for the day, but our principal is a dick." Mileena cracks a smile. "That's the understatement of the day. He's the reason I'm here in the first place." Tasha perks up, "Me, too! Well, actually, it's his demonic daughter." "We never did explain what we're all in trouble for", says Gio. Sky jokingly raises his hand.

"Ooh, ooh! I wanna go first!" he says childishly.

It makes Mileena laugh. She wanted to stay grumpy. Really, she did. These individuals just made it nearly impossible. So, why not give in?

"You're in detention every day. What did you do that was so terrible, brave knight?" she asks with a wink. Before he answers her question, Sky locks eyes with Rocky and gives him a quick warning.

"You said you were cool, right? Don't go bragging to all your little friends about our business."

Rocky rolls his eyes. "I don't talk to anybody from my class. They're *all* annoying."

"Ha! I like you, kid. Honestly, my story isn't really that long. About a year ago, I was caught behind the school in the middle of a uh, let's call it a 'transaction'. One of the football players was nervous about an upcoming game, and he knew I was holding. Of course, once we get caught, the guy takes off like a bullet. There's no use in my running too since I'm built like a biscuit."

"Oh, stop it, Blondie, you look fabulous", Tasha interjects with a smile. Sky's cheeks go a little pink.

"Well, aren't you just sweeter than a Georgia peach?"

The group giggles. Sky continues.

"Well, I'm brought to the office, lectured at, yada yada. They tried to get me to tell them who I was selling to, but I ain't no snitch. *However*, I've already got two strikes on my record. Plus, I was on the verge of turning eighteen at the time, so Mr. Charles brought up pressing charges. My uncle is practically on his knees *begging* him not to. So, in exchange for not sending me to jail or expelling me, I had to do three months of community service, write an essay on the dangers of drugs, and serve indefinite detention, basically until graduation." Sky scoffs, adding,

"Wanna know the funny part? The only reason my uncle wanted to keep me around was that he'd have nobody else to pawn his four kids on every time he left the house. Being my guardian adds to his monthly checks. Thanks, mom and dad. I'll be sure to send you postcards from hell."

Mileena swallows. Jeez. It really is the goofiest people dealing with the most crap. There's an awkward silence. Nobody knows how to respond. Sky's chestnut brown eyes darken for a second. As if nothing happened, Sky laughs it off and points at Mileena.

"Why are *you* here, your highness?"

Mileena's hands slap her thighs.

"Just gonna put me in the spotlight, huh?" "Yup." "Fine, but it's *really* stupid. Yesterday, the honor society and I were having a meeting in room 107. You know, the one with the best air-conditioning, that's right across the hall from the vending machine? We'd already gotten approval from Ms. Ronson. In the middle of our meeting, Mr. Charles barges in and tells us we have to leave. The student body wanted the room to discuss prom or something. I *tried* to tell him we had permission first but... he told us honor society wasn't as important. I got mad and called him a fascist, so he gave me detention. *Just* to put a smudge on my perfect record."

"He gave you detention just for calling him a fascist?" asks Rocky.

Mileena snorts.

"I might've thrown in 'dickface' in front of that 'fascist'. Still, old white men don't get reality checks as often as they should." Tasha hums in agreement. "Hmph. Period." Mileena then points at Gio.

"How about you? What's *your* story?"

Gio scratches behind his head.

"It's uh, it's kind of embarrassing, honestly."

The rest of the group waits quietly. Gio takes the hint that he can trust them.

"Okay. So uh, a couple of days ago, I saw a flier on one of the bulletin boards that there was somebody holding auditions for a new bass player for their band. Now, I've only lived here for about a year, but there's no gymnastics team like I had at my old school back in Indianapolis." "Wait, gymnastics? So you can do backflips and stuff?" Rocky interjects. Gio nods.

"And more", he replies with a wink. Rocky is positively beaming.

"Yo, that kicks ass!" Tasha gently smacks the boy on his forearm.

"Hey, only *we* get to swear. Watch your mouth", she orders sternly. Rocky wants to argue, but he's not disobeying Tasha.

"Anyway," Gio continues, "I also know how to play a little bass guitar. And since there's no gymnastic team, I figured I'd give this band thing a shot. I actually *nailed* the audition. But the lead guy, Louis, said I wasn't in until I did one more thing." "Which was what?" asks Mileena. Gio sighs.

"He said I had to pour oatmeal in the pool before the swim team's practice."

Mileena snorts embarrassingly loud as she and the others can't stop themselves from laughing.

"*Oatmeal?!*" she asks incredulously. "Regular or flavored?" asks Sky. Gio hangs his head, his bangs slightly obscuring his crystal blue eyes. Quietly he admits,

"Maple ginger."

The laughing only continues. For a full minute in fact. Sky actually has to clutch at his side when he starts getting cramps. Rocky nearly falls off the log before Tasha pulls him back up. Eventually, Mileena manages to ask,

"Wait, so did you do it? I feel like this would've been news around the school."

Gio shakes his head.

"Nope. Louis even provided me with a giant bucket full of the stuff. I dragged it to the pool and was *about* to do it. Until Coach Hall came in early and saw me with the bucket. I tried running away, but you know, slippery floors."

Sky slaps Gio on the back.

"That was the funniest thing I've heard in a long time, bro. So what happens to you now?" "Nothing. I only got one day of detention since I didn't actually put the oatmeal in the pool. Honestly, I'm glad I didn't. I think Louis just has a personal vendetta against the swim team."

After that, Mileena, Sky, Gio, and Rocky all look at Tasha.

"Just you now. C'mon." goads Sky.

Tasha begins lightly tugging at one of her locs.

"My story isn't funny like Gio's," she says. Sky shrugs. "What else are we gonna do?" "I agree. I definitely want to know why *you're* here." Rocky adds with special emphasis. Tasha falls silent for a moment.

"You don't have to if you really don't want to." Mileena offers.

Tasha's been nothing but gracious this whole time. Mileena would feel bad if they made her uncomfortable. However, Tasha shakes her head.

"No, it's okay. It just pisses me off to even think about it."

She's quiet for another moment before she begins.

"Yesterday, I was wearing a shirt that said 'Winnin' With My Melanin'. Real cute. Sparkly font and everything. And, while I was walking down the hall to class, freaking Catherine-Bethany Charles passed me and said, 'Yeah, right.' Now normally, I don't let shady little comments bother me, but that was obviously racist. So I turn to her and call her out like 'Excuse me? Care to elaborate?' She has the *nerve* to tell me, 'I just don't see how bad attitudes and nappy hair count as winning.'"

Mileena loudly gasps. She's never interacted with Catherine-Bethany before, but she's never heard anything pleasant about the principal's daughter either. Tasha scoffs as she continues,

"I should've just walked away. I know this. But I couldn't let that slide. So I tell her, 'Go season your chicken.' And you know what she says next? 'I bet you'd know all about chicken, wouldn't you? If you wanna talk stereotypes, at least *my* parents are around.'"

Mileena balls up her fists. The *audacity*! None of the boys looks too happy either. Especially Rocky. He looks like he wants to storm off and find Catherine-Bethany himself.

"Obviously, she took it too far when she made it personal, so I pushed her against a locker. Just a push. That's all. Mr. Charles showed up *just* in time to see me push her, but he conveniently didn't hear the things she said. I *tried* to let him know about her racist comments. Even had a couple of random people vouch for me, but he wouldn't hear it. All he saw was his precious little angel being 'assaulted' by an angry black woman."

Just talking about it has Tasha trembling with anger. Mileena can relate. Oh boy, could she relate.

"What's she even talking about?" asks Gio, "I mean, are your parents,... you know,...?"

Tasha gulps, slowly nodding in confirmation.

"Yeah. Dead." "What happened to them?" asks Rocky.

Tasha runs her hands through her locs.

"It was Winter Break during freshman year. They were driving home from the grocery store the night of a *really* bad snowstorm and uh... well, you can put the rest together. I guess Catherine-Bethany decided that was funny enough to use against me."

Everything falls silent once she's finished. Mileena knew it must've been bad if she was hesitant to share, but she didn't imagine this. There's a heaviness on everyone's face. Nothing but the sound of rustling leaves fills the air. Everyone knew Catherine-Bethany had a bit of a reputation, but that was just downright cruel. Tasha is such a sweet girl with a very likable personality. She absolutely did not deserve to be punished. After about a minute, Sky finally breaks the silence.

"I know we just met and everything, but I'm down to help you get revenge on her." "*Painful* revenge", adds Rocky. "Count me in, too," Mileena chimes in, "I'm half Japanese with straight A's, and I'm in an honor society. I've heard the things people *think* they say quietly about me. Even from my own family."

Sky brushes his fingers through his hair and says,

"I'm fat white trash who's been to juvie. Life isn't peachy for me either."

Rocky slumps his shoulders.

"I get made fun of *all* the time for being short. Also, strangers like to ask me if I speak Spanish or if I'm Mexican. Neither of those is true, but like, mind your business, y'know? It's so *annoying*."

Both Mileena and Tasha give the boy gentle shoulder pats. She can relate to him as well. The things that strangers (even relatives) think are appropriate to ask when dealing with race or nationality are laughable at best. Gio breaks up the tension by admitting,

"I can't eat a sandwich that's not cut diagonally."

The five all chuckle softly, but they can tell he actually has something relevant to add.

"My dad's been out of the picture as long as I can remember. After my mom and I moved here from Indiana last year, I lost contact with my ex-girlfriend and *all* of my old friends. Then my mom married a banker who has as much personality as a bag of flour, but he makes good money. Now she hardly pays attention to me but insists I be the best big brother to her new husband's daughter."

Mileena can't help the soft sigh that escapes her. Strangely, everyone airing their grievances with life and why they were in detention helps her feel a lot better.

"We've all got our crap", she says in a dry tone. Sky mimes raising a glass.

"To our crap!"

The group entertains him and toasts their imaginary glasses, which puts a genuine smile on Mileena's face. As Sky and Gio stand up from the boulder to stretch their legs, the rock itself wiggles a bit. Mileena catches a flash of something beige beneath the boulder and squints her eyes. There's something there. Something that isn't grass or dirt.

"What's that?" she asks.

The boys both look down. "What are you talking about?" asks Gio.

Curiosity getting the best of her, Mileena gets up from the log and walks over to the boulder. Right by Sky's foot, she gets a better look at what caught her eye. It's wood.

"There," she points out, "Think you big, strong men can move this rock out of the way?" Sky cracks his knuckles.

"Why of course, your highness. I'll gladly throw out my back for you." He jokes, but still bends down and starts pushing the boulder. Gio joins him. With great strain and a string of swear words, the two actually manage to shove the boulder on its side and roll it about two feet away. Excitedly, Rocky goes,

"Whoa! Check it out!"

Mileena is flabbergasted at what they've just uncovered. Standing at their feet, in the middle of an unknown area in Hillstone Park, lies a wooden trap door. Mileena puts her hands on her hips. *So many questions,* she thinks. She looks to her peers to gauge their reactions. Rocky looks ready to open it right away. Sky and Gio back away slightly, both nervous. Tasha seems curious yet cautious. Mileena is bouncing between all of these reactions herself, not quite sure how to feel. Rocky reaches down to grab the handle of the door when Mileena slaps his hand away.

"*What* do you think you're doing?!" "Don't you wanna see what's inside?" he asks.

Sky shakes his head.

"There's a trapdoor hidden under a big rock. I don't know about you, but to *me*, that screams 'red flag'."

Gio nods in agreement.

"I don't think whoever put this here wanted it to be found", he adds.

Once again, everyone looks to Tasha to see what she thinks. There's just something about her that makes Mileena trust her intuition. Tasha bites on her lip as she ponders what to do.

"Well, this *is* a government park. So technically, we wouldn't be trespassing."

Mileena, Sky, and Gio all purse their lips. She makes a valid point. It is weird that there's some sort of secret door in the middle of the woods. At the same time... there's a secret door in the middle of the woods! The only negative thing anyone's ever said about Hillstone Park is that areas off-trail are supposedly haunted. They've all been fine so far. As long as they stick together, they *should* be good. Making her decision, Mileena smirks.

"Let's just have a look." Sky scoffs at her. "*You* want to see what's in there, your highness?"

Mileena straightens her shoulders and puts her hands on her hips.

"Don't tell me our brave knight is scared", she says challengingly.

The blond doesn't say anything. Instead, he bows and gestures towards the door. Challenge accepted. Mileena walks up and pulls on the door handle, revealing a flight of wooden stairs leading down into pure darkness.

Chapter 5

Rocky

As it turns out, the staircase led to a tunnel. A narrow, concrete tunnel, merely five feet wide and God knows how long. It was dark. Dusty. Kind of creepy. But at the same time, really, *really* cool. Despite the oddness of the situation, Rocky Sartana Barragàn Castillo couldn't complain. Like, what were the chances of discovering whatever this place was? Since Rocky was the only one with a cellphone, its flashlight wasn't helping as much as they'd liked. They could only see directly in front of them with each step, so the group proceeded with caution. Right as they descended the stairs into the tunnel, the *gorgeous* red-haired girl, Tasha, grabbed his hand. She said it was to make sure she could keep track of him in the dark. Not that she would have to worry about losing him anyway. Where else would he be? Rocky absolutely snuck away from his class and crossed that raggedy bridge just to have a shot at speaking to her again.

He wasn't lying when he said he found his classmates annoying. Standing at a mere four feet nine, many of the other boys in his grade poked fun at him for being short. The ones who weren't making fun of his height were making comments about his mom. It's nothing new, unfortunately. Rocky's heard many people objectify his mother his entire life. She's beautiful. She's always been beautiful, so he does his best not to let it bother him. After all, he and his mother have been close since day one. Growing up with a single mother, Rocky learned young to appreciate all the hard work and effort Andrea Castillo put into providing for him. And he's eternally grateful to her for it.

Sadly, other than his mom, Rocky never quite formed a close bond with anyone else. At least, nobody long-term. He tended to keep his distance from other kids. While the majority of them played together and hung out in their little cliques, Rocky was perfectly fine at home playing video games or reading comic books. His favorite is Kid Estrella. Rocky has a friend online named Kenny, whom he talks to about all things Kid Estrella. He'd love to meet him in person. Unfortunately, Starfish, California, isn't exactly around the corner for a play date.

This day in particular was the first thing in a long time that Rocky's actually been looking forward to. He's always enjoyed life science, so when Ms. Davis proposed this field trip to Hillstone Park to get some firsthand experience with botany, Rocky was all for it. The fact that his mom volunteered to be an extra helping hand was nice, of course. However, his day was truly made when he saw who she brought along. High-Schoolers! *Cool* high-schoolers. Especially Tasha, though that goes without saying. Rocky hasn't had many crushes in his life, but he was absolutely taken with her. Those brown eyes. Those ruby red locs. Her smile. Her voice. Her take-charge attitude. Rocky just couldn't help himself. While everyone was running around in chaos trying to help Mr. Murphy, Rocky's feet had a mind of their own as he saw the teens sneaking away. If there was one thing Rocky *did* like about being short, it was that he was incredibly light on his feet. Growing up, he was a master at hide-and-seek. Was it incredibly risky that they were all going into uncharted territory and exploring an underground tunnel? Yes. But hey, his mom would probably be happy he's finally socializing.

None of the group say much as they continue on for about five minutes. Other than their footsteps, it's eerily quiet down there. Rocky looks behind him. Mileena is directly in the middle of their little huddle. Gio and Sky take up the rear. Then, of course, there was his future wife up front with him. Not only was Tasha a hottie, but the others seemed to follow her lead. Rocky was no different. After hearing about the girl who got her in trouble, he was ready to go to war for her.

"Maybe we should turn back," Gio says, breaking the silence, "We haven't found anything, and this dust is messing with my allergies."

Rocky smirks in his direction.

"If you go back and we find a giant stash of maple ginger oatmeal, you'll be sorryyyyy."

Gio rolls his eyes but laughs anyway.

"Very funny. You might wanna be careful, though. Your name is Rocky, but you don't look like you can punch anything."

Rocky snorts.

"Right, cuz you're the first person who's brought up that *ancient* movie to me. Besides," and he gestures to Sky, "We have our brave knight."

Sky laughs hardily.

"Lucky for you all, I *do* know how to box. Brave knight fears no evil!"

Tasha giggles, music to Rocky's ears. *She's seriously just perfect.*

"I'll remember you saying that if there's an ax murderer at the end of this tunnel," she jokes. "Mm-hm. You know *exactly* how that situation is gonna go for us minorities", adds Mileena.

Everyone laughs together, which Rocky appreciates. It helps ease the tension. They really have no idea what they're walking towards. Rocky's curiosity might be strong, but the anxiety of the unknown is absolutely there as well.

But I might never have this chance again. Let's see what we're in for.

Shortly after, the tunnel finally comes to an end as they come upon yet another old wooden door. Rocky looks up at Tasha and asks,

"Should we knock?"

Tasha shrugs. She lets go of Rocky's hand (much to his dismay) and gives the rickety door a single knock. The second her knuckles make contact, it opens slightly with a loud, grinding creek.

"Huh," she mutters.

With another shrug, Tasha pushes the door fully open and slowly steps inside. The others follow. Rocky wasn't sure what to expect down here, but it wasn't this. They're in a cellar the size of an average kitchen. There is a small window letting in some daylight, though not very much. It's also not big enough for any of them to fit through, so they still have to go back through the tunnel to exit. There is a rusty ladder leading to another trap door. Rocky wonders what it leads to, but they've gone far enough for one day. Keeping the flashlights on their cellphones, the five youngsters spread out as they explored the cellar. There are cobwebs everywhere, with shelves caked in thick layers of dust. Rocky strolls over to a cupboard. He opens it to find stacks of canned goods and other nonperishables.

"Wow. What the heck have we walked into?" he asks no one in particular. "We're in a park, right? Maybe this is an old ranger station or something." Gio suggests.

Tasha scratches her chin saying,

"You might be right. The question is, why is it obviously abandoned? Somebody *had* to put that boulder over the tunnel." "Someone who *clearly* doesn't want visitors", adds Mileena. Sky scoffs.

"Are you telling me we just stumbled onto a mystery? Where's a talking dog when you need one?" he jokes.

Rocky chuckles softly. However, they all bring up very valid points. Whatever basement they were in hasn't been touched in a *very* long time. And whoever was here last obviously wanted to make sure it wasn't easily found. Rocky and these high-schoolers just happened upon this place by accident. Just as he's about to say something else, an odd noise catches his attention. It's low and faint, but he can definitely hear it. *Bum-bum. Bum-bum. Bum-bum.* Rocky closes the door to the cupboard and crouches down to get a better listen. *Bum-bum. Bum-bum. Bum-bum.*

"You guys might think I'm crazy, but... I hear something."

The four older teens all look at Rocky with the expected looks of confusion and skepticism, but it doesn't matter. He *knows* he can hear it. Keeping low to the ground, Rocky walks in the direction of the noise. As he approaches a pile of wooden crates, the strange noise suddenly gets a little bit louder. *Bum-bum! Bum-bum! Bum-bum!* Tasha follows close behind him.

"He's right, you guys. There *is* a noise. It's coming from over here", she says.

Rocky can't help but smile. He was beginning to worry that he was actually imagining things. *Tasha, you're an angel.* Luckily, the crates seem to be empty, so Rocky has no issue pushing several of them to the side. With the crates out of the way, he finds a small wooden chest the size of a shoe box wrapped in old, thick chains. Suddenly, the noise begins to fill the entire room. *BUM-BUM! BUM-BUM! BUM-BUM! BUM-BUM!* There's no denying it now. Whatever is making that sound is clearly originating from this little chest. And if Rocky's not mistaken, it sounds eerily like a heartbeat. It's weird. *Too* weird.

"Okay. Brave Knight's not feeling so brave, now." Sky admits. Rocky nods his head.

"Yeah, me too. Maybe we should,-"

The boy stops mid-sentence. A small but noticeable green light emits from the chest's keyhole. Rocky can't look away. The light seems to put him in a sort of trance. Just five seconds ago, he was ready to call it quits and get the hell out of there. Now there's nothing but a strange, almost irresistible desire to *open this chest*. And apparently, he's not the only one feeling it. When Rocky turns around, Tasha, Sky, Gio, and Mileena are all fixated on the light as well. Their eyes are glazed over. It's clear that whatever's inside the box is hypnotizing them. But Rocky can't seem to care.

"Maybe,... just a peek?" Rocky suggests. Mileena nods slowly. "Yeah. Just a peek", she echoes. "We've already come this far", says Gio.

All of their voices are low and droning. Almost as if they were sleep-talking. Sky takes the box in his hands and yanks the chains off. They're already rusty and loose, so there's little resistance. Before he lifts the top of the chest, Rocky takes one more look at Tasha. Even under the box's spell, he still wants the final approval from her. Tasha places her hand on Rocky's shoulder, which makes his heart jackhammer in his chest.

"Do it," she whispers.

So he does. And when Rocky gently lifts the lid of the chest, nothing on earth could have prepared him for what they saw. Inside the small wooden chest was a heart. A *heart!* Not the cute shape one would see on Valentine's Day and the like. An anatomically correct and disturbingly human-looking glowing green heart. And the *bum-bum* they heard? It was because the heart was beating. On its own. Rocky should be freaking out. They should *all* be freaking out. Yet, the heart still had them entranced under its spell. The light begins to grow in intensity, encompassing the group and the entire room in an emerald-like glow. Succumbing to its will, Rocky, Tasha, Sky, Gio, and Mileena collectively reach a hand forward and each lay a finger on the heart. *ZAP*! Rocky feels a jolt of electricity course through his body the second they make contact with the organ. Bone-rattling shudders rack his entire being from head to toe, causing him to nearly jump out of his skin. Simultaneously, his vision shuts off like a switch. All he can see is fuzzy green light. This goes on for a frighteningly long ten seconds. Then, as suddenly as it happened, Rocky's vision comes back. He looks at the rest of the party. Their eyes fade from glowing green back to normal as well. Mileena shakes her head as she finally comes to.

"Okay, what the *heck* was that?!" she exclaims.

Rocky gasps. He feels his common sense return. There's a glowing beating heart in this box! And they *touched* it! *Gross*! He slams the lid of the chest shut and tosses it back into the pile of boxes.

"We shouldn't have come here," he whispers. Mileena throws up her hands.

"You're right, we shouldn't have! I don't know what kind of *freak* lives in a place like this, but I sure don't wanna be here when they get home."

Gio is already one step ahead of her as he runs to the door and dashes back into the tunnel. Sky and Mileena fall in step behind him. Rocky stands still trying to make his brain work. He's scared. They have no idea what touching that heart just did to them, but he can still feel waves of invisible energy bathing over him. None of it makes any sense!

"What's going to happen to me?" Rocky asks out loud.

He looks down at his hands. They haven't stopped trembling. Tasha lays a palm on his shoulder. It helps calm him down a little, though not as much as he'd like.

"C'mon. We've been away long enough by now", she says gently.

Rocky nods. Then a brand new fear comes to mind as he remembers a very important detail about their little outing.

"*Crap*! My mom's gonna kill me!"

Chapter 6

What Happens Next?

After Tasha and the rest of the group exit the tunnel, they don't even bother pushing the boulder back on top of the trap door. As far as she's concerned, whoever did that in the first place can deal with it. She shudders at the thought of what just happened. They found a beating, glowing green heart which hypnotized them into touching it! *Ew!* It was something straight out of some sci-fi or horror movie. Neither of which she was a fan of. Poor Rocky still hadn't let go of her hand. He was probably the most shaken out of all of them. Tasha could tell he was trying to put on a brave face since they allowed him to stick around. Now he was probably traumatized. Hell, they *all* were. None of them speaks a word the entire trek back. Everyone was too lost in thought. Evidenced when Gio seemed to have less of a problem crossing over the rickety bridge. Probably because he had the same question running in his mind on repeat that Tasha does: *What just happened?!*

After they cross the bridge, it's relatively easy to retrace their steps. As soon as they find the hill they come down from, Tasha ushers herself to the front. Rocky has stopped holding her hand, but he's still right by her side. Mileena is behind her with Sky and Gio on her left and right, respectively. Tasha figured the two boys would be arm in arm by now. But romance was probably out of the picture with what just went down in that cellar. So many questions. No answers. At least, none that she won't have to look for. Which she *really* doesn't want to. It's odd. There's still some aftereffects she can feel from touching the Heart. It feels like a shot of espresso was injected straight into her veins. She's jittery. Tense. Like, a coiled rattlesnake ready to strike. The other four seem to be experiencing more or less the same. But it's more than how they look. Tasha can literally feel whatever the Heart is doing to them. They were all now neurologically linked somehow. Tasha has always been intuitive, but this is different. It's direct. Almost intimate. Testing just to see if it was true, Tasha takes a deep breath and concentrates on her travel mates mentally. There's mostly fear, of course. But there are individual surface thoughts coming through also.Rocky is seesawing between dread and sadness. Possibly because he might not see this group again, Mileena is annoyed and full of regret, probably wishing she'd never come along. Gio is actively suppressing his anxiety, doing his best to keep up his chill demeanor. Sky is the happiest, relatively speaking. From the stress of his home life and daily boredom in detention, he told everyone about, this whole trip was likely the most excitement he's had in, well, ever. That makes Tasha smile a little. *There's always a silver lining,* she thinks. Rocky, noticing her smile, looks up at her.

"What's got you smiling after all of that?" he asks.

Tasha looks around at the others. *Can they pick up what I'm feeling the same way I am with them?* Rocky doesn't seem to. The other three are lost in their own thoughts. So maybe they do. Maybe they don't. Tasha shrugs.

"Don't worry about it," she says gently.

As Rocky starts to pout, Tasha reaches down and grabs hold of his hand again. In an instant, she can feel Rocky's anxiety subside a little. He goes red in the face and looks the other way as they hike uphill. If the Heart did indeed give her some sort of empathic link with these guys, Tasha finds she wouldn't mind so much. *I just hope that's the only thing it did to us.* While Tasha and the others were gone, Andrea was able to find the nearest park ranger and get them to help relocate Mr. Murphy to the park entrance. There, he was met with an ambulance and immediately taken to the hospital. Meanwhile, one of the kids saw Rocky sneak off and notified the other two teachers. Andrea had Ms. Davis take the rest of her class back down to the entrance as well. She knew her son and her detention students would most likely return to the very spot they left.

As Tasha and the gang get closer to the top of the hill, she spots Andrea talking with a park ranger. Probably describing to him what the group looked like in case he had to start a search. Before they approach, Tasha looks down at Rocky.

"Listen, I need you to do us a giant favor and *not* tell anyone about the Heart. Or that secret tunnel we found."

Rocky looks at her with uncertainty.

"I guess so. Why?" he asks. "Because," Tasha replies, "we have *no* idea what we came across or what that thing did to us. Until we have more answers, it's just better for everyone if we keep this a secret."

Rocky nods. She can tell he's being truthful. Good. The second Andrea sees them, her eyes squint and go dark. Tasha can't help but cringe. She's always liked Andrea. And she can see the pure disappointment in her eyes. Rocky's sweaty palm slips from her grasp as he catches his mother's eye.

"Good luck, little man." Sky whispers.

He was definitely going to need it. Rocky saunters over to his mother, who crosses her arms in the classic parental fashion.

"Rocky Sartana Barragàn Castillo, give me *one* good reason I shouldn't ground you until your eighteenth birthday!"

The boy just lowers his head.

"I'm sorry, Mom."

Andrea exhales through her nose and sets her dagger eyes on the teens. She may not be her mom, but Tasha still feels the need to grovel.

"I asked you four to do one thing. *One* thing! Don't act like jackasses, and everything would be fine! And what do you do? You sneak off while a teacher is hurt for over an hour and take my twelve-year-old son with you, doing God knows what?!"

Tasha winces. They were gone for over an hour? It certainly didn't feel like that long.

"If it helps, we didn't take him. He just followed us," says Gio.

Tasha puts up a hand.

"Rocky followed us, but we let him tag along anyway," she admits.

Andrea swears under her breath.

"Unbelievable. *Unbelievable!* Let's leave before I lose my job and possibly my freedom!"

She grabs Rocky by the sleeve of his shirt and begins stomping away with repressed fury. Tasha closes her eyes and sighs sadly. They'd had fun, yes. But at the cost of ticking off her favorite teacher.

"I guess this means we're not getting lunch," Sky says rhetorically.*

Indeed, lunch was not bought. In fact, the drive back to school is dead silent. No small talk. No questions. Not even any music. The second Andrea parks, Tasha, Gio, Sky, and Mileena all drag their feet to the building with no trace of enthusiasm. Andrea doesn't say a word as she drives away with Rocky. Tasha feels like crap for making her angry. Hanging out with these guys was fun, but was it worth it?

Back in the detention lounge, Mr. Charles was waiting for them with the box of their cellphones. He quickly returns their devices and goes about his business. After gathering their belongings, the four teens step into the hallway. None of them moves to leave just yet. Instead, they stand there staring at each other. It's so strange. Just a few hours ago, they were all complete strangers. Now they were acquaintances who had just gone through the weirdest bonding experience ever. Gio finally breaks the silence.

"So uh, like you told Rocky, maybe we should keep whatever that was to ourselves."

Mileena scoffs.

"I can do better than that. Just forget this whole thing ever happened, and I'll do the same." "No amount of therapy could make me forget what happened." Sky jokes.

None of them laugh. Instead, Tasha takes out her phone.

"Look, I think we should at least exchange numbers. We should be able to contact each other in case there's any more, uh, side effects."

It was the logical thing to do. Sky is the first to put his number in everyone's contacts. Then Gio. Then Mileena. Afterwards, she says,

"You make a lot of sense. However, do me a favor and try not to need me."

With that, she turns on a heel and is the first to walk away in a hurry. Tasha can't even be mad. She has every reason to be upset. With a friendly smile, Gio shakes hands with Tasha. Then, with Sky, his hand lingered for just a second longer.

"It's been the weirdest day ever, but uh, it was nice to meet you guys anyway. I'll see you around."

The dark-haired boy strolls away. But not before looking at Sky one last time. Sky bites his bottom lip as he lets out a nervous chuckle.

"Do you really know what we're feeling?" he asks.

Tasha shrugs.

"Kinda. Whatever the Heart did to us, it's a part of it," she answers. Sky looks at her with a shy grin.

"Any chance you got a read on that guy?" he asks her. Tasha sighs, but smiles. "Not like I *need* to, but yes. He likes you, too."

Sky puts his hands in his pockets and gestures his head to the front door.

"C'mon. I'll walk you out." "Aww. Thank you, brave knight."

As Sky and Tasha exit the school, the nighttime handyman passes them by. He was a bald, forty-something-year-old man with a prominent beer gut, a scraggly gray beard, and countless circles under his eyes as though he hadn't slept in years.

"See ya tomorrow, Mr. Mays," says Sky. "See ya tomorrow, smart ass," the handyman replies.

As Mr. Mays continues into the building, he stops for a second and looks at Tasha and Sky. There's an unreadable expression. Like he's searching for something in them, it makes Tasha feel uneasy. As soon as it happens, Mr. Mays shrugs and goes back to his business.

"Friend of yours?" asks Tasha. Sky shakes his head.

"Nah. Since I'm here all the time for detention, we pass by each other almost every day when he comes in for the night shift."

Tasha looks at the building one last time before she begins unlocking the chain on her bike.

"I'll see you later?" she says with uncertainty. Sky smiles at her. "Probably."*

Due to the day she had, Tasha pedaled home in record time. As soon as she steps through her front door, however, she begins to feel woozy. Lightheaded. A little dizzy.

"What the hell's going on?" she asks nobody.

It wasn't the sun that was making her feel like this. Or even the bike ride. No. She can tell. It's from the Heart. The jitters and tension earlier have now evolved into a sort of vertigo. A burst of nausea courses through Tasha's body. Sweat pours from her profusely. She looks as though she'd run a marathon. Her eyes roll to the back of her head as her vision goes fuzzy. Jasmine sent her a few text messages a while ago, but she can't even muster up the energy to respond.

"I... I need to lie down," she huffs.

Bree still isn't home yet, which is probably for the best. There's no way she wants Bree to see her like this. Let alone a doctor. They'd probably think she was on drugs. Tasha laughs to herself as she clumsily sways her way up the stairs. *Drugs would be easier to explain*. In reality, what takes fifteen seconds seems to take years for Tasha to make it upstairs. Her feet feel ten pounds heavier with every step. She nearly cries with relief as she finally makes it to her bedroom and flops face down on the bed. She doesn't even bother taking off her clothes or shoes. Bed was what she needed, what she *craved.* The clock on her nightstand reads six o'clock. Far from her usual bedtime, but today was an exception.

As Tasha closes her eyes, she can feel herself slipping from consciousness. *Sleep. I just... I just need some sleep.*

Though Tasha falls asleep almost instantaneously, her entire night is anything but restful. She subconsciously grips her sheets deathly tight as she's bombarded with *very* vivid dreams. She can sense the others. Sky. Gio. Mileena. Rocky. They're all asleep as well, and being assaulted with the same imagery. She can't make sense of them, of course, but there are a few that stick out in particular, like clips from a movie. Green light. A meteor shower. A train. An explosion. The woods. The bridge. A rundown cabin. Fireworks. Blood. Screaming. Cash. Angry yelling from unknown voices. More green light. More screaming. And every once in a while, between the seemingly random images, there's a figure. A dark, menacing figure. It seems to be a man made of black smoke and shadows. It's... *chilling.* The shadow man has no facial features. And yet, Tasha can feel it looking at her. *Directly* at her.

Chapter 7

The Human Flashlight

The next day,...

Rocky loudly yawns as he turns to the next page in his comic. He was finally catching up on the latest issue of Kid Estrella. A teenage hero with the power of cosmic energy, Kid Estrella was Rocky's all-time favorite fictional character. Especially since he was a mainstream Latin superhero, unfortunately, Rocky couldn't keep focus on his comics as he pondered the last twenty-four hours.

Yesterday, after receiving the expected scalding from his mother, Rocky began feeling a little off. He was dizzy, lightheaded, and on the verge of puking. Deciding to skip dinner, he went to bed shockingly early at 730. And when he did, he was hit with strange, vivid, partially violent dreams. And the weirdest part was that he was sure the older teens he hung out with yesterday were experiencing the same phenomenon. Tasha. Sky. Gio. Mileena. Rocky wishes he could see them, though he has no way of contacting any of them. As part of his punishment, Andrea confiscated his phone, laptop, and game console until further notice. Rocky feels bad. He rarely gets in trouble with his mom. Despite wanting to confide in her, Rocky keeps his promise and doesn't tell her what happened in that basement. It's more than just avoiding extra punishment. He doesn't want her to freak out. Was his impulsive decision to sneak off worth it? Yes. But at a cost.

After a night of rough sleep and no phone or video games to occupy his mind, Rocky had felt a little more restless than usual. He even periodically did a few jumping jacks or simply walked around the house just to expend some energy. Andrea at one point even asks him, "What's gotten into you? Are you really this helpless without your devices?" Rocky doesn't really answer her. Of course, it's not his lack of devices driving him nuts.

Well, not entirely. He knows what it is. The Heart did something to him physically. He's still short, unfortunately, but he can tell a drastic change has happened to his body. *I just wish I knew what it was.*

Around 8 pm, Rocky exits his room to grab some water when a familiar scent hits his nostrils. Vanilla-scented perfume. It's his mom's go-to fragrance when she has a rare night out. Or a date. Rocky crosses the hall to his mother's room. Sure enough, she's looking in the mirror, applying eyeliner and burgundy lipstick. She's also wearing an off-shoulder, tight knee-length orange dress, black stiletto heels, and gold hoop earrings. She looks nice. A little *too* nice. Rocky clears his throat to catch her attention.

"Where do you think you're going, young lady?" he asks with a cheeky smirk.

Without looking away from the mirror, Andrea replies,

"Out. Remember, I told you I had a date planned with that repairman a few days ago." "Wait, that's today?" "*Yes*, it's today. And since you're going to be thirteen this year, I figured you're finally old enough to be home alone."

Rocky begins to smile when Andrea gives him a pointed look.

"Don't start celebrating just yet, *mijo*. Your phone and console are still on lockdown. Also, I *was* going to order you a pizza for tonight, but since you got yourself grounded, you gotta fend for yourself."

Rocky crosses his arms.

"Fine. But if you bring this guy home, I'm calling him 'new dad'." "Which is exactly why I'm *never* introducing you two, even if tonight goes well."

Rocky can't help but chuckle. He enjoys giving her a hard time once in a while.

"I love you too, Mom."

Andrea sighs as she puts down her eyeliner.

"And I love you."

She walks over, bends down, and gives him a quick hug.

"I'll allow you to watch TV while I'm gone. Just don't stay up too late." "That goes for you, too." "Don't push it, Rocky. You're already on thin ice."

Andrea pats him on the head, grabs her purse, and then heads downstairs. Rocky follows her and watches as she leaves. It feels a little odd being home alone. The last time she went on a date, he was ten years old and still needed a babysitter. He was glad not to need one now. Though it doesn't change that he was still bugged about her putting herself back out there. Unfortunately, his mother has never had the best luck with men.

Especially his father. Wherever he is, Andrea rolls down her window and blows Rocky a kiss as she starts the car. He "catches" the kiss and puts it in his pocket. It was their routine anytime she went somewhere, ever since he was a toddler. It's corny for sure, but it will probably continue well into his adulthood. Rocky waves goodbye to her as she drives off. He continues to stand on the porch for a while after Andrea's car is out of sight. He looks up at the nighttime sky and shivers. Something about the darkness of it reminds him of the shadowy figure he saw in his dreams. Despite all of the other weird things he saw, this... whatever it was, creeped him out the most. Was it even real? Shivering at the thought of the shadow creature, Rocky quickly goes back into the house. He was getting hungry. **

Rocky wasn't too concerned about not getting pizza. If there was one thing he loved other than Kid Estrella, it was cooking. As long as he could remember, Rocky used to sit in front of the television with his eyes glued to the cooking channel. Eventually, after asking his mother over and over again for permission, he was allowed to recreate some of the dishes he saw. And as it turned out, he was a natural to the point where more often than not, Rocky would be the one happily making dinner for him and his mom. He's thought about joining the home-ed classes at his school, but the last thing he wants is something else to be made fun of for. It's a shame. He's quite good at what he does. Deciding to keep things simple, Rocky chops up some vegetables and leftover chicken tenders to make an easy stir fry. He has his mother's playlist of nineties hip-hop playing for background noise as he gets to work. He loves listening to old music. Once Rocky is done dicing onions and jalapenos, he thinks about adding some potatoes to the mix. He dances over to the pantry and reaches down where the sack of potatoes is further back in the dark. As soon as his hand makes contact with the darkness, *sheen.* The palm of his hand brightens.

"Whoa!" Rocky shouts.

He jumps back, his heart pounding like a hammer. Looking down at his hands, his palms are both glowing with a brilliant white light radiating off his hands.

"This is nothing. This is *nothing*. I'm hallucinating." Rocky says to himself.

Womp! An orb of white light the size of a baseball rises from his hands. It floats in front of his eyes, illuminating every food item in the pantry before him.

"Wait a darn minute,..." Rocky mumbles while squinting his eyes. Experimentally, he reaches up to touch the orb. There's no weight or solidity, but it does feel warm. *Am I crazy or-?* Rocky slowly moves his hand to the right. The orb floats to the right. Rocky uses the same hand and gingerly swipes it left. The orb goes left. A surge of giddiness hits him. He can't help smiling. The orb came from and was responding *to him*! An excited laugh escapes Rocky as he lowers his hand and the light fades away.

"I'm just like Kid Estrella!" he exclaims.

Feeling confident, Rocky shoots both of his hands up. His hands glow again, this time producing wide flashlight-like beams.

"Nice!" he yells.

He slowly walks around the kitchen, shining his hand lights on various objects. There was no denying his reality. He was creating light from his bare hands! With a flick of his wrist on his right hand, the beam of light switches from white to red.

"What the-?"

He flicks his wrist again. The light turns yellow. Another flick. Blue. And another. Green. Blue. Pink. Purple. He does the same experiment with his left wrist. Blue. Yellow. Orange. Green. Rocky laughs almost manically. This was so much *fun*! He closes his fists, and his hands return to normal. They feel a little hot, but overall, nothing too serious. Was he suffering from radiation poisoning after touching that Heart? Who cares?! He's got a cool, unique ability out of it, so it seems! Brimming with excitement, Rocky switches off the kitchen light and stands there in the dark. With a deep breath, he holds out his hands, willing for them to glow. They do, nearly blinding his own eyes before he holds them further away from his face. *Uum,... Orb?* he thinks. *Womp.* The baseball-sized orb from earlier floats from his palm and hovers in the air, shedding five feet of white light in the dark room. With a thought, Rocky makes it turn red. Yellow. Blue.

"*Sweet*! Now let's see..."

Rocky closes his eyes and brings his arms to his sides. He concentrates, this time imagining multiple orbs to come into existence. An uncomfortable brightness hits his closed eyelids. When Rocky opens them, his jaw drops. There are at least a dozen multicolored orbs floating in circles around his body like a swarm of prismatic fireflies. It's a beautiful sight to behold, even if it is testing his retinas. Rocky closes his fists and the orbs blink away. He switches the main kitchen light back on, remembering what he was doing before. The stove was still on and his food was going to burn if he didn't get back to it.

After dinner, while Rocky cleans everything, his brain is a beehive of thoughts. He has superpowers! His mom is going to kill him for not telling her. He has superpowers! Touching the Heart did *way* more than he expected. He has superpowers! What's going on with Tasha and the others? He has superpowers! But most importantly, *he has super-*

powers! This was real! *WOW!* Rocky's curiosity burns inside him and completely takes over. There's no *way* he can sit around the house all night after this discovery. Damn his mom for taking away his phone! He needs answers. And he's not going to find them in this kitchen. Knowing his mother won't be home for at least a few hours, Rocky gets an idea. A reckless idea.

"If I hurry, I should be able to catch the last bus," he says to himself.

Lucky for him, minors thirteen and under get to ride for free. He grabs his shoes and his house key. If anyone thought they were going to give him a hard time, they had a face full of blinding lights to deal with. Rocky leaves the house and runs to the nearest bus stop. It was time to take another trip to Hillstone Park.

Chapter 8
Run, Run, Run!

Gio sighs as he brushes his wet curls from his eyes. He thought a long, hot shower would've helped more after the crappy sleep he'd gotten the night before. It did, but not as much as he'd hoped. Dreams don't usually stick with Gio, but this one... *Yikes.* Everything was too weird to make sense of as is, but that shadow thing gave him chills every time he thought about it. Something told him what he saw wasn't just a dream. And the Heart was right in the middle of it all.

It was doing something to him. To everyone, Gio was with us yesterday. He was a little skeptical when Tasha told them she felt some sort of empathic link. Though after getting woozy and passing out far earlier than usual, Gio was thinking maybe she was right. Everything was seemingly normal when he woke up this morning. And yet, he could tell his body had gone through some type of metamorphosis. He just doesn't know how yet. Gio looks down at his phone. Despite everyone besides Rocky sharing their numbers yesterday, he hasn't received any messages yet. Perhaps they were all processing like he is. Still, it would be nice if he heard from any of them. Especially a certain blond with a great sense of humor. Gio grins as he bites his lip.

In the beginning, he was simply enjoying Sky's obvious flirting. After having to break up with his ex-girlfriend Tina due to the move, Gio was simply happy to get some attention. It wasn't until the "brave knight" helped him cross the bridge that Gio began entertaining thoughts of "maybe" towards the senior. The guy seemed to bag on his own body a lot, but he was definitely cute. And funny. And surprisingly chivalrous. *If* Gio were to actually engage his first time pursuing another guy, Sky was certainly a viable option.

As Gio gets dressed in a simple band tee with black shorts, he hears a drawer opening behind him. Gio turns around and sees a certain four-year-old in a ladybug onesie rummaging through his nightstand, where he keeps his various jewelry. She holds up a chain necklace with a treble clef pendant and puts it in her mouth.

"Phoebe, *no*!" he yells.

He quickly runs over and snatches the necklace away before she accidentally chokes on it.

"My neckie!" she squeals. "No, *mine*! Now get out of here!" Gio exclaims.

Phoebe pouts at him.

"Meanie!" she spits back.

She runs out of his room, no doubt going to tattle his mom or her father. Gio kicks his bare foot at his dresser and immediately regrets it. This was seriously the last thing he needed. Sure enough, his mother Ava appears in his doorway a minute later.

"What's the problem now?" she asks exasperatedly. "Mom, I didn't do anything!" Gio replies, "She's the one who came into my room and tried to put one of my necklaces in her mouth!"

"Giovanni, she's four. You can't be so mean to her." "I wasn't being mean, Mom. I just don't want her slobbering all over my jewelry!"

Ava pinches the bridge of her nose.

"Gio, you act like you don't want her around at *all*. She's your sister." "Stepsister! *Step!*" "Enough! I'm not having this conversation with you again."

As Ava turns around to leave, Gio slams his door behind her.

"Hardly a conversation in the first place", he mumbles to himself.

Gio was perfectly fine being an only child for sixteen and a half years. He never asked to become a big brother out of nowhere. Just like he never asked to be taken away from Indianapolis. His old friends, Greg and Dylan. His Tina. Coach Johnson and the rest of the gymnastics team. His old bedroom, where he drew on the walls as a toddler. His old backyard, where he nailed his first backflip. *None* of that was asked for! But as long as Ava Carano isn't single at forty anymore, who cares what he wants, right? Frustrated, Gio flops on his bed and begins browsing for more possible band auditions. Hopefully, the next one doesn't involve getting himself in trouble again. As Gio scrolls through various pages, a sudden ping goes off in his brain. *Rocky*. Something is telling him the young boy is doing something he isn't supposed to be doing. Gio sits up against his headrest. The Link.

Whatever invisible connection that formed between the five of them was telling Gio that the little guy might be in trouble. He closes his eyes, deciding to focus in on the signal. Just to make sure he isn't going crazy. Flash! A fuzzy image projects itself in Gio's mind. He can see Rocky at the top of the hill where Mr. Murphy hurt himself yesterday. He's holding a flashlight, stepping over the railing.

Is he-? Is he actually trying to go back to where we-?!... Oh, crap! Gio's eyes snap open.

"Okay. I'm a believer." he whispers.

A notification from Gio's phone catches his attention. He looks down and sees he got a text message from someone he didn't expect.

Mileena- Maybe I'm going crazy, but I think something is going on with Rocky

Gio hurries and replies.

Me- I literally just saw him in my head. He's in the woods

Mileena- So I'm not going crazy after all?

Tasha- No. I saw it too

Me- What the hell is happening to us?

Tasha- I dont know but we can talk about that later

Mileena- I hate to say it but I agree. Someone should probably check on Rocky tho Sky- I thought u didnt wanna be involved, ur highness

Mileena- I dont, but im not heartless. Id offer to go but Im grocery shopping with my dad right now

Sky- im stuck babysitting but Im really wrried abt little man

Tasha- I am too. I can get on my bike and go to hillstone right now. Gio, can you com with me?

Gio pauses. He's worried of course, but what were they about to walk into? If Rocky was trying to find his way back to the secret door, what if whoever left the Heart was waiting this time? And he's out there alone. At *night.* What makes him think he can do that? Why is Rocky so confident that he can go exploring by himself? Was he crazy?! Gio is scared. He doesn't want to go out there. That experience in the basement freaked him out hardcore. And now he was going through changes because of it.

"I could just say no. Make up an excuse. This isn't my problem, right?.... Right?"

Gio grunts in frustration and punches an imaginary target. No. He couldn't live with himself if Tasha went solo and came across trouble. Or worse, if Rocky got hurt and he could've helped. These were nice people. Good people.

"*Crap*!" he growls.

Me- Yeah. On my way

Tasha- Thx so much. Meet me by the park entrance. I'm leaving now

Sky- Pls be careful u 2

Mileena- and keep us posted

Tasha- will do

Me- I'm gonna kill that kid

Gio slides on a pair of socks, his steel-toe shoes, and a blue windbreaker. *Please don't make me regret this!* he thinks.

As Gio exits his bedroom and goes to the kitchen, where the side door is, he hears his mother.

"Going somewhere?"

Gio turns around. His mother is standing next to his stepdad, Kevin. With his bifocal glasses, tight pursed lips, and middle-parted gray-blond hair, Kevin McFadden was the poster child for generic bankers.

"Having a Saturday night out on the town there, Giovanni?" he asks with his annoyingly perky voice. Gio scoffs.

"Yeah, something like that." "You gonna tell us where?" his mom asks.

Gio rolls his eyes. Suddenly, she cares about his whereabouts? He relents,

"With some new friends. That's what you wanted for me, right?" "You know, young man, I'm not liking this new attitude of yours. You get yourself in detention, you don't try to get along with your sister, you-"*Step!*" Gio interrupts, "She's my stepsister! Yell at me later, but I gotta go!"

Before his mother can say another word, Gio storms out. He doesn't have time to deal with her right now. He's got to help Rocky! Walking from the side of the house to the front, Gio snatches up the wooden baseball bat leaning against Phoebe's tricycle. Just in case he comes across something... unpleasant. As Gio begins to lightly jog down the street, it suddenly hits him that Hillstone Park is *not* within walking distance.

"Dangit!" he curses, "I'm such an *idiot*! What am I supposed to do, just run there?"

Suddenly, a jolt of energy shocks his system, which makes Gio gasp. He stops jogging for a second. He feels weird. Like his adrenaline is kicking in, only doubled. His pulse increases *far* past normal, like the beating wings of a hummingbird. There's a buzzing in his ear. The muscles in his legs contract. Gio crouches down, hands touching the sidewalk.

He should be concerned, but oddly, he isn't. This wasn't like yesterday's uncomfortable jitters from touching the Heart. No, this... this felt kind of good. Like he was getting the best kind of energy burst, he's an arrow notched on the string of a bow pulled back tight. Ready to just. Let. Loose. Gio's brain tells him what to do. *Run*. And run he does. As soon as Gio takes off, his feet carry him down the street in a matter of seconds. He banks left, continuing forward at an inhuman pace. There are a few cars driving ahead of him. The speed limit sign says twenty-five. *Run!* Gio bursts forward, his shoes barely touching the pavement as he sprints like a gazelle. Gio is greeted with the hilarious shock of a woman driving her SUV at the speed limit as he casually passes it. On *foot*! It feels amazing! The rush! The pure, electrifying *rush*! Gio smiles ear to ear as he decides to give it all he's got. Boom! Like shifting gears in a race car, Gio goes full throttle, and the edge of his vision begins to blur. The fastest any human has recorded running is roughly thirty miles per hour. Countless marathon runners and Olympic sprinters train like crazy to reach those parameters. And here is Giovanni Carano going at *least* that! But it's not just speed that Gio's got. Despite having only been to Hillstone Park once, he somehow instinctively knows exactly where to go. Like a built-in GPS leading him straight to Tasha. Every twist and turn, he makes with ease. Every sharp turn, every curve, he's able to maintain his momentum. What would have been a fifteen to twenty-minute drive to Hillstone Park takes Gio roughly six and a half minutes on foot. It isn't until he finally reaches the edge of the parking lot that he begins losing steam. In fact, the second he sees the "visitor parking" sign, the jolt that "activated" Gio's speed seems to burn out entirely. He begins to slow to a light jog, then nearly collapses against a random SUV. Gio wheezes harshly as he leans against the vehicle. His legs almost give out on him, but he maintains himself. He's covered head to toe in sweat. Never before has he felt so exhausted. And yet, even while struggling to regain his breath, Gio smiles. He even starts to breathlessly laugh. He finally figured out what the Heart did to him. He's fast. *Very* fast.

Chapter 9
Hide N Seek

Tasha looks down at her phone in confusion as she turns another corner on her bike.

Gio- im here

She left before him, and she's riding her bike. How did he get there before her? Did he get a ride? When Tasha arrives at the Hillstone parking lot a few minutes later, she sees Gio doing stretches by a black SUV. She locks her bike on a light pole and approaches the junior.

"Hey", he greets, breathing heavily.

"Hey", she greets back, "Why are you breathing like that? Are you okay?"

Gio's eyes light up with an excited smile.

"Me? Oh, I'm *great.* You'll never believe this, but I just ran all the way here."

Tasha raises an eyebrow.

"You *ran*? And you beat me here? How?" she asks.

Gio points at the treeline in the distance.

"The Heart. You were right, Tasha. It *did* do something extra for us. I was leaving my house to come meet you, and before I knew it, I just got this burst of energy that made me run fast. Like, *crazy* fast. Speeding ticket fast!"

Tasha scratches the bridge of her nose. Even though she didn't witness it, she believes him. Seeing Gio excited about this new ability of his brings a smile to her face.

"So you have superspeed", she states. Gio shakes his head. "It's more of, I don't know, an energy boost, I think. Like, I don't think I could run over water or dodge bullets, but I can give a car a run for its money", he explains.

"Ohhh, I get it. You basically have a super shot of adrenaline." "Exactly! I can't lie, it felt *awesome!* But there's a limit to it. My whole body almost gave out when I got here."

Tasha looks at the park entrance. It's dark. And it's only early spring, so the nights are still a little brisk. Little Rocky was out there all by himself for God knows what reason. She has no clue what they're walking into, but she has a bad feeling they're not going to like what they find. Again.

"You got enough left in you to help me find Rocky?" she asks.

Gio exhales through his nose.

"I sure hope so", he says. Tasha hesitantly steps forward. "You scared?" asks Gio. Tasha nods. "Hell yeah", she replies. And she keeps walking ahead.*

Tasha grows more and more nervous with every step she and Gio take through the forest. They were there after hours, which meant little to no chance of running into any park rangers in case they got in trouble. It was also the middle of the night. If not for the flashlights on their phones and the glow of the full moon, they wouldn't be able to see at all. To make matters worse, the majority of Hillstone had no phone reception. Tasha and Gio let their link take over as they try to sense Rocky's location. It feels like a built-in locator right in the center of her brain, which would be much cooler if not for their current situation. It's also eerily quiet, which makes Tasha feel even more uncomfortable. Other than the sounds of their shoes crunching on the leaves, there's no other noise going on in the background. She figured there'd at least be crickets chirping or owls hooting. But there's nothing. Just a void of silence. Tasha gulps nervously.

"This is how horror movies start, you know. As a black woman, my chances don't look too hot", she says. Just to break the silence.

Gio chuckles softly as he gives his bat a light swing.

"Well, I've got a weapon and enhanced speed. I'll make sure you don't become a stereotype."

Tasha chuckles with him.

"I definitely appreciate that. I'm not completely defenseless, though." "Oh yeah? How so?" "My dad was in the special forces most of his adult life. He had a lot of CQC training under his belt, so he taught my sister and me everything he knew when we were little."

Gio smirks at her with raised eyebrows.

"Shoot. Remind me not to get on *your* bad side."

Tasha smiles, grateful for the company.

"Thanks again for coming with me. I *really* didn't want to look for Rocky solo." Gio shrugs. "You're good. Besides, it's getting me out of the house", he says casually.

Not long after reaching the bottom of the hill, their radar sense begins tingling, indicating that Rocky wasn't too far ahead.

"So, any chance you got something'extra' as well?" Gio asks. Tasha shakes her head.

"Not really. I spent most of the day in my room just trying to make sense of everything. However, I'm thinking Rocky also got an 'extra' and that's why he felt brave enough to come out here."

Before Gio can respond, the tingling sensation intensifies. *He's close,* she thinks, *but where?* The distant sound of crashing water lets her know they're nearing the bridge. Just as the area comes into view, a hushed voice whispers,

"Turn out your lights!"

"Rocky?" Tasha asks out loud. "Shhhh! Just do it *now!"* he insists.

Tasha and Gio immediately click off their lights. In the darkness, she can feel Rocky's presence, but he's nowhere to be seen. "Where are you?" she asks. "Over here," he answers. She pinpoints his voice to a tree, but she still doesn't see him. Suddenly, *womp!* A small wave of light sprouts from the ground, and Rocky appears before her very eyes. He's crouched down, clutching the roots for dear life with panicked eyes. Tasha and Gio slowly creep their way over and crouch next to him.

"Rocky, what's going on? And were you just *invisible*?" asks Gio.

The younger boy nods in confirmation.

"Yes. It's a side effect of my powers." "Powers?" Gio asks. "Never mind that. What are you *doing* out here?!" Tasha demands.

Rocky groans,

"I came out looking for answers, okay? I was almost at the big rock when something popped out of the trap door and chased me across the bridge. I've been hiding over here ever since." "What do you mean, something chased you?"

Rocky shivers with fear. He looks her in the eyes.

"I think it's the monster." he whispers.

Tasha's entire body seizes all movement. She knows what he means. Damn it, she knows what he means. She and Gio look at each other. He's just as freaked. Tasha puts a hand on Rocky's shoulder.

"Stay right here", she instructs.

Tasha rises from her crouched position and gestures for Gio to join her. The brunet double-hand grips his bat and slowly follows. The two teens tiptoe to the edge of the bridge, then freeze like a deer in headlights. On the other side of the gorge, under the light of the full moon, is the very thing Tasha was hoping she'd never see. The shadowy figure from her dreams. All of their dreams. It was real. And, she can already tell, *it's not* friendly. It looks like the outline of a human, but there's no body. Just a specter of dark, swirling, black and gray. Tasha's breath comes in shudders. If they can see it, it can definitely see *them*. Not daring to take her eyes off the figure, Tasha grabs Gio's wrist.

"You got your energy back?" she asks. "If I didn't before, I surely got it now", he replies.

The shadow figure begins shifting from a humanoid form to an increasingly large cloud-like state. From one hundred feet away, an inhuman, scratchy voice shouts,

"I SEE YOU!" Tasha's eyes go wide. "Oh sh-!"

Before she can finish her swear, the shadow monster begins flying across the bridge directly towards them at an alarmingly fast rate. Quickly, Tasha turns to Gio.

"You gotta get Rocky out of here." "Wait, but what about-?" "Your bat's not gonna do anything to a cloud! We know how to find each other, now *go!*"

Hesitantly, Gio does as she commands. Within five seconds, he tosses Rocky's small frame onto his back and dashes away. She can hear the younger boy protesting, but Gio is already gone in the blink of an eye. Tasha would be impressed... if she wasn't about to die. Knowing the monster had no chance of catching the boys, Tasha made a run for it in a separate direction. Just like she thought, the shadow goes after her instead.

"Now what, genius?!" she berates herself.

An ear-piercing howl erupts from the monster as it pursues her. Tasha screams as she dips and dives through the trees, running as fast as she can. It's right on her tail! God only knows what's going to happen when it inevitably catches her. Twigs and bushes scratch at her face and legs. It stings, but none of that matters. She just has to *get away*! SNAP! The loud pop of branches snapping fills the air as the monster easily breaks through them to get to her.

"*YOU CAN'T ESCAPE ME, GIRL!*" she hears the shadow call out.

It sounds unnatural. Like the voice filter on someone in witness protection on tv. Tasha can feel herself tearing up as she keeps running. Her lungs are working overtime. Her shins are on fire. Other than her bike riding and occasional fight training, she was never much of an athlete. *Gio was wrong. I'm about to become a stereotype after all.* Tasha's fear is only further confirmed when her foot gets caught in a patch of slippery mud. With a loud yelp, she loses her footing and tumbles onto the forest floor, rolling hard into a nearby elm. The shadow monster is a mere fifteen feet away and closing in fast. A pair of smoky arms emerges from its cloudy form, reaching out for her. With a scream, Tasha instinctively raises her arms to her face. The monster's smoky hands wrap their gnarly fingers around her calves, roughly pulling her closer. Tasha claws desperately at the ground, only for clumps of dirt and leaves to fall through her fingers. She tries to kick herself free, but the monster has a vice-like grip on her legs, dragging her as though she weighed nothing.

God, I wish I were stronger! Then, something strange happens. As Tasha reaches out and grabs hold of a rather large set of roots, suddenly the monster's shadowy arms are having a harder time pulling her towards itself.

"*What the-?*" it asks out loud.

Tasha looks down at her hands. She's got a firm grip and is holding steadfast. Something electrifying courses through her muscles. She feels empowered. Stronger.

Do I have a chance after all? Wanting to know if this was true, Tasha yanks herself forward and actually manages to pull her legs out of the monster's grip. The shadow monster pauses for a second, clearly confused. Tasha uses this moment to fully break free and scramble to her feet. The monster moves to try to close in on her again.

"Get *back!*" Tasha yells, swinging her arm to try to right hook her attacker.

Her fist goes through its smoky form and right into the trunk of a tree. *Bam!* The impact hurts her knuckles, but oddly not as much as she expected. In fact, she hits the tree so hard that it begins to shake as if struck by an SUV and not a regular human girl. The shaking causes a flurry of leaves and a few loose branches to snap and fall from above. Tasha somersaults out of the way as the falling objects seem to catch the monster off guard and actually make contact with its head. This allows Tasha to take advantage and run away at last. She dashes in a straight line and doesn't dare to look back, using every ounce of willpower to put as much distance as possible between her and the creature.

After about a minute, Tasha realizes the monster is no longer behind her. But it doesn't matter. She doesn't plan to stop moving until she absolutely can't take another step. Luckily, she quickly finds the bottom of the hill and begins making her way up. The steepness of said hill forces her to finally slow down and realize how worn out she is. With a few more agonizing strides, Tasha makes it to the top before collapsing onto the grass. She almost cries, but she manages to fight off the incoming tears. *Not now, girl.* For a moment,

Tasha just lies on the ground and looks up at the stars in the sky. She made it. By some miracle, she was still alive. Part of her wonders if she dreamed what just happened, but the full throbbing pain in her knuckles from punching the tree reminds her otherwise. Tasha stares at her hand. It should be bloody splinters from how hard she hit the tree, but she's rather alright. It seems her 'extra' was increased strength, and it arrived in the nick of time to save her life.

"I have superpowers", Tasha says to herself.

She huffs a tired laugh. Her lips tug themselves into a smile. Always with the silver lining, she was.

After her breathing slows back to normal, Tasha stands up and steps over the railing back to the official trail. She taps into the Link to try to find the boys. It tells her they're not too far ahead. Sure enough, after about another minute of walking, she can hear their voices before they come into view.

"Gio, we *have* to go back for her!" "Rocky, she told me to get you to safety!" "Dude, that *thing* could be torturing her or something!" "I know that kid, but-" "I'm *not* a kid, Gio!" "*Not* the point, Rocky!"

Tasha clears her throat to catch their attention. As soon as Rocky sees her, he runs up and hugs her waist.

"Oh my God! I thought you were a goner!" he cries.

Tasha gently pets him on the head.

"I thought I was, too. But then *my* extra came in and saved me", she says.

Rocky quickly lets go of her and backs up a little.

"You have a power, too? What is it?" he asks.

Tasha looks at Gio. He hasn't said anything yet, but he looks relieved to see her as well.

"I'll explain on the way. But first,"

With a mighty swing, Tasha smacks Rocky hard upside the head.

"OW!" "The next time you think about going into the woods alone, *don't*!"

Chapter 10

Happy Birthday, Hero

Thankfully, there's no sign of the shadow monster for the rest of the trip back. As the trio gets closer to the entrance, Tasha asks,

"I think I'm ready to talk now. Rocky, what exactly made you come out here?" "Yeah, dude. You had us all pretty worried." Gio adds.

Rocky nervously scratches at his hair.

"Long story short, I was in the kitchen making dinner when my 'extra' activated. Turns out, your boy is a human light show! Check this out."

The boy holds out his hands and *sheen*. His palms light, and three torch-sized orbs of various colors begin circling around their heads. It's pretty, yes. But also *incredibly* bizarre. Tasha shakes her head.

"Wait a minute. Flashlight hands and glow balls, I get, but invisibility? How does that correlate?" she asks. Rocky holds up a hand.

"One, *please* don't call them 'glow balls'. Two, vision is based on light, right? Well, when that *thing* popped up out of nowhere, I guess my powers kinda went into autopilot to 'hide' me."

Tasha shakes her head.

"Huh. That's impressive. Still, you shouldn't have gone off on your own like that", she says.

Rocky shoves his hands in his pockets.

"I know, I know. It's just, I was already going kinda stir stir-crazy all day. And after I discovered my power, I just... I don't know. I felt like I needed to *do* something. Besides, it's not like I know how to contact any of you."

Tasha sighs but decides to drop the subject for now. What's important is that they were all safe for now.

"So, Tasha, how exactly did you get away?" Gio asks, changing the subject. Tasha exhales, still processing the fact that she *almost died*.

"It's super weird. I tried outrunning that thing, but that didn't work out so well. I tripped and fell, and when it grabbed me, I managed to grab hold of some roots and pull myself free. Then boom, I punched a tree so hard it made a bunch of branches fall on that thing so I could get away."

Gio looks puzzled as he hears her reply.

"You pulled yourself free *and* punched a tree that hard? How?" he asks. Rocky smacks the middle of his forehead.

"Isn't it obvious? She's got super strength," he replies, "I think that's pretty awesome."

Tasha smiles at the compliment.

"Thanks. It *was* pretty cool now that I think about it. I would've liked to have been able to fly away or something, but I can work with this."

After finally making it back to the main parking lot where cell reception was accessible again, Tasha texts the group chat.

Me- We got Rocky, but something major happened

Sky- wats goin on?

Mileena- yeah what do you mean by major?

Me- We're about to take Rocky back to his house. I think y'all should come too if ur able Mileena- you got Rocky, right? you sure all of us need to be there?

Me- yes. I know u don't want this more than any of us but trust me this is important Mileena- ...

Sky- cmon ur highness. U r part of this just as much as we r

Mileena- fine

Sky- any chance I can get a ride?

Mileena- yeah. I'm finally home, so I'll borrow my dad's car

Sky- thx ur highness

Mileena- whatevr

After everyone shares addresses and such, Gio offers to pay for a taxi to take them back to the Castillo house. The three of them are exhausted from all the running and terror. While in the back of the car, Tasha notices another 'extra' happening before her very eyes. The minor scratches and bruises she received while running away from the shadow monster were all gone. Her intuition told her it was another bonus they all shared from their Link. *I wonder how much damage this can cause.*

Once they arrive at Rocky's house, Tasha tips the cab driver and lays her bike on the front porch. Rocky leads her and Gio inside, where he rewards them for their help by making peanut butter and jelly sandwiches with potato chips and apple juice. Always a classic. While they're all eating in content, the front door opens. Andrea strolls in, rolling her eyes and sighing as she walks into the kitchen.

"Hey, baby. How was your-?"

The woman pauses as she sees two extra guests in her house.

"Rocky, what are these two doing here?" she asks. "Mom! You're early." Rocky says in surprise. Andrea puts her hands on her hips.

"Yeah. I'm early", she says through her teeth.

Tasha gulps nervously. Rocky told them his mom was on a date and wouldn't be home until late. She was probably still upset with them from yesterday, which made things even more awkward. Rocky's mouth opens to say something when Sky and Mileena step through the front door as well.

"Knock knock! We got here as soon as we could." He and Mileena freeze upon seeing Andrea.

"Crap", Mileena mutters.

Andrea's eyes squint at her son.

"Rocky Sartana Barragán Castillo, I hope you know how to build a time machine. Because if you don't have a good explanation for this, you are *not* leaving this house until the year 3000!"

Rocky's face flushes with sheer embarrassment. He looks on the verge of a panic attack. Tasha places a hand on his tiny shoulder to try to calm him down. What else could they do? She looks from Rocky, to Gio, to Mileena, to Sky. There's not much of a choice. They need to tell her. With a tired sigh, Tasha relents.

"Ms. Castillo... Andrea... there's something you need to know."

Andrea leans against the counter.

"I'm listening."

Moving from the kitchen to the living room couch, Tasha, Rocky, Sky, Gio, and Mileena each take turns explaining the last 24 hours to Andrea. Starting from when they snuck off. Finding the bridge. The trapdoor leading to the basement. Discovering the Heart. Touching the Heart and feeling its aftereffects. The odd dreams they all shared. Rocky is the first to learn about his power. He's not excited about letting his mom know he snuck out of the house and ventured into Hillstone Park alone. Fortunately, that gets overshadowed when he, Tasha, and Gio recount the shadow monster attack. Once Tasha finally wraps up with her daring escape, everything goes quiet. Andrea sits there the entire time just listening. Other than her eyebrows going up a few times, her face stayed neutral as she absorbed the information. Tasha wrings her hands together, waiting for a response. She knows they must sound insane, like something straight out of Rocky's comic books. Tasha is still having a hard time believing it herself. After about a minute, Andrea leans forward. With a long, tired sigh, she looks over to Sky and Mileena.

"Do either of you have anything... extra yet?" she asks. They shake their heads' no'. Then she looks back at Tasha and Gio.

"You saved my son's life tonight. Thank you."

Tasha smiles gently. It hadn't really hit her until now. She helped save someone's life. Wow. What a feeling.

"You're welcome", she replies. Gio shrugs. "I was just following her lead." Rocky gives Gio's shoulder a light smack.

"Don't be modest, dude. You totally saved my ass." At the same time, Tasha and Andrea both go,

"*Language!*" Everyone gets a little laugh from that.

"I gotta say, Andrea, you're being weirdly chill about all this", says Sky.

The woman clicks her tongue.

"Oh believe me, I'm just covering it up well. I am absolutely *not* chill about *any* of this. However, I'm tired and you're all still alive, so that's the important thing. And yes, you can trust me to keep everything between us."

Mileena awkwardly raises her hand.

"Not to be a downer or anything, but what if that *thing* strikes again?" she asks.

Sky chuckles as he puts an arm around her shoulder.

"Then we'd better hope our 'extras' pop up asap", he says with a smile. Mileena groans at that.

"He's not wrong, y'know," says Andrea, "If this *thing*, this,... Boogeyman decides that he wants to come after you again, you ought to have whatever you can to defend yourself."

Gio scratches his chin in thought.

"So far, we've got Rocky's lights, me running fast, and Tasha's strength."

Rocky giggles with glee.

"This is so *awesome,* isn't it? I can't wait to see what your 'extras' are gonna be."

Sky grins in anticipation. Mileena isn't as excited. Andrea stands up from the couch and addresses the group.

"In the meantime, I suggest you all go home and get some rest. Stay in contact and watch each other's backs. If anything else happens, don't be afraid to come to me."

Tasha could almost cry. Andrea reminds her a lot of her own mom. The woman gives a stark glare at Rocky, who shrinks into himself. Little man was probably about to be in even more trouble. Taking this as their cue to leave, Tasha looks at the clock on the wall. It's 12:01. Just past midnight. Tasha Simone was officially eighteen years old. After tonight, she can't wait to finally have some sister time with Bree on her first day as a grownup. It's been ages since they simply hung out. Mileena gestures her head toward the front door.

"C'mon. I'll give you all a ride home", she offers. Before they all leave, Rocky runs over and holds his hand out to Tasha.

"Thanks again for saving me. You're a hero."

Tasha grins as she swats his hand away and gives him a proper hug. After putting Rocky and Andrea's info in their phones, the four teens take their leave in the Janes' green Dodge Neon. While the boys are in the backseat talking, Tasha leans her head against the passenger side window. Other than the Boogeyman, she keeps thinking about Rocky calling her a hero. She likes the way it makes her feel. *Hero. I start my birthday as a hero.*

While stopped at a red light, Tasha notices Mileena looking at her. Her green eyes soften as she says,

"Happy birthday."

Tasha is a little surprised to say the least.

"How'd you know?" she asks. Mileena shrugs.

"This weird Link thing, I guess. I can't exactly read your mind, but-" "Surface level stuff. I know."

In the back, Sky and Gio stop their conversation as they hear the news. Sky leans forward and gives Tasha a rough shoulder pat.

"No way! How old are you?" he asks. Tasha chuckles. "Eighteen," she answers. Sky grins ear to ear.

"Nice! I welcome you to the legal adult club. We have brochures and snacks, oh fearless leader."

Tasha can't help but laugh.

"I'm not fearless. But thank you, brave knight."

She catches Gio smirking in the rearview mirror when he says,

"Funny how you only denied being fearless."

The next day,...

It's one o'clock on a Sunday afternoon, and Rocky has been a very busy boy. As punishment for his antics last night, Andrea woke him up early and immediately got him to work. She presented him with a list of everything she needed done around the house. Clean his bedroom. Wipe down the bathroom. Vacuum the living room. Dust the ceiling fans. Take out the trash. Sweep the front porch. Organize the spice rack. Load all the laundry into the washing machine. Then, finally, mop the kitchen floor. Once he's finished with everything, Rocky flops down in a chair at the kitchen table. He's tired, but he doesn't regret a thing. He was still jazzed with the knowledge that he and his new friends had superpowers! Unfortunately, they also seemed to have a villain, but hey, pros and cons. And knowing he can create light from his very being is an absolute *pro.*

As Rocky sits thinking about everything, he is suddenly hit with a wave of sadness. Only, it's not from him. He looks out the window. One of his new friends is not having a good time. But who? Rocky closes his eyes. Despite everything else, the weirdest thing to him was the Link. From what Rocky gathered, it was like a mental radio activated by strong emotions. It can communicate vague, simple thoughts and even images, according to Gio. Having powers was cool and everything, but if it wasn't for the Link, Rocky probably wouldn't be sitting here in this chair thinking about it. He shudders at the thought of the Boogeyman. They got lucky last night. Who knows what's going to happen in the future? Rocky is startled out of his thoughts by his mother placing a glass of ice-cold lemonade in front of him.

"Good work. You've earned this," she says.

Rocky thanks her with a nod and starts chugging the drink. To his surprise, she also slides over his cellphone.

"Considering what happened, I'm allowing you to have this back. But you have to promise me that from now on, you'll tell me *everything*."

Rocky nods.

"I promise. Thanks, Mom."

He looks down at his phone and sees there are actually a few texts from the group chat.

Tasha- hey

Gio- hey bday girl

Sky- how r u? U good?

Tasha- could use some company actually. Original plan kinda fell through

Gio- dang that sucks. Moms dragging me to church atm so maybe l8r?

Sky- i cant leave my house right now. Babysitting again. I h8 my uncle

Mileena- i'm on my way to work. Im sorry

Tasha- its ok

Sky- r u sure? I feel bad

Tasha- it is what it is

Rocky quickly puts together the sadness he felt was definitely from Tasha. He can't have that. Not on her birthday! A girl like this deserves nothing but the best at all times!

Me- u can come over here if you want. I'll make food

Tasha- you cook?

Me- all the time. If u want, of course. No pressure. Ur an adult. Do u like steak? I can do something else.

Tasha- lol, steak is fine. medium please

Suddenly bursting with a second wind of energy, Rocky hops up from his chair and opens the fridge.

"What's gotten into you?" asks Andrea. "Tasha is coming over. I offered to make her dinner for her birthday." he replies.

Andrea furrows her eyebrows.

"You just told her she could come over without asking me first?" "Mom, c'mon! It's *Tasha!*"

Within the next twenty minutes, Rocky whips up a simple but expertly made dinner of steaks with mashed potatoes and sauteed broccoli. Just as he's done portioning plates, Tasha arrives. He and Andrea greet her with 'happy birthdays' and 'congratulations' and the like. As Rocky sets their plates at the table, Andrea gives him and Tasha cola while she opens a bottle of pink chardonnay for herself. It's her go-to drink. As the three dig in, Tasha's pleasurable hums of approval when she takes her first bite warm Rocky's heart. It's not often he actually gets to make food for people other than his mom. However, he can still detect a deep sadness radiating from her. It feels heavy. Like an invisible weighted blanket, only not in a comfortable way.

"So uh, what's going on?" he asks. "Yeah," Andrea adds, "It's the big one-eight for you. Did you not have any other plans?"

Tasha chews on her steak for a few seconds before answering.

"My sister Bree and I were supposed to have this big girls' day out. We were gonna get our nails done, some facials, buy me some new clothes, and go out to eat. I was *so* excited."

She takes a sip of her drink and continues.

"This morning, I woke up to a text from Bree saying she had to come in to work today because somebody quit. Now normally I wouldn't care so much, but she *promised* this day for us. Instead, she left some money for me to go do whatever I wanted. I want to be grateful but,... Our parents are gone. They're not here to see me turn eighteen. And all I wanted was,..."

Tasha stops, biting on her lip as she chokes back tears. Without a word, Andrea stands up from her chair, walks over to Tasha, and gives her a warm hug.

"Listen *mija*, you're the reason my boy is still here. As far as I'm concerned, that makes you family now. You can spend your birthday with us."

Tasha sniffles, wiping away a tear from her glistening brown eyes.

"Thanks, you two. You really didn't have to do this for me", she says. Rocky slams his hand on the table.

"Are you kidding me? Of *course* we do", he counters.

Andrea looks Tasha in the eye and says,

"I was eighteen years old when I met Rocky's father, Enrique. I was young, dumb, and in love with a man who didn't show his true colors until after I got pregnant."

Rocky crosses his arms. He's never met his father, but he's heard enough to never want to.

"Dear old dad hasn't been around since I was born. Prematurely, by the way", he says. Tasha gasps.

"Really?" she asks incredulously. Andrea nods.

"Yup. By almost an entire month. He was so tiny when he was born that the doctors were actually afraid for his health. So, I wanted to name him after somebody strong and persistent for good luck. And *yes*, I am a big fan of the movies. Therefore,..." Andrea gestures towards her son, who grins proudly as he adjusts his glasses.

Tasha's sadness slowly ebbs away, and at last, she smiles.

"I'd say it worked."

Chapter 11

Don't Upset Your Waitress

Sizzle Bay was a local diner in downtown Olligrove known for its barbecue rib platters and homemade strawberry lemonade. Mileena rolls her eyes as she walks through the front doors. She'd been working there for the past year or so as a waitress. With her parents separated, Mileena decided to get a job to make some extra money for herself. Going from a two-income household to one meant no more allowances. Despite being an introvert at heart who hates interacting with the general public, most days weren't that bad for Mileena. She knows how to put on a smile, fake laugh at a customer's corny jokes, and act like everything is wonderful. Today was not one of those days. Not only did she have the unpleasant experience of dreaming about the Boogeyman, but now she's also waiting in dread to see what her "extra" was going to be. Mileena thinks the other four are nice enough people, but she really wants nothing to do with *any* of this. Her grandfather's funeral was in a couple of days. Wasn't that bad enough? Superpowers and a Boogeyman were the last thing she needed.

As Mileena clocks in, her favorite coworker, Dawn, slides up beside her.

"Hey, Milly. You good?"

Dawn was a tall, black college student with a fluffy afro and the face and body of a runway model. Mileena sighs as she clips her hair into a ponytail.

"Not really, but hey, gotta get the coins", she replies. Dawn nods slowly. "Oh. Right. The funeral", she says with empathy. Mileena pins on her nametag and ties an apron around her waist.

"Among other things, but I'll be alright. It's Sunday, so we'll probably be too busy for me to think about it."

Dawn gives the girl a reassuring pat on the shoulder.

"That's the spirit. Make that money, girl. Lord knows I need to. It's almost my wifey's and my anniversary." "Aww. Tell Courtney I said 'hi'." "Of course. Now, let's go. The lunch rush is starting any second."

For the next two hours, Mileena's shift goes as expected. Lots of families and some elderly folk come pouring in after church, ordering everything under the sun. Mileena and Dawn are the only two servers scheduled, so the two young women have their hands full, to say the least. Normally, crowds like this would mean lots of tips for Mileena, but Sundays were always the worst for non-tippers. At least a quarter of the guests would offer "blessings" or even bible verses instead, which did nothing to brighten Mileena's already sour mood. Around 3 pm, once the rush finally dies down, Mileena sits down at an empty table to take a quick breather. So far, she'd only made about twenty dollars in tips, even though several parties had bills totaling sixty and above.

"Cheap bible thumpers", she mutters to herself.

As Dawn walks by with a tray of sizzling hot food, Mileena notices her heading right towards a mopped area that hadn't had a wet floor sign placed yet. This was a disaster waiting to happen!

"Dawn, wait!!" she calls out, but it's too late.

Dawn's right foot lands in the puddle and causes her to fumble. Mileena reaches out a hand. *Don't fall!* she wills. Suddenly, a small green spark flashes from Mileena's fingers. By some miracle, Dawn doesn't fall and drop the tray. Everything is still intact. Dawn shakes her head as she regains her composure.

"Whew. That was a close one", she says to herself, and she goes back to delivering the order.

Mileena looks down at her hands. The green spark snakes between her fingers before fading away. *What did I just do?* Great. Her "extra" showed up while she was at work, of all places. But what was it exactly? Mileena looks around nervously. Luckily, it doesn't seem like anyone saw her. Quickly, she gets up to go grab the wet floor sign.

Some time later, while wiping down counters, her manager, Rodney, approaches her.

"Hey, can you help me grab some things from the freezer really quickly? Tony and Gus are up to their ears in tickets in the kitchen." Mileena nods. "Sure."

Bless the cooks and everything they do. In the deep freezer, while helping Rodney grab bags of cheese sticks and onion rings, a tower of boxes heavy with meat starts swaying concerningly. Mileena keeps her eye on them. Whoever stocked up last didn't line them up correctly. As Rodney grabs a case of chicken nuggets, he backs up directly into the makeshift tower, causing a box on top to slide over. Twenty pounds of frozen meat was going to hit Rodney right on his skull! *Move!* she thinks. Once again, a small green spark ignites from Mileena's palm. The box shifts the other direction, plopping loudly next to Rodney's shoes.

"Oh my! Guess I got kinda lucky there", he says with a small laugh. "Yeah,... Lucky." Mileena mumbles.

She puts her hands on her hips. Once was a coincidence. Twice was a pattern. The green energy coming from her must somehow affect her surroundings. Was her "extra" the ability to conjure good juju? *I sure could use some.*

While taking her official break, Mileena ponders whether or not to text the group chat. Tasha, Gio, and Rocky all have their "extras". Should she keep to herself the way she wants to, or go ahead and indulge in this weirdness? After all, nobody forced her to go exploring the woods with them. Sky was right. She was a part of the fray whether she liked it or not. Eventually, Dawn comes up to her table with a nervous look on her face.

"I'm sorry, Mil. This next customer on rotation is yours." "What's so bad about 'em?" "Well, I think he's been drinking a little bit."

Mileena groans. She *despises* dealing with drunk customers.

"You hate me, don't you?" "Yup."

Mileena laughs at the joke, but the moment of brevity is short-lived. While approaching her assigned table, she can already tell this is going to be a pain in the butt. Her customer seemed to be in his late fifties to early sixties. He had a patchy white beard, a dusty army jacket, dirty talon-like fingernails, and smelled like whiskey and bad breath. Mileena suppresses a shudder as she introduces herself. The old creep is blatantly leering at her while he orders his root beer. Gross. Mileena knows she's pretty, but she's also very clearly a teenager. Men like him make her skin crawl. Part of her wants to ask Rodney if she can just go home early. When she brings the creep his root beer, he has the nerve to try to touch her hand as he takes the glass. Mileena snatches her arm back in disgust.

"Relax, young lady. I'm not gonna hurt ya." Creep says.

Mileena pinches the bridge of her nose. Trying her best not to snap.

"Sir, that's inappropriate. Now, will you please place your order?"

Creep has the nerve to look offended that she doesn't feel like putting up with his blatant harassment.

"Nuh uh, young lady. *I'm* the customer, and you're not going to get smart with me." Mileena crosses her arms in defiance. "Sir, nobody's getting smart with you."

Creep slams his hand on the table like a petulant child.

"They told me the light-skinned ones were supposed to be nicer. Before speaking to me, Pookie, you need to fix your damn attitude!"

Mileena has officially had enough.

"You know what, there are a *lot* of things I can tell you that *you* need to fix, but we'd be here all day!"

Some of the other guests are looking at the altercation, but at this point, Mileena doesn't care. Job or no job, she refuses to put up with disrespect, sexual harassment, or racism. The creep smacks his lips in anger.

"What ugly behavior from such a pretty lady! Get me your supervisor, *now*!" he demands.

Instead, Mileena puts her hands behind her back and grins mischievously.

"Let me show you a trick," she says.

Deciding to put her extra to use, she snaps her fingers behind her back and thinks, *Embarrass yourself.* Creep begins to say something else when he starts to cough harshly. So harsh in fact that his dentures fly right out of his mouth and into his root beer. The man's eyes go wide in horror as Mileena and several other guests begin laughing out loud at him. Creep grabs his soda-drenched dentures out of the glass and runs out the door. Mileena is still laughing when Rodney appears.

"Hey, what happened here?" he asks.

Mileena smirks as her laughter calms down. That entire interaction just made her day a little brighter.

"Oh nothing, boss. He just had a little bit of bad luck is all."

Six o'clock hits, which is music to Mileena's ears. After the incident with Creepy McDrunkard, the rest of her shift is fairly uneventful. She says goodbye to Dawn, who's still on the clock for another two hours. Her father had to use the car today, so she was left on her own to walk home. Mileena sighs. Her total amount of gratuities for the day added up to about 50 dollars. Hardly enough to put a dent in the deposit she needed to buy a car for herself. Mileena pulls out her phone. She really does feel bad about not being able to help Tasha celebrate her birthday. She'd felt some of her sadness earlier from the Link before she clocked in. Good thing Rocky offered to have her over. Even if Mileena didn't have to work, there's not much she could've done personally. *I still could've done something, maybe.* There weren't any new messages in the group chat yet, which means they were all probably occupied. Half of Mileena wants to go straight home and wallow in her dread. The other half is thinking about giving the others a chance socially. Before the freaky thing with the Heart, they were all having a pretty good time just hanging out. As Mileena comes upon a convenience store, she nearly has a heart attack. The old creep from earlier is leaning against the side of the building. Cigarette in one hand and a bottle of bourbon in the other. Mileena stops in her tracks, praying to god that he hadn't noticed her. She isn't so lucky.

"Hey! It's *you*! C'mere!" he yells.

He's definitely been drinking much more since she last saw him. God knows what he's trying to do to her. Not wanting to find out, Mileena starts running across the street.

"Get over here! I wanna talk to ya!"

Struck with fear, Mileena dashes to the other side of the road at full speed. Once she reaches the sidewalk, she turns around to see if he's still on her trail. Creep is stumbling in the middle of the street. He can barely take a step without stumbling, but he's for sure trying to pursue her.

"I said I wanna talk to you, tramp!"

Mileena's jaw drops. *What did he just call me?!* Wanting to teach this jerk a lesson, Mileena balls her fist and focuses on her new ability. *Get hit!* she wills. The green energy from before springs from her fist. Next thing she knows, a red pickup truck driving in a completely separate lane swerves right in Creep's direction. *BAM*! With a loud honk, the truck plows right into the man, knocking him several away. He's not dead, but he's not feeling good. *Was that too much?* she wonders. As the driver hops out of his truck to check on Creep, the old man swats his hands away, pounding angrily on the asphalt when he sees his bottle of alcohol has shattered. Mileena smirks as she turns around and continues walking home. *Nah. Just karma.*

Chapter 12

A Total Vibe

There's a lot on Sky's mind as he takes another bite of his fifth chocolate bar. He knows stress eating is a horrible habit, but it's better than his old method of calming down. Since Sky shares a bedroom with a nine year old girl, he tries to stay respectful. After keeping his eye on his uncle's offspring all day and not being able to go see Tasha for her birthday, Sky figured he could be a bad noodle for the night. He devours the rest of the chocolate bar and lets the wrapper fall out of his window. Living in a three-bedroom house with five other people was a little stressful. Sky shared one room with Piper, Uncle Paxton's oldest and the only girl. Pierce, Perry, and Parker, the five-year-old triplets, shared the other room. Uncle Paxton kept the master bedroom for himself. Needless to say, it felt a little cramped every day. Currently, Piper and her brothers were in the living room watching cartoons while Uncle Paxton was taking a nap. Sky grumbles to himself. Uncle Paxton hadn't had an actual job in years. Outside of collecting government checks for him and his children, most days he was either wasting away in front of the TV or going around town making his money in... other ways. Those other ways used to occasionally involve Sky which was why he had a record. Luckily, after almost getting expelled, Uncle Paxton hadn't roped Sky into helping him anymore. Good. Sky *hated* interacting with his Uncle's dealer anyway. The guy was a complete tool. These days, Sky spends much of his time as a semi-permanent babysitter.

As he shuts his window, Sky gets a notification on his phone. He's shocked to see it's from Mileena to the group chat.

Mileena- Just figured I'd let you guys know my "extra" came today

Tasha- Really? What is it?

Mileena- It's a little hard to explain but basically I can make things happen

Rocky- huh?

Me- yeah, what does that mean, ur highness?

Mileena- i think it's probability manipulation. You know, luck

Gio- sounds interesting

Me- yea it duz. ur gonna have to show us u know

Rocky- yeah I wanna see!

Mileena- lol maybe. You guys have a good night. Also happy birthday again, Tasha

Tasha- Thanks M. Btw, you guys HAVE to try Rocky's cooking. He's amazing

Rocky- :)

Me- hell yea brothr!

Sky is happy that Mileena seems to be warming up to them a little, but he's also a little jealous. He's the only one who's "extra" who hasn't shown up yet. What was it going to be? *Something cool, I hope!*

Some time later, Sky's stomach starts growling. Snack time. He walks past all the little gremlins, hoping they don't need anything. Lord only knows what Uncle Paxton would do if Sky ever moved out. He's eighteen and a senior with graduation right around the corner. Despite what most may assume, Sky actually has steady grades and a 3.5 GPA. He hasn't given much thought about college, but perhaps he should. He'd probably only miss Piper. She's the sole member of the house spawn who remembers to show him gratitude sometimes. Searching through the cabinets in the kitchen is depressing. There are some cans of ravioli, a roll of crackers, a case of microwaveable ramen, and a jar of unopened pickles. Sky makes a note to himself to remind his uncle to go grocery shopping. *Which means I'm going grocery shopping*, he thinks. Sky chuckles to himself. It's a joke. Everything's a joke. Not in the mood for noodles or crackers, Sky grabs the pickle jar. It was brand new, so the lid was naturally giving him a little bit of resistance. Sky strains as he tries and fails at twisting the top off.

"What do they do, superglue these things on?" he asks out loud. "Budge, dammit!"

As Sky presses his fingers into the glass, he feels an odd sensation pulse through his arms. It runs from his biceps, through his forearms, and into the palm of his hands, making the jar noticeably vibrate. The glass makes an odd humming noise, which makes Sky stare at it wide-eyed. *What the -?* He quickly sets the jar down on the counter and recoils his hands. It's no longer vibrating. Sky looks down at his hands. They're trembling, though not from fear or anxiety. He can feel it. It's his 'extra' finally emerging! Sky smiles to himself. About time something makes his day better. He takes a deep breath, focusing on the trembling feeling in his hands. Feeling experimental, he places them on the countertop. The wooden surface begins to shake softly, gingerly bouncing the pickle jar. Sky can't help the excited laugh that erupts from him.

"What are you doing?" a little girl's voice asks.

Sky immediately snatches his hands away from the counter and turns around. Skinny, brown haired Piper is standing in front of him with an empty bowl in her hand. Did she see him? Hopefully not. Clearing his throat, Sky replies,

"Nothin'. Do you need something?" "Yeah. Is Daddy still sleeping? He said we could have some cereal, but I'm still hungry."

Sky rolls his eyes. Just because she's nine doesn't mean cereal was enough for dinner.

"Don't worry, I'll take care of it. Just hold tight for a bit, and I'll order pizza." Piper smiles at him and puts her bowl in the sink. "Thank you."

Piper goes back to the living room, where the three boys are now arguing about which show to watch next. Sky demands them to shut up and walks out the front door.

The Harrises live in eastern Olligrove on the bottom floor of Frankdale Apartments, the city's main area for public housing. While not a cesspool for crime, the area certainly looks the part. Litter. Graffiti. Broken glass is decorating parts of the sidewalk. Loud neighbors yelling and swearing at each other all hours of the night. It was paradise. At the moment, Sky doesn't care about any of that. He was a new superpower to test out. After placing an online order for pizza using his uncle's credit card, Sky loops around the back of the building to the lot next door. There's a rusty old convertible with no wheels next to a dumpster that's been collecting dust for some time. Ideal target to see how far Sky can take his ability. He looks back and forth to make sure nobody is around. The coast seems clear. He rubs his hands together, takes a deep breath, and puts his fingers on the hood of the car. Nothing happens at first.

"C'mon, car. Give me a little shimmy", he whispers.

He presses down on his fingertips, willing for the energy to pulse through. *Brrrrrrrrr-rrrt.* The hood of the car begins vibrating like a large phone. *Hell yeah!* he thinks excitedly. Sky presses his fingers down harder, wanting to know just how strong he could make this thing shake. *Rtatatatatatata!* A loud, metallic rattle rings in the air as the vibrations travel from the hood to the rest of the vehicle.

"Oh, *now* we're talking!" he exclaims.

Giving his power even more juice, Sky pushes his hands firmly into the hood. The entire vehicle begins to shake in a concerningly violent fashion. Suddenly, *bam!* All of the glass from the doors and side-view mirrors completely shatters. The windshield in particular explodes outward, covering the asphalt around the car in shimmering shards. Luckily, it's mostly little bits that fly past Sky, though he does receive a few slash marks on his face and arms in the process. There's also an uncomfortable, recoiling feeling jolting its way through his arms. Almost as if the strength of the vibrations he created caused some kickback. Sky hisses as he caresses his knuckles.

"My power has a bit of a drawback. Fantastic."

Deciding that was enough for now, Sky jogs away from the old car and back to his apartment before anyone sees what just made all the noise he caused.

Sky is in the bathroom, tending to his minor cuts, when he notices something else happening. He barely has to wipe away at the cuts on his skin, as they seem to slowly but surely seal shut before his eyes. Right. Tasha did say the same thing happened to her after she escaped the Boogeyman. Part of him wonders if their healing applies only to minor injuries like these. *What happens if Boogeyman returns and wants to chop my leg off or something?* Sky shakes his head. Thinking like that wasn't going to help. He pulls out his phone, intent on sharing his discovery with the group chat, when he hears a knock on the front door. Throwing away the paper towels he was using to clean himself, Sky exits the bathroom to answer the door. If it was the pizza guy, he'd sure gotten there in record time. When Sky opens the door, his heart jumps in his throat. It's not the pizza guy standing in Sky's doorway. Rather, it's Gio, panting and sweating.

"Hey", he huffs tiredly. "Uhhh, hey. Not that I'm not happy to see you, but uh, what're you doing here?" asks Sky.

Gio looks Sky up and down, which is making his chest do a weird, fluttery thing that hasn't happened since Sky first kissed a boy.

"The Link. You hurt yourself. I felt it. I wanted to make sure you were okay, so I uh... ran over." Gio answers.

Sky crosses his arms and grins.

"*All* the way from your house?" he asks. Gio nods. "Wow. Your speed really is impressive. I never told you where I lived, y'know. I guess you and Tasha were right about the Link having GPS or something."

Gio starts to blush.

"Yeah, 'or something'. So uh, *did* you hurt yourself?" he asks. Sky nods.

"Yeah, but only a little." "Oh. So you're fine now?" "Yup. Totally fine." "Cool." "Cool."

For a second, the two of them just stand there. It's hard to make eye contact. Gio is so naturally handsome with those bright blue eyes and adorable curly hair. Sky couldn't help flirting with him as much as he did during detention, but that was only because he was pretty sure they wouldn't see each other again. As outgoing as Sky is, he's actually quite hesitant when it comes to pursuing guys. It was bad enough that he felt too fat and poor to be of value to *anyone*, but being gay on top of that sometimes made him even more discouraged. Gio clears his throat.

"Ahem. If you're fine, I guess I can run back home. Though uh, I used up all my energy to book it here", he admits.

Sky shakes his head, knocking away his other thoughts.

"Do you wanna rest up here and hang for a bit? We got pizza on the way and I can fill you in on what just happened." Sky offers.

Gio smirks at him, which is doing nothing to stop the fluttering in Sky's chest.

"Bet."

Chapter 13

Friends? Friends.

Spending her birthday with the Castillos had lifted Tasha's spirits by a long shot. She, Andrea, and Rocky spent the rest of the day swapping childhood stories and learning more about each other. It was so sweet learning that the first time Rocky made a cake was at seven years old as a Mother's Day gift. Andrea, it turns out, was actually born in Florida. She'd moved to Illinois after graduating high school and attended Chicago State University for her teaching degree. While there, she met her future ex-boyfriend, Ernesto, and took up permanent residence in Olligrove. She tries to take her and Rocky to visit Florida at least once a year. Easier said than done with a teacher's salary. Bree apologized to Tasha for skipping out on her birthday later that night, but by then, Tasha was over it. Mostly.

The following Monday goes by rather uneventfully. Other than a message from Sky letting everyone know his 'extra' finally came, none of the five said much else to each other. They don't even see each other during school hours since everyone has different schedules. It's strange. Tasha had only known them for a few days, and yet, she misses them. Now that they all officially have their powers, what is the next step?

After Monday was over, Tuesday began in an odd way. When Tasha awoke, she felt a wave of sorrow smack her in the face. Similar to the one she had herself just days ago. Using her senses to pinpoint the source, the Link tells her it's Mileena. Tasha texts her directly rather than the group chat. There's no response.

The last bell of the day rings. School was over. Tasha sighs. She should be going home, or at the very least make plans to hang out with Jasmine. Instead, she was waiting in the hallway for a certain junior while everyone else rushed to the exit. After a minute or two,

Tasha finally catches a glimpse of Gio and beckons him over. The boy smiles as he notices her and strolls in her direction.

"What's up, fearless leader?" he greets.

Tasha smiles back.

"Hey. I was hoping to catch you and Sky." "What for?" "It's about Mileena. You're both juniors, right? Have you seen or heard from her at all?"

Gio shakes his head. "Nope. We have a couple of classes together, but she didn't show up today. I know she's really sad about something, though."

Tasha sighs.

"Yeah. This Link thing feels like a blessing and a curse. Like, I'm invading her privacy or something", she says.

Gio puts his hands in his pockets.

"I know what you mean. I ran to Sky's house the other day when I felt him get hurt."

Tasha raises her eyebrow.

"*I* didn't feel that. I wonder why *you* did", she says with a coy grin.

Gio's face flushes red.

"I guess the Link can be more specific than we thought." "Right. And just why would a specific string form between the two of you?" "Tasha, quit it. This is all new for me and I'm-" "Calm down, Gio. I'm just messing with you. I know Sky's your first guy crush, but it's nothing you need to rush into. No pun intended."

Gio turns his head.

"How'd you know he's my first guy crush?"

Tasha answers him by tapping her temple. Gio chuckles.

"Okay, fair enough. Anyway, I'm pretty sure Sky's on his way to daily detention, so we won't be able to see him for a few hours", he points out.

Tasha puts her hands on her hips as she thinks for a second.

"Hmm. Well, I'm gonna text Rocky to see if Andrea can bring him with me to go check on Mileena when Sky's available. Do you wanna come with?"

Gio nods.

"Yeah. I like her." "Me, too. But maybe you should hang out here until Sky gets out of detention. That way, you both could meet us there. *Together.*"

Gio laughs.

"You're enjoying this a little too much", he jokes. Tasha giggles.

"Of *course* I am. I already have your ship name, too; Skio." "*Ew,* Tasha!" "Skio! Skio! Skio!"

She turns around and walks away laughing. Gio is shaking his head, but he's also not making a move to leave. In the meantime, Tasha goes to the coffee shop with Jasmine to get her second espresso of the day. It's different hanging out with Jasmine now. It's normal. Almost too normal. Her friend is dishing out the latest gossip she's heard about some celebrity. Meanwhile, Tasha can't quite focus on what Jasmine is saying. She's too busy thinking about everything that has happened over the past few days. The Heart. Her strength. Her new (friends?) and the scary monster who was still out there. But that was the thing. The Boogeyman wasn't a monster. It may have been dark while she was out there, but Tasha saw the outline of a human being before it attacked. The Boogeyman has to be a product of the Heart as well. But then why was he hostile? What does he have to gain? Tasha tries her best to listen to Jasmine, but there's just far too much occupying her brain. Things she can't even discuss with Bree, let alone Jasmine. Tasha gently lets her know she's headed home early. She needs to be with her group. They're all so different, but who else would understand her current circumstances?

It's around 6 pm when everyone is finally able to convene. Andrea drives her and Rocky to pick up Tasha from her house. Then they go to the school and grab Sky and Gio. It's not hard to find Mileena. The Link directs them right to the Jane household. Tasha feels Mileena's sadness the closer they get. The boys do as well. It's all over their faces. It's almost uncomfortable just how intimate their Link is. Automatically knowing exactly what one another is going through emotionally, as well as innately having each other's location, is a little... intense.

As Andrea pulls into the driveway, a particular signal burns in Tasha's mind. *Loss.* Mileena was feeling loss. Tasha almost feels a tear fall from her eye. Looking in the rearview mirror, she can see Sky and Gio coming to the same realization. Rocky even wipes his eyes. Andrea clears her throat as she parks the car.

"I'll wait here while you all talk to her", she says.

Tasha nods as she gets out of the car. The boys follow suit. She feels a little nervous knocking on the front door. Mileena might get weirded out by this uncalled-for visit. A bald, middle-aged black man with bifocals and a thick gray beard answers the door. He's clearly bewildered at the sight of Tasha and the others.

"Um, can I help you?" he asks hesitantly. Tasha straightens up her posture and tries to give a warm smile.

"Uh, hi, um, Mr. Jane, I'm guessing?" "I am." "Oh. Good. Uh, can we see Mileena, please?" Mr. Jane sighs.

"Look, you four seem nice and all, but we just got home from a funeral about an hour ago. So if you're wondering why she wasn't at school today, that's why." "Gosh. I'm sorry for your loss. We didn't know. But can we please still see her?" asks Tasha. "Just for a moment, sir", adds Rocky. Mr. Jane steps aside.

"I suppose. Her room is the first door on the left upstairs." "Thanks, sir."

Tasha leads the way upstairs. Before she can even knock on the bedroom door, it opens with a swing. Mileena is standing there with crossed arms and slightly red eyes. It was obvious she'd been crying a lot today. Mileena sniffles.

"What the hell are *you* all doing here?"

Her tone doesn't affect Tasha. She knows all too well how Mileena is feeling. Vulnerable, and angry about being vulnerable.

"We wanted to check on you since you didn't show up at school today", she softly explains. "We felt your sadness, but we didn't know you had a funeral today", says Gio. Mileena scoffs.

"You 'felt my sadness', huh? And you still came over here. Why? It's not like we're *actually* friends. We were only together because of detention."

Tasha can almost taste the bitterness from Mileena. It was like biting right into a lemon peel. None of them says anything. Mileena was right. Their coming together was a sheer coincidence, which culminated in a *remarkably* strange series of events. Eventually, Sky steps forward.

"It doesn't matter", he says with a gentle smile,

"I for one don't give a darn how we met. Brave knight took an oath to protect you, your highness, so you're stuck with me."

Mileena looks at him with an unreadable expression. She doesn't say anything, but the bitter energy is slowly receding. Rocky steps up as well.

"Me, too." Then Gio. "And me."

Tasha opens her arms, silently asking for Mileena's permission. The other girl consents and lets Tasha give her a hug.

"It was my grandfather." Mileena says into Tasha's shirt, "We weren't super close, but he was always nice to me. I handled the service just fine, but it was after that really sucked. My parents are divorced and our families never really liked each other anyway, so... my mom told me and my dad that we shouldn't come to the repass."

All Tasha can say is,

"Damn."

Mileena stops hugging her, wiping away another tear.

"Pretty screwed up, huh? I'm sorry for being so rude. Clearly, I get it from my mother", she says with a resentful chuckle. Tasha shakes her head.

"You've got nothing to apologize for. I just want you to know that we *can* be your friends. If you want."

Mileena looks off to the side.

"I need some time alone", she whispers. Then she looks at the group again and smiles. "But thank you for coming. I mean it." "You're welcome, your highness", says Rocky. Sky ruffles the spikes in the boy's hair.

"Nah, little man, that's *my* line."

Everyone laughs a little before Tasha gestures for them to leave. As Sky, Gio, and Rocky descend the stairs, Tasha looks back at Mileena.

"Are you sure you're going to be okay?" she asks. Mileena nods.

As Tasha joins the others outside, heading back to the car, she can feel a pair of eyes on her. Before she opens the door, she takes one look back at the house. Mileena is looking at her from her bedroom window. She waves. Tasha waves back.

Mileena sits on the edge of her bed once Andrea's car is gone. Crazy how four random strangers she met last week helped lift her spirits better than almost anyone in her family. As a biracial young woman, Mileena heard it all growing up. Half-breed. Blasian. Jap-negro. Mix and match. Just to name a few. Mileena had to learn from a very young age to grow thick skin. To her cousins on her father's side, they interpreted this as Mileena being "uppity" or "boujee". Simply because she refused to put up with insults, that made her "too good for them". It was almost worse on her mother's side. There, she was seen as some sort of science experiment. She was even judged for wearing box braids once, as if she were appropriating her own culture. It was exhausting just existing sometimes.

Some time later, as Mileena tries to think of what to do with herself, she hears a familiar voice coming from downstairs.

"Good evening, Terrance."

Mileena's head drops. Great. Her mother is here.

"Jesus, Val, you sound like we weren't married for fifteen years." "Yes. And now we're not. I'm here to give Mileena something." "Oh, is that right? Trying to make our daughter feel even worse?" "I just buried my father today, Terrance! Don't you *dare* guilt-trip me!"

Mileena angrily grips her pillow. They'd been arguing like this almost nonstop during the divorce. Part of her wonders why they were ever together in the first place.

"She's in her room", her father says.

Mileena anxiously waits as she hears her mother's footsteps ascend the stairs. She hasn't seen her much since the split. While not a cold woman, Valerie Yoshida can be distant. Whatever magical, motherly instinct supposedly sparks in some women when they have kids never quite showed up in her. There was care, sure, but Mileena could tell early on a harsh reality; her mother never wanted to be one. Valerie steps into Mileena's room, still looking prim and proper from the funeral with her pearl necklace, red lipstick, and tight up-do, holding a long rectangular case.

"Hello, Mileena. I apologize for earlier. Surely, you understand why you and your father at the repass might've seemed... inappropriate", she says.

Mileena tries her best not to roll her eyes.

"No, I get it. Family discourse and all that. What's in there?" she asks.

Valerie taps on the latch of the case, giving her a stiff smile.

"This is something personal your *sofu* wanted you to have before he passed. He said the two of you used to take lessons together when you were younger."

Mileena's eyes brighten up. She knows *exactly* what's in there. Valerie sets down the case and gives her daughter a short hug.

"I really am sorry, Mileena. No matter what, I still love you."

Mileena has mixed feelings. She can tell her mom's apology is genuine, but it doesn't change the fact that there's always been a wall between them. Rather than say anything, she hugs her mom back. Valerie gives a curt nod and takes her leave. Once her mother is out of the room, Mileena goes back to smiling as she holds the case in her hands. She can't believe she'd forgotten about a hobby she loved as a child. Feeling more amped up than she had in forever, Mileena takes out her phone and shoots a message to the group chat.

Me- I have an idea. We should get together tomorrow and practice

Rocky- Practice what?

Me- Our powers

Tasha- You actually want to do that?

Sky- im shockd ur highness.

Gio- me too. Why the change of heart?

Me- Are we friends or not?

Sky- u tell me ;)

Rocky- I've been dying to use my powers again! Can we pls? PLS?!?!

Tasha- The Boogeyman is still out there. We need to learn anyway.

Gio- Im down

Sky- hell yeh!

Rocky- YAYYYYY!!!!

Tasha- lets do it then. And yes, Mileena, we ARE friends

Me- good :)

Chapter 14

Superpower Show and Tell

Rocky can hardly contain himself. Ever since the group agreed to finally come together and test out their powers, he was practically bursting with excitement. Rocky was barely able to get to sleep, let alone get through the school day. His teachers had to snap him out of daydreaming multiple times. How could he pay attention? Rocky had admittedly been experimenting privately in his room since the night in the kitchen, and he was *itching* to show the others what he could do. He also wanted to see everyone else's abilities in action. Who *cares* about the Industrial Revolution or the difference between chlorophyll and chloroplasts? He has more important things to do!

Rocky is bouncing on his heels outside Olligrove Middle School, waiting for his mom to pick him up. Sky texted them a good meeting place for their little venture earlier that morning, so they were all heading there directly after school. The moment he sees his mom's Volvo pull up, Rocky practically dives into the front seat.

"Are you ready for this?" Andrea asks with a smile. "Heck yeah, I am!"

"Now listen, I know you're excited and all, but your power is *extremely* risky." "Sure, Mom." "I'm serious, Rocky. We're trying to keep everything under wraps, but your lights can *easily* be noticed. I just want you to use your head, okay?"

Rocky pauses. She was right. He got so caught up in the revelation of his new power that he never considered what would happen if the wrong person saw him in the act. Any exposure could change his and his mother's lives forever, ruining any chance of normalcy. Rocky couldn't live with himself if that happened. Not after all she has done for him.

"I'll be careful. I promise, Mom." "Good." Then she smirks at him.

"I'm excited, too, by the way. I want to see this for myself."

Andrea drives them to the edge of Olligrove, where the avenues of businesses and residences begin thinning out into more rural territory. As Andrea turns into a rather empty parking lot, Rocky recognizes where they are. Superstar Megamart. Or rather, what *used* to be Superstar Megamart. Rocky remembers his mother taking him there multiple times when he was younger. It was a local shop that, for a time, was the go-to place for groceries and toys. Unfortunately, as more franchises popped up over the years and online shopping became a thing, Superstar Megamart grew more and more irrelevant and closed its doors for good two years ago.

Andrea drives the car all the way to the back of the building, where a mile-wide parking lot awaited them. It's empty, spacious, and completely out of sight from the already sparsely used road. Outside of Hillstone Park, this was the most remote location in Olligrove where they could safely demonstrate their powers. As Andrea parks, she and Rocky exit the vehicle and stand near the trunk. Rocky goes back to bouncing with excitement.

"I *seriously* can't wait that much longer. Weren't they supposed to meet us here?" he asks.

Andrea shrugs. The two of them stand there for five agonizingly long minutes when at last, Rocky sees a green Dodge Neon coming in from the horizon. They were finally here! The Neon parks right next to the Volvo. Mileena exits the car first, looking much more cheerful than she had been yesterday.

"Sorry, we're a little late. I had to pick up some ammo", she says. "Ammo? For what?" asks Andrea.

Tasha emerges from the passenger side, handing Mileena a black recurve bow and a bundle of arrows.

"A gift from my *sofu*, RIP. He and I used to practice together when I was a kid, so I figured it'd be nice to learn again since we're targets of some stupid shadow thing." "Although," Sky starts as he gets out of the car, "Not sure what good that's gonna do. From what you guys told us, he's basically a cloud." Mileena shrugs. "Can't hurt to try anyway. After all, I'm lucky."

Finally, Gio exits the car as well.

"We could use all the luck we can get. You guys haven't seen that thing yet. It was,..." "Nightmare fuel." Tasha finishes. Rocky shudders.

"Yeah, it was. But screw that! I wanna get to it! *Now!"*

Andrea puts her hands on her hips.

"Alright. All of you, show me what you got."

Since Rocky was the most enthusiastic and the one who discovered his powers first, he began the demonstrations. He stands a good ten feet away from the group and holds up his arms.

"Let there be *light*!"

Shing. Rocky's hands illuminate. He starts off small, shedding just enough to highlight his face. His friends clap and nod with mild grins. They seem entertained but not too impressed yet. Seeing this, Rocky concentrates and produces a flash on par with vehicular high beams. Everyone quickly shields their eyes.

"Jesus, little man! I enjoy having sight!" yells Sky.

Rocky shakes his hands, flickering out the lights. There's an uncomfortable heat radiating from his palms, so he blows on them to cool them down.

"Sorry about that. I was seeing how much wattage I could put into that. I gotta be careful though. It burns my hands." "That was cool and all, but show us those orbs you made," says Tasha. "Yeah, and your invisibility!" Gio adds.

Andrea, Sky, and Mileena look at him expectantly. Rocky nervously tugs on the sleeve of his T-shirt. He wasn't used to this much attention.

"Okay, okay. Here it goes."

With his hands cooled down, Rocky spreads his arms open. Four basketball-sized glowing globes appear. Like a maestro conducting an orchestra, Rocky waves his hands and directs the orbs above the heads of his friends, each with their own color. Red for Tasha, yellow for Sky, blue for Gio, and green for Mileena. The teens all stare at the orbs in awe. Tasha reaches up to touch hers, her fingers phasing right through it. Rocky clenches his fist, willing the orbs to return as they orbit around his body.

"You're like a star projector." Andrea compliments.

Rocky grins and turns all the orbs violet. His mother's favorite color. She gasps and claps her hands over her heart. The orbs are dismissed, and everyone claps with more enthusiasm this time.

"And for the big finale, Rocky Castillo will disappear before your very eyes!" he announces.

This sub-element of his "extra" was trickier than his flashlight hands or glowing orbs. When he first turned invisible, it happened automatically and out of fear. Rocky closes his eyes, stands completely still, and focuses. He keeps his mind on one word and one word only: *disappear.* The air around him begins to shimmer and warp until finally, *presto.*

"Holy crap he actually did it!" he hears his mother yell.

Rocky opens his eyes and sees everyone turning their heads to try to find him. He grins an unseen grin. As long as he kept focus (which was easier said than done for a twelve-year-old boy), he was indeed invisible. Using his naturally light stride, Rocky tiptoes right behind Tasha and pokes her in the back. The redhead screams in surprise and pushes him clear off his feet and onto the ground, breaking his focus and rendering him visible once again. Tasha laughs in good spirits and helps him up. Everyone cheers and gives Rocky pats on the back.

"I'll admit it. That's pretty incredible, Rocky." Tasha says with a smile. Rocky fist pumps the air. Tasha just called him incredible! *This is the greatest day of my life!*

Next up was Gio.

"I've only done this twice now, but my power is basically a *massive* adrenaline boost. When I was running to Hillstone Park and to Sky's place, I was going *crazy* fast", he explains.

"Sure did! When he dashed away with me on his back, it felt like I was riding a go-kart." Rocky adds. "Yup. The problem, though, is that I get *exhausted* afterwards. Like, I actually lost all feeling in my legs for a second after that first time. I could barely stand."

Mileena snaps her fingers.

"You're like a cheetah." "A cheetah?" "Yeah. They're the world's fastest land animals, but they can only be that fast in short, controlled bursts. And every time they go full force, their bodies need time to cool down or else they risk overheating and going into shock. It's the same with you. Your body almost gave out on you because you used your adrenaline boost all at once."

After her explanation, Gio nods.

"Wow. I think you're right", he says. Andrea looks at her car, then back at Gio.

"If you trust me, I've got an idea."

Gio stretches and limbers up as Andrea revs the engine of her car. The idea was for her to drive directly behind him as he ran around the parking lot at different speeds. That way, he could switch back and forth between his normal jogging and activating his boost, so he doesn't get wiped out so quickly. Of course, there was the risk of him getting run over if he wasn't careful, so Gio does his best to keep focused. He starts off at a light jog, Andrea gingerly driving her car, merely four feet behind him at cruising speed. After about fifteen seconds, she honks to give him the signal to boost up. Gio flips the proverbial switch in himself, feeling the energy of the Heart surging through his body. His heart rate increases. His lungs go to work. His feet almost have a mind of their own as he dashes forward. He feels like a human bolt of lightning as he leaves Andrea's car in the dust, clearing to the other side of the massive concrete ocean that was the Megamart parking lot in ten seconds. Andrea speeds up, gaining on him. He knows he can outrun her, but that wasn't the point of the exercise. With another honk, she signals for him to slow down. With a deep inhale through his nose, Gio wills himself to dial it back, returning to a normal pace. He feels a little tired, but not concerningly so. *I can do this,* he thinks. They continue the cycle of acceleration and deceleration in a circle around the parking lot for three more turns.

"Alright, Gio, I'm gonna go a little faster now! I want you to show me the fastest you can go with whatever you have left!" Andrea calls out.

Gio gives her a thumbs up. He's getting fatigued, but he can feel the exercise working. Flipping his switch back on, Gio takes off at full force, running in a straight line across the lot. He can hear the *vroooom* of Andrea's car as she shifts gears and pursues him. Despite Gio's incredible speed, she's gaining. And fast*! Is she crazy!* He thinks. There's a tingling in the back of his skull as Andrea's car gets closer and closer.

"Mom, what're you doing?!" he hears Rocky yell.

VROOOOOOOOM!! Her vehicle was directly behind him! On some form of instinct, Gio directs every ounce of energy in his legs and makes a jump for it. With the momentum built up from his speed, Gio leaps over seven feet in the air, executing a seamless backflip. He lands in a crouched position as the car skids to a halt in front of him.

"YO, THAT WAS AMAZING!!!" Sky yells from a distance.

Gio's emotions see-saw between excitement and terror as he realizes what he just did. Andrea steps out of the car with an evil grin on her face and says,

"I knew it."

Gio shakes his curls out of his face as he sits down on the ground, panting like a dog.

"Knew *what*?! You just tried to run me over!" he exclaims between breaths.

Andrea walks over and reaches out a hand. Gio grabs hold and hoists himself up.

"I mean, I knew I wasn't *going* to run you over. I figured your adrenaline boost also amplifies your situational awareness. Plus, it helps that you're already a gymnast."

Gio can't help but smile.

"You're crazy, you know that?" Andrea chuckles. "It worked."

As the two rejoin the others, Gio is met with shoulder pats and fist bumps.

"You got *hops*, dude!" says Rocky. "Seeing you run was already awesome, but that *backflip*! So good." Tasha compliments. "I agree. I'm *thoroughly* impressed", adds Mileena.

Sky hugs Gio from behind and gives him a friendly shake.

"Man, you need to enter the Olympics! You're amazing, Gio", he says.

Gio looks at Sky from behind, feeling all the blood rush to his cheeks. Sky smiling at him in awe with those big, doe brown eyes of his was doing funny things to Gio's chest. He licks his lips and replies,

"I'm pretty sure that would be cheating, but thanks."

Remembering there were still other people around, Gio gently slides out of Sky's embrace, but keeps smiling at him all the same. He then takes a seat on the trunk of Mileena's car to rest.

Tasha was next in rotation. She walks to the front of the group and shrugs.

"My powers showed up in self-defense like Rocky. I haven't really tried anything since that night, to be honest." "What exactly happened again? In detail", asks Andrea.

Tasha scrunches her face, recalling her encounter with the Boogeyman.

"Um, I remember when he grabbed me, I got scared and wished I was stronger. Next thing I know, I grab hold of some roots and miraculously pull myself free. When he couldn't drag me anymore, I tried to hit him and ended up punching a tree. But I hit it so hard, I made a bunch of twigs and branches fall as a distraction so I could get away."

"Soooo what, are you super strong or something?" asks Mileena. Tasha shrugs again. Andrea looks from Tasha to her Volvo and back again.

"Show us," she suggests.

Tasha nervously bites her lip as she approaches the car. She feels like her regular self. Not someone who can casually lift a car with their bare hands. Giving it a shot, Tasha squats down, grabs the bumper of the car, and tries pulling it up. As expected, the vehicle doesn't move, and a quick rush of pain shoots up her arms and back for trying. Tasha yanks her hands away from the bumper and curses under her breath. She'd been hoping what happened back in the forest wasn't just a fluke. Tasha stands back up, slapping her arms at her sides.

"I don't know what I'm missing," she mutters.

"This might sound stupid, but maybe you have to activate it," says Rocky. "True. You did say you wished you were stronger the moment it happened, right? Try it now." Andrea adds.

Tasha almost smacks her forehead. Of course! That *had* to be the trigger. Feeling more confident this time, she bends back down and grabs hold of the bumper. She closes her eyes and thinks really hard on one word: *Lift*! As she pulls, the same rush from the other night strikes her body like an invisible bolt of lightning. She can feel it. The power. The pure, unadulterated *power*! With a loud grunt, Tasha once again pulls up. *Creeeeaaaak.* The car actually begins to move! When Tasha opens her eyes, she can see her own hands lifting the back end of the Neon as the rear wheels raise two feet off the ground. It's heavy, of course, but a bearable kind of heavy. Feeling giddy and experimental, she exerts a little more force. Her arms are trembling, and sweat is raining from her brow, but she continues to raise the nearly 3-ton vehicle. Lo and behold, Tasha has the entire back end of Andrea's Volvo just about eye level. Her friends all erupt into loud applause, watching her.

"Alright!" "Wow!" "She really did it!" "Okay, Supergirl!"

Tasha smirks pridefully. What she can do is absolutely impressive. But also absolutely beginning to hurt. As she continues holding up the back of the car, a sharp, intense headache makes itself known in her frontal cortex. She hisses at the sensation, wondering why this is happening. Then it dawns on her. Her super strength not only has to be activated, but also produces a rather harsh strain, like a pulled muscle. As carefully as she can, Tasha slowly lowers the car back to the ground and nearly collapses as her body returns to normal. The muscles in her arms are throbbing in protest, but still she smiles as she catches her breath. If her powers were like a muscle, then she'd have to train them like such.

"Have I made my point?" she asks rhetorically as she rejoins the group. Sky gives her a fist bump.

"Super strength looks good on you, fearless leader. On that note, I think it's *my* turn now." *

Sky doesn't want to risk breaking more car windows. So, in order to properly demonstrate his ability, he walks over to the dumpster behind the building and drags an empty, dented oil drum over. Though the metal scraping against the concrete is *not* a pleasant sound in the ears. Luckily, it's empty and easy enough to drag. Planting it down in front of the group, Sky places his hands on both sides of the drum.

"So let me get this straight; you touch things and make them... vibrate?" asks Mileena with a hint of skepticism. Sky looks at her.

"It's cooler than it sounds. And a little more dangerous. Remember how I told you I shattered a windshield?"

Mileena raises her hands in mock surrender.

"Fair enough. Go on."

Sky closes his eyes and concentrates. He had to be careful not to put too much power and hurt his arms like last time. He feels the energy ripple through his fingertips into the metal of the drum, giving it a low but clearly visible rumble. There's a loud *tink tink tink tink* noise as the drum quakes in place on the ground.

"Dude, I *gotta* see what that feels like!" says Rocky.

Before anyone can stop him, the young boy reaches out and touches the drum. The moment Rocky's hand makes contact, his entire body locks up, and he yelps. Rocky yanks his hand away with a shudder.

"Holy *crap*! That felt like a joy buzzer on crack!" he exclaims. Sky grins at him and ceases the vibrations.

"That was me holding back, too. The reason that the windshield broke is cuz I rattled the car *that* intensely." "How does that work, exactly?" asks Gio.

"I think it's more than just vibrating," Mileena replies, "If I'm not mistaken, you have the ability to magnify oscillation."

Tasha turns her head in confusion.

"What does that mean for us non-straight-A students?" "Basically, Sky gave the car such an extreme shock in movement that the resonance broke the glass."

Sky looks down at his hands, feeling the tingling sensation subside.

"We'll see if I can break more than just glass in the future."

Last but certainly not least for the demonstrations was Mileena. As she grabs her bow and arrows, Rocky asks,

"You said your power was luck-bending or something like that, right? What's the bow for?" Mileena grins as she nocks an arrow on the string.

"Well, since *my* power is a little harder to explain, I figured I'd just show you. I haven't shot in years, but now's as good a time as any."

Without even thinking, all the technique Mileena learned from her *sofu* floods her brain. She places the end of the arrow between her middle and index fingers and draws the string back. Spine straight. Feet shoulder-width apart. Thumb just below her jaw. All systems go.

"Somebody give me a target", Mileena says with a smirk.

Despite her hesitation just days before, she can't deny feeling emboldened to show her new friends what she can do. Andrea points at a streetlight above one of the empty parking spaces not too far from where they're standing.

"Let's make it interesting. Hit the bulb of that thing."

Mileena nods, takes a deep breath, and lets the arrow fly. *Twing!* The arrow embarrassingly flies to the far right and clambers onto the ground.

"Uhhh, nice shot?" Sky jokes. Mileena nocks another arrow.

"I told you, I haven't shot in years. Besides, I just wanted to make my point before I used my power. Now watch *this.*"

With more confidence this time, Mileena internally awakens her ability. Everyone notices the green spark ignite from her finger. It travels up the arrow, landing at the point with an emerald glow before it disappears. *Twing!* This time, the arrow soars directly at the forty-foot-high streetlight. *Ksssh!* The arrow shatters the glass bulb before falling to the ground. *Bullseye*! As the group applauds and cheers for her, Mileena feels a swell of pride bubbling in her chest. She feels bad for fighting this before. This was good. Helpful. Heck, it was *fun*!

For the next half hour or so, the five youths spend their time using their abilities individually, with Andrea checking on them periodically. Rocky switches between lengthening his invisibility and seeing just how many glowing orbs he could create before his hands got too hot. So far, his limit was a dozen. Gio continued doing as many laps as he could around the parking lot at different speeds. Tasha lifts the back end of Andrea's car again several times, seeing how long she can sustain holding it off the ground before she gets a headache. She does four reps for approximately 30 seconds each before it becomes too much for her head to handle. Afterwards, she also begins practicing some of the close quarter combat her father used to teach. She's a little rusty at first due to being out of practice for some time. But after a while, she's performing perfect sweep kicks and roundhouses just like she used to. While Sky tests his vibrations at different levels on the oil drum, he discovers an interesting effect. By concentrating on a particular spot, the drum indents almost violently into itself. A neat trick he takes a mental note of. Mileena used her luck energy to execute more trick shots. After all of the streetlights in the parking lot were taken out, she decides to be a little mischievous. As Gio runs by her during one of his laps, Mileena snaps her fingers and thinks, *Trip. Harmlessly.* Suddenly, Gio's shoes come undone, and he rolls like a tumbleweed. He's unscathed, but still a little dirty. Gio swears at her but still laughs about it. Eventually, Andrea gives everyone a holler.

"I think that's enough for today! Lunch is on me! For real this time!"

Chapter 15
Let's Do This

After their thrilling but tiring practice session, Andrea takes everyone to Pizza Castle for a well-earned lunch. Gio looks around the booth they've settled in. Rocky is directly across from him between Andrea and Tasha. Mileena is on Gio's left. Sky, his right. While Rocky is busy gushing over Tasha, Andrea discusses theories with Mileena about her abilities. Meanwhile, Gio finds himself scooching closer to Sky, their legs pressed against one another. Gio decides to be bold and brushes his fingers over Sky's hand under the table. Sky gives Gio his trademark smirk, which makes the chest flutters return with a vengeance. Gio tries playing it cool by not giving Sky direct eye contact. He's still got a lot to think about, but he knows this unspoken thing between them can't stay unspoken much longer. Not that it was much of a secret anyway.

"Earth to Gio!" someone says, catching his attention.

Gio shakes his head out of his own thoughts. It was Andrea.

"I'm sorry, what?" he asks. "I asked if you wanted anything different or if you're good with two pepperoni and one supreme", she reiterates. Gio nods. "Oh. Yeah, sure, that's fine." Andrea stands up from the booth.

"I'll let you talk amongst yourselves for a bit while I go place our order."

As Andrea walks away, Rocky slams his hand on the table.

"I just wanna say, you guys are the *coolest*! I loved seeing what everyone could do!"

Gio can't help smiling at the boy's infectious energy. It certainly lights up the room.

"Yeah. Me, too", he adds. Sky begins rubbing at his wrists, which have grown red from his power use.

"Anybody wanna trade 'extras'? Making things vibrate is cool and all, but the recoil is killing me."

Mileena snaps her fingers as an idea comes to mind.

"I have a thought about that. You should get those compression sleeve things that the gym bros and athletes wear", she suggests.

Sky gasps in a fake dramatic fashion.

"Are you calling me fat, your highness?" he asks jokingly. Mileena rolls her eyes.

"They're supposed to help support muscles and prevent overextension, which is basically what your power does, the more you increase it. And yes, I am calling you fat."

The group shares a small but hearty laugh. Gio's enjoying this. They're just hanging out and telling jokes. Then his brain reminds him why they're all together in the first place, and he stops smiling. Ever the perceptive one, Tasha looks at him and asks,

"What's going on, Gio?"

Gio leans forward on the table with his elbows.

"I don't mean to be a buzzkill or anything, but what're we supposed to do now about our... situation?" "You mean the Boogeyman, don't you?" she asks.

Gio nods silently. Rocky pushes his glasses against his nose and says,

"I say we go back to that tunnel. There *have* to be more clues there about the Boogeyman or the Heart." "You're joking, right? We *barely* got away last time," says Gio.

Rocky gestures to everybody at the table.

"Yeah, but that was before *everyone* got their powers. If he shows up, we can kick his butt now!"

Mileena drums her fingers on the table.

"You know you sound insane, right? We have *one* practice session, and suddenly you're ready to play hero?" "It's not about being a hero! It's about getting some answers, and for some reason, I'm the only one trying to do that!"

The table goes quiet. Rocky had a point. For someone so young, he sure had a lot of initiative. He went off on his own in the middle of the night to try to find that basement. Meanwhile, Gio and the rest of them sat around worrying. Rocky looks at Tasha.

"What do *you* think?" he asks. Gio, Mileena, and Sky all look at her expectantly as well. Tasha slaps her hands on her legs.

"Once again, you're all looking to *me* for the final say-so?"

Sky nods. "Yup."

Tasha doesn't say anything at first. Just runs her hand through her locs with a heavy sigh. She then reaches into her backpack, pulls out her sketchbook, and sets it on the table. Before anyone can ask why, Tasha flips the book open to her last few entries. There are six whole pages of the Boogeyman, hand-drawn in scarily good detail. The most recent piece has the Boogeyman in his full, cloudy form, reaching out with clawed hands. Gio is uncomfortable just looking at it. Softly, Tasha speaks up,

"I've been drawing these almost every day since that night. Rocky's right. We need answers. But, nobody should do anything they don't want to do."

To everyone's surprise, Mileena is the first to put her hand in.

"I *don't* want to do this. Let me make that perfectly clear. But, I also don't want to bury my head in the sand anymore."

Sky puts his hand in next.

"I'm not turning this down and letting you make me look bad."

Gio looks at Mileena with her hesitant but willing resolve. Rocky, giddy and ready for action. Tasha, gentle yet strong. Finally, to Sky, who Gio can see is asking him with his eyes, *Please?* Without even thinking, Gio reaches forward and grabs Sky's hand. His entire body flushes with heat, realizing everyone can see. He knows there's not a hint of judgment. But he's still nervous about making his move in public. However, the nervousness pales in comparison to just how *right* his hand feels in Sky's. Gio smiles at the blond. With a deep breath, Gio says,

"Let's do this." And in his mind, he's not just talking about going back to Hillstone.

It took some heavy convincing for Andrea to let Rocky participate in this idea, but they all figured now was as good a time as any while there was still daylight. It was just past 4 pm. The sun was still up, but they had limited time before it began to set. They eat every slice of pizza, rest for a bit, then drive to Hillstone Park. Gio shakes his head as they pull into the parking lot and exit Mileena's car. Andrea parks right next to them. She's fussing over Rocky as he makes his way to the group.

"Just stay in the back and go invisible if a fight breaks out." "I will, Mom." "And try not to blind yourself or anyone else." "I won't, Mom." "And *please* don't break your glasses. Prescriptions cost, Rocky." "I *know*, Mom!"

Gio stifles a giggle. It's cute how much of a fuss Andrea is making over her superpowered son. He doubts his own mother would do the same. Rocky practically hides behind Gio after Andrea says something about his hair. The woman crosses her arms, squinting her eyes at Tasha in particular.

"I'm trusting you to keep my baby safe. If *anything* happens to him, you won't have to worry about the Boogeyman coming after you. Am I clear?"

Gio gulps. She's not exaggerating.

"He's in safe hands with us. Promise," says Tasha. Andrea nods.

"Good. I'll stay here, but keep in contact with me so I'm not losing my mind worrying." "Cell reception gets spotty the deeper we go into the forest. We'll do our best."

Andrea returns to her car and turns on her music. Gio feels bad. He knows she wants to come along, but she's the only one of them with no powers. If a fight did happen, there'd be nothing she could do. Mileena opens the trunk of her car and grabs the case with her bow and arrows. It's still daytime with a chance of running into park rangers, so she's keeping them in the case for the time being, so as not to attract attention. Gio grabs his wooden baseball bat from last time. That was less likely to be questioned. They were all about as prepared as they could be. Several groups of people, both entering and exiting the park, pass them by. *Lucky normies,* Gio thinks. They had no idea the rumors about this place were true. With a sense of dread weighing on their shoulders, Tasha, Gio, Rocky, Mileena, and Sky walk single file into Hillstone Park. It's relatively easy to find the same off-beaten path as before. To pass the time on their thirty-minute walk up the hill, over the barrier, and down the slope to the secret bridge, Sky manages to keep small talk going. To keep their minds off of impending doom, he asks them all simple questions. Tasha's favorite color? Turquoise. Rocky's favorite dish to cook? Chorizo con huevos. What was Mileena's Halloween costume plan later this year? Malibu Barbie. Gio's snack of choice? Candied walnuts and cheese cubes. Gio can't articulate enough in his mind how grateful he is for Sky doing what he's doing. If it was quiet the entire time, he might've come to his senses and run back home.

As the group come upon the stupid, rickety bridge, Gio hesitates. Tasha, Mileena, and Rocky all cross without a second thought. And yet, once again, the heights. The sounds of the crashing river below. They make Gio's bowels turn to mush. He tightens his grip on his bat, willing himself to get it together. Sky appears beside Gio and grabs his free hand.

"C'mon. I gotcha," he assures with a gentle smile.

Gio happily takes Sky's hand, and the two young men gingerly make their way across the bridge.

"I'm really glad you're here," says Gio. "I kinda have to be." Sky replies. "I meant here with... with me." Gio reiterates.

Sky stops walking for a second and looks into Gio's eyes with unexpected intensity.

"Listen, Gio, I know I'm Mr. Jokey Joke, but I can't handle this not being real."

Gio shakes his head.

"Sky, I *promise* you, it's real. I wouldn't take your hand if I didn't mean it." "But you're like, new to the whole guy thing, right? Well, I'm not. I've been played before by pretty boys who are too good-looking to take me seriously. It's basically a gay rite of passage."

Gio closes his eyes. He knows plenty of people find him conventionally attractive. It's been a thing ever since he hit puberty. He's never thought much of it or let it get to his head, so for Sky to think Gio is too good-looking to take him seriously is both flattering and sad. And also not true. Couldn't Sky know how he felt through the Link? In the spur of the moment, Gio embraces Sky with a hug. Sky returns the hug with a squeeze that cracks Gio's back in all the right places.

"You're a pretty boy too, Sky." Gio whispers.

He feels the warmth of Sky's body as the other boy laughs.

"Aw. You know how to make a girl feel special," he jokes.

"You guys coming or what?!" they hear Mileena yell from a distance.

"Get a room or get your butts in gear!"

Gio and Sky chuckle as they continue on, their fingers intertwined. After crossing the bridge and descending more hills, the group finally made it to the clover field clearing. They're able to easily locate the area with the trap door. Only this time, instead of a single boulder, there were three massive boulders the size of an outdoor generator, as well as the rotted log cluttering the way. Mileena crosses her arms.

"Boogeyman clearly doesn't want us to get back in," she says. Sky cracks his knuckles.

"We can take care of this. Tasha, mind helping me out?" "Sure."

Tasha squats down, grabs the bottom of one of the boulders, and activates her strength. She's able to lift it, though not without some considerable strain on her end. Quickly, she tosses it a few feet over to the side with a heavy thud. She repeats the process with the other two boulders before her head starts screaming in pain, forcing her to rest. At the same time, Sky crouches down and grabs hold of the log, imbuing it with his vibrational power. The log bounces up and down, noticeably shifting but still covering the trapdoor. Sky grunts as he significantly increases the vibration.

"Move, you stupid thing!" Sky growls in frustration.

Next thing he knows, *boom!* The log is sent rolling away, a good five or six feet, clearing the way.

"Whoa!" Rocky exclaims. Sky winces, rubbing his arms as they recover. Mileena gives him and Tasha pats on the back.

"Impressive. Do you two feel okay?" she asks. Sky gives his arms a shake.

"A little uncomfortable from the kickback, but I'll be fine. You, Tasha?" Tasha wipes some sweat from her brow.

"I'm good. My power just gives me headaches if I strain too much."

As her headache fades away, Tasha bends down and opens the trap door.

"Are we ready for this?" she asks. The group shake their heads. Tasha sighs.

"Me either. Let's go."

Chapter 16

The Unusual Suspect

Nobody is particularly excited to be back in the dark, dusty concrete tunnel. Although this time, it's much easier to see thanks to Rocky. The boy summons an orb of white light to follow them and act as their torch. With every step she takes, Tasha wonders if coming back here was the right decision. It may have been Rocky's idea, but for some reason, the others are all counting on *her* to lead them. Tasha doesn't know how or why she ended up in this position, but she's determined to do her best regardless.

At the moment, she can feel the fear and uncertainty radiating from everyone without even using the Link. Sky isn't even asking trivial questions anymore. *C'mon, Tasha. Raise morale or something,* she thinks to herself. Then she grins as she comes up with an idea.

"Hey Rocky, can you do something for me?"

Rocky's eyes light up as he holds the orb closer to his face.

"Literally *anything* for you", he replies.

Tasha chuckles. It's obvious he has a crush on her, but she doesn't mind. He's the least most obnoxious twelve year old she's ever met.

"You're the comic book expert. Why don't you come up with codenames for us?" she suggests. Rocky does a happy little skip.

"Hell yeah! I was hoping for a moment like this! For you, Mileena, I've got the perfect codename: Karma."

Mileena hums in approval.

"Wow. That *is* perfect." "Thanks. Now for Sky,-" "I swear, little man, if you name me 'Vibrator', I will rattle your bones apart."

The whole group snorts with laughter.

"No, but seriously, whatcha got for me, dude?" asks Sky. Rocky hums then snaps his fingers.

"How about Shakedown?" "Ha! I like it!" "What about me? I was thinking 'Cheetah' for myself", says Gio. Rocky shakes his head.

"If your powers were more animal-like, then maybe. But I've got something better for you." "Oh yeah? What?" "Pace. Since your speed comes from adrenaline." "Oooh. Dang, you're good."

Tasha smiles to herself. Not only was her idea working, but she was getting excited about her own potential codename.

"So, what do you have for me, Rocky? Heavyweight? *Please* say it's not Heavyweight." "That's pretty funny, actually, but no. I think your codename should be Angel."

Tasha nearly stops in her footsteps. That was a little unexpected. Though not unwelcome.

"Angel? You really think so?" she says. Rocky just smirks at her.

"You're powerful and you hit hard, so yeah. And I do mean the other definition too because you're obviously-."

The boy turns beet red and slaps his hand over his mouth before he can finish his sentence. This makes Tasha smile even more. She finds the name and Rocky's reasoning all very flattering.

"So what's *your* name gonna be, Rocky?" asks Mileena.

"Well, since Kid Estrella is already taken, I was thinking of something like 'Beacon' or 'The Torch'. Maybe even 'Shining Devil'."

Tasha gently pats him on the shoulder.

"Sorry, Rocky, but you're more of a light switch than a devil," she says with a giggle. Rocky looks offended for a second, then brightens back up.

"You're right, Tasha! I *am* a light switch! Off and on. Which makes me..."

Rocky waves his hands and makes them gleam with blinding light.

"A Luminator! *The* Luminator!"

"Ah, you made your point! Shut it off, Luminator!" Gio exclaims. Rocky giggles mischievously.

Tasha smiles, internally giving herself a pat on the back. She can feel all of them gaining some confidence. Including herself. Karma, Pace, Shakedown, The Luminator, and her. *I'm the mighty Angel... Man, that sounds dorky.*

A few moments later, the group reaches the wooden door at the end of the tunnel. The door's handle is wrapped in chains. Sky vibrates them loose enough to yank off. Rocky steps in first, closing his fist to dismiss his orb. It's odd. There's something different about the cellar this time around. As Tasha, Mileena, Sky, and Gio file in, they all can tell whoever owns this place did something drastic. Tasha turns to her peers and says,

"The Heart's not here anymore." "You're right. We'd probably sense the hell out of that thing the closer we got, but... there's nothing", says Mileena.

Tasha puts her hands on her hips. The thing was freaky and gross, but the fact that the Heart has been rehidden is highly concerning. Gio points to the rusty ladder in the corner of the room.

"We should see where that goes," he suggests. Rocky nods. "On it."

Before he can move to climb, Tasha grabs the collar of Rocky's shirt and pulls him back.

"No way. We don't know what's up there, and your mom told us to keep you safe, so you do *not* go first."

Tasha walks to the base of the ladder and looks up. It's not that tall. Ten feet or so. But it's dark at the top. There's no telling what's waiting for them. It's making her stomach do cartwheels. She *really* doesn't want to be there. Tasha grabs hold and climbs before she can change her mind.

As Tasha reaches the top of the ladder, she's met with the wooden floor of a narrow, empty closet space. There's a door with slits in front of her. Through the slits, she can see another lock on the outside. *Let's get this over with.* With a quick, "*Hyah*!", Tasha chambers her right leg and kicks the door wide open. Easy work. As Tasha steps out, she's greeted with what looks like the inside of a small log cabin. There's not much around to look at. A metallic desk. A circular table with four chairs. A two-seater navy blue sofa. Hardwood floors. A ceiling fan. Mini fridge next to the desk. And an extensive map of Hillstone Park on the far-right wall. There are cobwebs and dirt all over everything, but also a strange sense that someone had been there lately. Tasha purses her lips.

"A cabin in the woods. I'd probably find this funny if it wasn't so creepy", she says to herself.

Tasha walks a few steps into the space, taking a further look around. There's an ashtray on the little table, with three disturbingly fresh-looking cigarette butts. She looks down at the ground. There are boot prints in the dust here and there throughout the house.

"Everything okay up there or have you become a stereotype?!" Gio shouts from below. Tasha rolls her eyes.

"Yeah! Come on up!" she calls back.

One by one, Gio, Mileena, Sky, and Rocky climb up the ladder and out of the closet. Sky looks around, scratching his head in confusion.

"Where the *hell* are we?" he asks. "I think Gio was right last time," Tasha replies,

"See that map by the desk? This is probably an old ranger station."

Mileena shrugs. "I guess that explains the tunnel. We're technically still in the park. Maybe it's an emergency escape route or something." "So whoever the Boogeyman is uses this place as his supervillain hideout", adds Rocky.

He's a little too enthusiastic about that revelation for Tasha's comfort. She walks over to the desk to see if she can find anything.

"He's been here recently. Watch your backs." she warns.

Gio double grips his bat. Mileena knocks an arrow. Sky cracks his knuckles. Rocky's hands light up. The four of them stay close as Tasha inspects the desk. She finds a drawer underneath and pulls it open. Inside, she finds a single Polaroid photo. Tasha gingerly grabs it to get a closer look. It's a decades old picture showing a group of four young adults. The first is a black man with braided cornrows, brown eyes, and a soul patch. He has his arms around the waist of a short, blond woman throwing up the middle finger. They were clearly a couple. Next to them was a tall, good-looking rocker type with wavy black hair down to his waist and a beer can in each hand. The last person is a dorky-looking guy with a hook-shaped nose, slumped shoulders, and an *awful* middle-part haircut. He has a cigarette hanging out of the side of his mouth, but it just makes him look like a try-hard. Tasha chuckles softly to herself. Sky, who notices her staring at the picture, walks over and asks,

"Who's that?"

Tasha shrugs. "It was in this drawer. I don't know who these people are, though." she replies. The others gather around and take turns looking at the picture. Sky's eyes widen as he points at the dorky guy.

"Holy *crap!* I'm pretty sure that's Mr. Charles!" he exclaims. Mileena gasps in confirmation. "Whoa, you're right! That's totally him and his stupid face!" "Mr. Charles? You mean the 'Dickface fascist'?" asks Rocky. "The very same." she replies.

Tasha brings the picture closer to her face. It was true! This photo was of a twenty-something Isaac Charles, now principal of Olligrove High. Tasha looks from the photo to her group.

"This *can't be a* coincidence," she says, "Either he's involved with the Boogeyman or,..."

Gio snorts.

"No. Nuh uh. There's no way you're suggesting our principal is what, a *supervillain*?"

Tasha looks him dead in the eye. "Yes, that's *exactly* what I'm saying."

Before anyone else responds, a sharp, cold feeling creeps up the back of Tasha's neck. It was a frightening, ominous feeling. Like the suspense of an approaching jump scare in a horror movie. Or the pause right before a roller coaster drops from the top of the tracks. Only that was more fun. This was not. Tasha shivers, and so do her friends. Something bad was about to happen. Right. Now.

"We need to leave," Tasha warns quietly.

Eeeeeeeek. The five all bunch together as the sound of the front door opening fills the room. There's still some daylight outside, but as the door slowly opens further, all they can see is a mass of black, gray smoke filling the doorway. It was him! He was *there!* The Boogeyman! The top half of a humanoid shape emerges from the cloudy form, stretching unnaturally into the living room. It has no facial features, but they can all tell he's staring right at them. With its deep, warbly voice, it croons,

"I'm *going to enjoy this far more than I should."*

Nobody has time to process their fear as the creature goes in for the attack. Two smoky arms reach out with lightning speed, expanding in shape and mass, and take a wide arched swing. *Wham!* Both Sky and Rocky are knocked into the right wall. The arms take another swing at Mileena, who thankfully reacts on time and yells,

"Miss!"

Green energy erupts from her fingers. The arms soar right over her but go for Gio instead. On instinct, the young man does a backflip and dodges. Before Boogeyman can make another attack, Tasha springs into action and grabs the chair by the desk. She gathers her might and sends the chair flying straight into the Boogeyman's face. It doesn't seem to hurt him much, but he is stunned for three seconds. It's all Mileena needs. In those three seconds, she pours her luck energy into her bow and fires a green-lit arrow into the Boogeyman's chest area. The smoky figure grunts in pain for a second, but then he laughs as the arrow is pushed out of his body and onto the ground. Tasha swears to herself. Of *course,* this thing can reduce damage. Why make it easy for them? In the blink of an eye, the Boogeyman slinks its way over to Sky. Its fingers morph into slinky, shadowy tendrils that wrap around Sky's torso. Gio rushes forward, bat in hand. Another lashing tendril ejects itself from the Boogeyman's back and swipes Gio's ankle, tripping him hard on his back. Tasha runs forward, particularly focusing on increasing the strength of her fists. She throws a right hook at the monster's side, but all it does is phase right through it and cause her to trip as well. The Boogeyman's creepy, tentacle-like hands remain firmly grasped on Sky. With a determined grunt, Sky grabs hold of the very being constricting him and sends a powerful wave of vibrations. The Boogeyman's form ripples as it's stunned from the shock. Recovering from his slam against the wall, Rocky forms a red glowing orb in his palm and throws it at their opponent. It goes through him like everything else.

"Rocky, no! Disappear!" Tasha yells.

Rocky somersaults out of the way and turns invisible. Shaking off the effects of Sky's vibrations, the Boogeyman turns around and looks at Tasha. Before it can retaliate, Tasha grips the bottom of the sofa, focuses, and lifts it in front of her like a shield. The Boogeyman grabs the couch from her hands and *BAM!* He slams it violently back on the floor, nearly splitting it in half. However, he's distracted long enough for Mileena to fire another luck-embedded arrow. *Twing!* It hits the target its right shoulder. The Boogeyman turns and growls in fury at her. He lashes out, now intent on wrapping his tendrils around her. Mileena screams in fear, her fingers fumbling to grab another arrow. Luckily, Gio intercepts and knocks the tendril away with his bat. Boogeyman sprouts several more shadowy tendrils, but Gio's speed and reaction time allow him to block every strike. Tasha can barely see how fast Gio's swinging. He almost looks like an anime swordsman, which would be cooler under better circumstances. Tasha shakes her head. This was insane! They've been holding ground, but they can't keep this up. She can feel herself draining from her power usage, so she's sure the others are as well. With a deep breath, Tasha puts her remaining energy into one more burst of power. With a loud grunt, she grabs one half of the split sofa, raises it above her head, and throws it as hard as she can. *WOMP!* It smacks into the Boogeyman so hard that the impact shoves the monster through the kitchen window in a spray of broken glass. Exhaustion is rapidly taking hold of Tasha's body and her head is killing her, but there's no time for that!

"Everybody out! *Now*!" she commands. Her friends follow her lead as she bolts out the front door and into the woods. As they distance themselves from the cabin, they can hear Boogeyman already recovering to pursue them. Being the heftiest, Sky is having a harder time keeping up. As Mileena, Rocky, and Gio all push forward at full speed, Sky falls further and further behind. No. Tasha is determined to get them *all* out of here! She turns around and links their arms together as they run.

"C'mon, brave knight! You can do this!" she encourages. Sky is beet red and wheezing like an asthmatic.

"I think I peed a little!!" he huffs.

Tasha rolls her eyes. Even in the face of danger, he's still got jokes.

"GET YOUR ASSES BACK HERE!" the monster demands.

Tasha feels herself about to cry. It was *still* after them! As she looks back, she can see the threatening, black cloud gaining on them alarmingly fast. She's out of energy! So was Sky! Just as the loathsome creature gets within ten feet, a flurry of colored orbs hurtle past Tasha's head and right into the Boogeyman's face. Boogeyman roars in frustration and flies in the opposite direction, clawing at its face as it disappears into the distance. Tasha looks ahead and sees Rocky, Gio, and Mileena running back to them. On the verge of tears, Tasha grabs Rocky and pulls him into a tight hug.

"Nice aim, Rocky", she compliments. Rocky hugs her back. "You save my life, I save yours."

After the hug, Tasha looks around at her circle. They're all panting heavily and covered in sweat, but they were alive and in one piece. Tasha clears her throat and proclaims,

"We are *never* coming back to that tunnel or that house again! Understood?!"

Gio, Sky, Mileena, and Rocky all murmur their agreements. Tasha nods. "Good. Now let's go."

Because they left from the front of the house rather than back through the tunnel, Tasha and her friends were all in unfamiliar territory. Luckily, they quickly found a dirt path after descending countless more hills. Tasha was ready to fall asleep right there on the

forest floor. Between their practice session, the walk and the fight, everyone was beat. Sky doesn't even have it in him to make any more jokes. It was about 6pm according to Tasha's phone. The sun was almost set. As Rocky texts his mom to let her know they're on their way back, a thought occurs to Sky now that he had a second to think.

"Question: Where did Boogeyman come from?" "What do you mean?" asks Tasha.

"I mean, that place looked pretty uninhabited. Like, obviously, he was there recently, but it didn't seem like he *lived* there, ya know what I mean? Plus, he came in through the front door. So I'm thinking, from where?"

Mileena looks at him with mild shock.

"Didn't take you for the detective type", she says with a smirk. Sky chuckles.

"Don't act *too* surprised. I'm goofy, not dumb." he retorts.

Gio scratches the back of his neck and says, "Maybe we'll get lucky and find out once we reach the end of this road."

Unfortunately, they have no such luck. After ten more minutes of walking, the group reaches a second parking lot on the other side of Hillstone Park. With multiple vehicles about, there's sadly no way of knowing which one could belong to the Boogeyman. Back to square one.

Chapter 17

Friday Night Creepin'

Any scratches and bruises sustained from the battle are fully healed by the time everyone reaches the Castillo house. While seated at the kitchen table, Andrea graciously provides the teens with some much-needed water. Once Sky and the others explain to Andrea about their encounter with the Boogeyman, she grabs a bottle of tequila from her freezer and drinks straight from the bottle. Sky is a little taken aback seeing a teacher doing this. Then again, her son just fought a monster.

"So," she begins after she puts the bottle down, "What I'm hearing is that my boss is a supervillain with a hideout in the middle of the woods."

"We *think* he is," Mileena clarifies, "There were three other people in that picture with him." "Well, even if it's not him, he's involved in some way. It's the most we've got to go on," adds Tasha.

"Any chance you grabbed that photo on your way out?" Andrea asks.

Tasha puts her face in her hands and groans. Clearly, she hadn't. Sky pats her on the back.

"Don't sweat it, fearless leader. I'm pretty sure the only thing on our minds was 'Holy crap, we're gonna die!'"

Andrea takes another giant gulp of tequila.

"It's okay, Mom. We actually kicked his ass a little bit", her son chimes in. With a scoff, Gio replies, "Hardly. That thing was *way* stronger than I thought. We did okay at best."

Andrea puts down the bottle and clears her throat.

"First of all, Rocky, you're getting a little too comfortable cursing around me, so watch yourself. Secondly, you need to get more evidence. Isaac Charles is a *major* prick, but supervillain is a *big* accusation." "Well, we can't go back for that picture, that's for damn sure," says Mileena. Sky grins as he comes up with an idea.

"Sounds like it's time for a good old-fashioned stakeout."

He looks over to Tasha to see what she thinks. She sighs, contemplating this course of action. Then Sky adds,

"Unless somebody has a better idea outside of going back." "I would rather eat drywall than go back," says Rocky. Tasha looks around the table.

"Fine. Raise your hand if you're up for a stakeout." Everyone raises their hands. "Good. We'll take tomorrow to rest, meet up Friday after school, then take it from there."

Sky yawns.

"As fun as this has been, I'm ready to call it a night. We should probably head home." "Aww. You guys have to go already?" Rocky asks sadly. Andrea puts a hand on his shoulder.

"I'll excuse you from school tomorrow since you had a rough day, but you *still* have homework to do", she reminds him. Rocky slumps in his chair, groaning dramatically. Tasha chuckles and gives him a friendly head scratch.

"It'll be alright, Rocky. We have work to catch up on, too." she says. That makes him smile.

The teens say goodbye to the Castillos as Mileena drives them home. Sky is the first to be dropped off. Before he exits the car, Gio takes his hand and gives it a kiss which makes him giddy. Sky borderline proposes to him right there. Cute, funny, a gymnast, a musician, *and* a gentleman? Sky *still* can't believe his crush is reciprocated.

** Thursday goes by rather nicely. Sky goes to school, serves his daily detention, but then is met with a lovely surprise afterwards. Gio and Mileena greet him at the front steps and invite him to the Caffeine Commute for a hangout. Tasha is occupied elsewhere with her friend Jasmine. Rocky simply plays video games at all day. Hanging out at the coffee shop is a very welcome change of pace. For once, Sky was spending time with his new friends without talks of the Boogeyman or their powers. They simply chatted, made jokes, exchanged stories, and enjoyed the springtime air. Sky feels bad for being flat broke and unable to contribute, but Mileena is gracious enough to foot the bill. After a while, she heads out to catch up on her chores, leaving Sky to walk Gio back home. Sky keeps his composure for the most part. He and Gio hold hands as they walk and continue to make casual conversation. However, his stomach is still doing flips every time

Gio makes direct eye contact. They get some looks from strangers here and there, which is also nerve-racking. Sky isn't used to eyes being on him. Once they reach the front porch of Gio's house, Sky considers kissing him. He chickens out at the last second. Gio takes it in stride, letting Sky know that he's still nervous, too. Sky goes home that night wanting to slap himself for not kissing Gio. They're on the verge of actually starting something, and yet he can't seem to get out of his own way.

Friday arrives at last. The day Sky engages in amateur sleuthing. After sitting through another dreadfully long and dull detention, Sky bolts out of the room and nearly bumps into Mr. Mays.

"Whoa, smartass. You got a date or something?" he asks, his voice more hoarse than usual. Sky grins as he collects himself.

"Kind of. Do you?" "Get outta here." "Getting!"

He laughs to himself, heading straight to Andrea's classroom. She had to stay behind to grade papers, so she messaged the teens earlier to meet there when the time came. Tasha, Gio, and Rocky, who'd been picked up a little earlier, were all present. Mileena shows up a minute later, only with a deep frown on her face.

"Hey. What's wrong?" asks Tasha. Mileena sighs. "My friend Dawn called in sick, so I've gotta cover her shift tonight." "Well, can't somebody else do it?" asks Rocky, but Mileena shakes her head. "Dawn's my favorite coworker, and I owe her one. I know this is asking a lot, but... can one of you please stay with me? This Boogeyman crap still has me shook, and I don't want to be by myself."

The others look around at each other. "Well, we don't really need *all* of us to spy on Mr. Charles", says Sky.

Tasha smiles gently and raises her hand. "I got you, girl. Will your manager be upset with me just sitting at a table the whole time?" "Nah. I'll just let him know you're a friend of mine. Some people bring their kids to work and do that same thing anyway."

Rocky smiles and links his arms between Sky and Gio.

"That means it's boys' night for us", he says excitedly. "Just don't do anything stupid," Andrea warns, "If Isaac catches you, it's gonna be really hard to explain the situation. It doesn't pay great, but I'd *really* like to keep my job."

Rocky laughs mischievously.

"No worries, Mom. Total stealth mode."

Mileena tosses her car keys to Sky. Even though he doesn't have a cars, he's the only other person in the group with a permit.

"Sounds like a plan."

After waiting a little while longer, Tasha and Mileena leave together to go to Sizzle Bay. Thanks to Catherine-Bethany also being in her class, Andrea easily manages to find her information and give Sky the Charles' home address. Sky drives him, Gio, and Rocky to said location just as the sun sets around 6pm. The Charles family lived in a three-story house on one of the nicer blocks in the neighborhood. The complete opposite of where Sky resides. He laughs to himself as he parks near the curb two houses down.

"What's so funny?" asks Rocky. Sky turns off the car and rolls up the windows. "I just expected Mr. Charles' place to be a fiery hell pit since he's the devil and all." Gio laughs at his joke.

"Who knows? Maybe we'll get lucky and see his horns after he takes off that *stupid* toupee."

Sky and Rocky both laugh in reply. The boys then quiet down as the front door to Charles' house opens. They see Isaac letting out the family's golden retriever to go potty before closing the door.

"What exactly are we looking for again?" asks Rocky. "I don't know, honestly. Just to find something, *anything* to indicate he's the Boogeyman." Sky replies. Gio crosses his arms. "I'm already bored. You sure we shouldn't sneak in or something?" he asks.

Sky shakes his head. "*Way* too risky. Besides, I remembered to bring you something." "Oh yeah? What?"

Sky reaches into his backpack and pulls out a pack of candied walnuts and a bag of cheddar cheese cubes. Gio's eyes twinkle with excitement.

"A You remembered." "Of course I did." Rocky pretends to gag in the back seat. "You two are giving me diabetes."

It's 8:05 pm. Two *long* hours have passed. The sun is no longer out. The streetlights have clicked on in the dim of night. Other than letting out the dog and Mrs. Charles coming home from whatever her job was, nothing noteworthy happens while watching the house. Rocky brought along his tablet to play mobile games, but he quickly grew bored with them after the first hour. Sky and Gio mostly listened to music from Gio's phone. Not much is said as the two take turns with the binoculars Rocky provided. Where he got them from was a mystery. Sky looks in the backseat to check on the kid, finding things to be a bit too quiet. The boy was softly snoring against the window. Sky smiles at himself.

"Luminator decided it's naptime," he says with a laugh. Gio yawns. "I can't blame him. Stakeouts are *way* more exciting on TV."

Sky realizes they are essentially alone again, with Rocky asleep. Gio is sitting right across from him. Looking at Sky with those crystal blue eyes and that impossibly perfect mop of curly hair. Sky bites his lip, thinking, *I really want to kiss you*. Gio smirks, leaning forward a bit.

"You can, y'know," he says. Sky shakes his head. "Can what?" he asks, his face turning pink. Gio rolls his eyes. "The Link, Sky. I know what you're feeling, remember?" he points out.

Sky suddenly feels the urge to open the car door and run away. Instead, he retreats as much as he can into his seat. Gio sighs with frustration and turns off his music.

"What is it, Sky? We've been dancing around each other for the past week since we met. I know you know I like you back, but you keep pulling away from me. What's the problem?"

Sky grips the steering wheel. He's impressed by Gio's straightforward approach. However, it's about time Sky comes clean with him.

"Chris Spinner," he whispers. "Who's Chris Spinner?" asks Gio.

Sky grips the steering wheel tighter, the mere mention of that name bringing back some old anger.

"Gio, I've known I was gay since middle school, but I hadn't really done anything until tenth grade. There was this guy. Chris Spinner. He's one of the football jocks, but sometimes he'd meet me behind the cafeteria building to 'partake' if you know what I mean. He knew I was holding. Anyway, Chris is really cute. Athletic. Charismatic. A lot like you, actually. We used to just make small talk while we smoked, then go our separate ways. As time went on, I started getting into him, like an idiot. One day, I invited him over to my house. Just to hang out. To my surprise, he said yes. So while we were in my room and um, elevated if you will, at one point Chris asked me if I was gay. I told him yes. I asked if he was, too. He looks at me and says, 'Maybe.' In the heat of the moment, I kissed him."

Sky pauses, gauging Gio's reaction. Gio gestures for Sky to continue. So he does.

"Some stuff went down that night, but uh, I'll spare you those details. Now, I was *fully* delusional. Absolutely head over heels, thinking this fat slob miraculously landed a hot football player. But alas, my luck dried up like the Sahara. After that night in my room, Chris stopped meeting me outside for smoke sessions. He completely ghosts me and pretends not to see me when we pass each other in the halls. In my head, I'm thinking maybe he's just nervous about being with me or too scared to come out."

Sky squeezes his eyes closed, feeling the hot approach of tears building with the next part of his story.

"A couple of weeks later, I start seeing Chris walking down the halls with one of his other teammates,... holding hands. In public. I'm still in denial, thinking there's no way he's dating one of his teammates. It gets to the point where one day, I actually wait by the football field after one of his practices to try and catch him. I manage to get Chris in private and I tell him, 'Hey, don't take this the wrong way, but... I'm kinda afraid you only fooled around with me as an experiment.' Chris looks me dead in the eye and says, 'Aw. Don't be afraid."

Sky covers his eyes, not wanting Gio to see him on the verge of crying.

"Chris Spinner got to become a 'gay icon' among his team with his hot new boyfrien d,... because of me. Hooray."

Gio grabs Sky's hands and lowers them away from his face.

"Sky, listen to me; what Chris did was cruel and disgusting, but *I'm not him.* The reason I've been so hesitant is because... well, I've never had someone affect me so quickly the way you do. Girl *or* guy. You're really funny. And you're also kind, protective, and brave, and it kills me that you don't think you're cute just because you're a bigger guy. If anyone's lucky, *I* am."

For once, Sky is speechless. Gio is 100 percent serious. No Link. No flirting. No bull. Sky sniffles, smiling again.

"I'm sorry, man. I guess I thought I was over the Chris thing."

Gio takes Sky's hand.

"Heartbreak is messy. All you can do is try to push through it, and find someone who would *never* do that to you."

Sky bites his lip, struggling to maintain eye contact. "There's not a lot going on in my life to inspire faith, bro." he says. Gio just scoots closer, pressing their foreheads together.

"Well, you've got superpowers now. And you've got Tasha, and Mileena, Rocky, An drea,... and me."

Sky can't take the tension anymore. He puts a finger under Gio's chin and *finally* makes lip contact. It's a smooch that lasts for a millisecond, but it lights Sky's entire body like a river of warm fire. He chuckles, basking in the surreal moment he's been wanting for over a week. Gio chuckles with him, brushing his hair out of his face. "Took you long enough, dummy." "Blame my inner saboteur. He's a straight-up menace."

Suddenly, Rocky's eyes snap open as he up sits straight. "I'm up, I swear!"

Sky and Gio chuckle some more, gently letting each other go.

"Total stealth mode, little man." Sky jokes. Rocky rubs the sleep out of his eyes. "Yeah, whatever. Has anything happened yet?" he asks. Gio takes the binoculars and grins.

"Nothing with Mr. Charles, but I do see something *very* interesting with his daughter."

Sky grabs the binoculars from Gio to see for himself. On the second floor, leaning out her bedroom window was Catherine-Bethany Charles. She was a thin, generically pretty girl with shoulder-length brown hair and a beauty mark under her left eye. She was currently smoking a cigarette and waving the smoke out into the night air. Sky shakes his head.

"Looks like somebody didn't pay attention in health class." Rocky leans up to see what they're talking about and immediately grimaces.

"*That's* the girl that got Tasha in trouble?" he asks with a surprising amount of menace. Sky nods.

"Yup. I wish we could get revenge for our girl somehow." Rocky grins evilly and says, "Allow me."

With a snap of his fingers, he creates a tiny but powerfully bright white orb in his hands and directs it out the window. It soars from the car right into Catherine-Bethany's eyes. She screams, dropping the cigarette from her hand to the ground below. They all witness her mother rush into her room to see the cause of the noise and sniff the air. Sky can't make out what's said, but the girl is clearly being scolded for the cigarette. Her mom grabs her by the arm and yanks her out of the room. The three boys have a fit of side-stitching laughter. That just made Sky's entire night. Well, that and finally kissing Gio. Yeah. That was *very* nice.

Chapter 18
Lemonade

Mileena looks down at her phone and smiles. Sky sent a message to the group chat letting them know that Rocky just helped get Catherine-Bethany in trouble during their watch. Good. She might not have known her for long, but Mileena would bring all kinds of bad luck to anyone who hurt Tasha's feelings. Rodney, her manager, snaps his fingers, getting her attention.

"Hey, put the phone away. Table 3 is asking for refills and we just had an 8-top walk-in", he informs her.

Mileena complies, straightening her apron and grabbing a tray. Friday nights were always busy at Sizzle Bay, but she didn't mind. Unlike Sunday shifts, she actually manages to get decent tips on Fridays. Plus, being busy helped keep her mind occupied. Mileena does her best to suppress thoughts of the Boogeyman as she carries on with her tasks, but it's only helping so much. It was one thing to see it in her dreams and to hear about it from her friends. But seeing that thing in person was a *whole* different ball game. As far as superpowers granted by the Heart, the Boogeyman hit the jackpot. Mileena would be impressed if it weren't so terrifying. *Thank God for Tasha,* she thinks to herself. She has no clue how willing she'd be to participate in exploring abandoned tunnels and fighting shadow monsters if Tasha wasn't so natural at bringing them all together. Mileena looks over at the corner booth where Tasha was sitting. She was stirring her straw in her lemonade while absentmindedly staring off into the distance. Mileena takes a second to tune into the Link, just to see if she feels anything. She gets a ping. There's sadness. Remembrance. And a craving for cheesecake. Mileena takes note of that.

Thirty-five minutes pass by before Mileena can finally take her break. After checking out a family of six, she heads to the kitchen to grab something special from the cooler. A piece of cheesecake with raspberries and a brown sugar topping. Mileena takes the piece and sits down at the booth with Tasha, presenting it to her with a grin. Tasha's eyes brighten up at the sight of her dessert.

"Aww. How'd you know I was,...? Nevermind. Of course." The two girls giggle as Tasha digs in. The Link took some getting used to at first, but it definitely has its perks.

"So, how's your shift so far?" Tasha asks in between bites. Mileena shrugs, flipping her ponytail over her shoulder. "Busy, but it's fine. I should get at *least* a hundred or so in tips by the end of the night. What's up with you, though?"

Tasha puts down her fork and points at her glass of lemonade. Mileena is naturally confused.

"What's wrong? Is it nasty? I can get you something else", she offers. Tasha chuckles, shaking her head no.

"Nah, girl, it's good. *Real* good. It's just... My mom *loved* her some lemonade. It was her favorite drink on a hot summer day. It's been almost four years since my parents died, and sometimes, the most random things make me think about them."

Mileena looks at the glass. It's so mundane. Just a glass of lemonade. A basic mixture of lemon juice, sugar, and ice water. Funny how such a seemingly little thing can ignite something so major in a person's mind. Despite their issues separately, Mileena still has both of her parents in her life. She felt bad enough losing her *sofu*. The potential grief over her parents' leaving this world would probably ruin her. Mileena looks at Tasha and asks,

"How?" "How what?" "How are you still so,... I don't know, spirited and uplifting?" Tasha wipes away a single tear, managing a smile.

"Because I have to. Everything I am, it came from them."

Tasha holds out her hands, nodding for Mileena to grab them. When she does, she closes her eyes and is hit with imagery. There's a handsome, light-skinned black man with curly red hair. Tasha's father, Rick. He's showing a five-year-old Tasha how to kick a punching bag. He gives her a high five after a successful push kick. Then, there's a beautiful, curvy, dark skinned black woman with a shaved head, twisting Tasha's hair. Her mother, Shanté. She's playing smooth jazz and singing to her. Tasha rolls her eyes at first, but then she sings along. After that, there's Tasha's finger painting on the front porch while her mom watches. A smile on her face and a glass of lemonade in her hand.

There are quick flashes of other memories from Tasha's life with her parents. Birthdays. Cookouts. Shopping. Christmases. Car rides. Dinners. Lastly, Mileema sees a memory of Tasha's mom and dad waking her up for her first day of freshman year. The year that they passed away. Tasha is shockingly happy waking up, giving them both big hugs. Mileena softly lets go of Tasha's hands, feeling herself tear up from seeing such beautiful memories. Mileena sniffles, wiping away several tears.

"You obviously have a better connection to this Link than any of us, ya showoff."

They laugh together. A heavy chunk of the sadness has shifted away into something lighter and clearer. Gratitude. Catching her breath, Tasha says,

"You know, I am *so* glad to have another girl on this team of ours." Mileena snaps her fingers in agreement. "Two girls of *color* at that." "Damn right."

Tasha grabs her lemonade and finally takes a sip.

"So tell me, *Karma*, how far do you think your powers can go?" she asks. Mileena drums her fingers on the table.

"Good question. My ability seems to have three important factors: area, intent, and focus. It's about who or what is around me, what I'm trying to do, and how much I'm concentrating to make it happen. Truth is, I really have no idea how extreme I can get. What about you, *Angel*? Think you'll be benchpressing semi-trucks in the future?"

Tasha takes a napkin and plays with it between her fingers. "Time will tell."

After her downtime was over, Mileena was hard at work for the remainder of her time. Tables are served. Counters are wiped. All side work completed. The clock strikes 9:30pm. Mileena's shift was finally over. After counting her drawer and collecting her tips for the night, Mileena heads over to the table with Tasha, sighing with relief as she sits down.

"Man, I'm tired. Any word from the boys?" she asks as she lets her hair down. Tasha purses her lips.

"Nope. Other than getting CB in trouble, they said nothing else has happened all night." "Crap. Maybe they should just call it in." "Yeah, you're probably right."

Just then, Rodney approaches the table.

"Alright Mil, you're good to go. Just do me a favor and take that garbage out with you on your way." "Okay. Night, Rodney." "Goodnight, Mileena and friend."

Mileena clocks out, grabs said garbage bag, and exits the back door with Tasha right behind her. As soon as the two girls step outside into the night, they begin feeling cold drops of water hit their skin. A thundering crack echoes through the sky, instantly giving way to rain. Mileena groans as she quickly runs over to the dumpster and throws the bag inside.

"Aw man, I didn't know it was supposed to rain tonight! I *hate* getting my hair wet!" she laments. Tasha closes her eyes and smiles as the raindrops pelt her face.

"It's spring, girl. Rain happens at any time, and I *love* it", she says. Mileena rolls her eyes. "C'mon, let's just get out of here before-"

Both Mileena and Tasha pause. As the rain continues to pour, Mileena feels an *awful* sense of dread in the back of her neck. The same tension she felt back at the cabin when,... *Oh no.*

"Tasha... h-h-he's here", she whispers. On cue, Tasha balls her fists. Mileena's eyes dart left and right. It was dark in the alley with nothing but a dim light above the back door of the restaurant. They can't call for help. They'd be putting her coworkers in danger. Mileena gulps nervously. All five of them fought him at once last time, and they still barely escaped. How were they going to fare with just the two of them? Mileena stands back to back with Tasha, feeling her heartbeat increase to max pace. She's already uncomfortable from the rain, but at the moment, that doesn't matter. Everything is eerily silent, so Tasha decides to goad their stalker.

"We know you're here! Come on out, you punk!"

Mileena wants to object, but an ear piercing,

"*PEEK-A-BOO!*" erupts from the darkness.

WHAP! An elongated, shadowy hand springs forward and backhands Tasha. Even with her increased durability, the impact hits her hard enough to knock her off her feet.

"Ahhhh!!!!" She barely has time to scream before she's flung backward and makes contact with the brick wall. *CHOK!* The poor girl slides down to the wet ground, unconscious.

Mileena is paralyzed with fear. She can't move! She can't do *anything! WOOSH!* The Boogeyman's shadowy form beelines right for her, wrapping its horrible, semi-tangible tendrils around her entire body. Mileena screams as she's lifted two feet off the ground, face to face with the faceless monster.

"It's *not safe for little girls to be alone at night! There are monsters out here!"*

His horrible, warbly voice sends shivers down Mileena's spine.

Someone! Anyone! HELP ME!!! She tries to scream again, but the tendrils snake around her neck. The more she tries to wriggle out of its grasp, the tighter it gets. Mileena kicks and kicks with all her might, but her feet simply go right through its body. This wasn't fair! He could touch her, but she can barely touch him? What horrible luck. *Wait a minute,... Luck!* Mileena tries to activate her ability. To do what? *Anything!* Her hands spark the green energy, but the Boogeyman violently shakes her, making her lose focus.

"No tricks! Just stay still and this'll be over quicker!"

Mileena feels herself getting lightheaded. She can't breathe! She's constricted like an anaconda! She's going to die if she doesn't do something! Mileena's eyes go down, seeing Tasha's limp body begin to stir. She was gaining consciousness, but not fast enough. Boogeyman was going to kill them.

No! Not Tasha, or Sky, or Gio, or Rocky, and most importantly,... NOT ME! Mileena squeezes her eyes shut, concentrating with everything in her. The luck energy begins to spark again. This time, her hands crackle like a firecracker and the spark flies straight up in the air before disappearing. The Boogeyman is visibly confused and loosens his grip by the slightest margin, which is all Mileena needs. With all the focus she can muster, Mileena thinks,

STRIKE! The storming clouds above seem to answer her call. With a bone rattling thunderclap, a white zigzagging pattern cracks down from the Sky and *KRAKOOM!* The mighty lightning bolt smites Mileena's attacker, both blinding and slightly deafening her in the process. She drops from her two-foot suspension, gasping for air as pure electricity barrages the creature. He howls in agony.

"YAHHHHH!!!!!!"

Mileena's eyes are blurry, but she sees it. The Boogeyman's smoky appearance dissipates, revealing the obscure outline of an actual human being. She can't tell who it is from the fuzziness of her vision, but she can see him turn tail and run away down the other side of the alley. Mileena curses, slamming her fist into a puddle. They were *this* close to figuring out who it was! She lies there on the ground for a moment as the rain continues. She's soaked, exhausted, and scared, but also proud of herself for that display of power. Mileena groans, dragging herself over to Tasha, who was coming to at last. The other girl blinks, looking left and right.

"Mileena,... did you do that?" she asks. Mileena forces herself to get on her feet. There's some dizziness, but she's stable. She reaches down and helps Tasha stand as well.

"I did! I freaking did that!"

Tasha gives her a tight hug, which feels a little odd and squishy while they're still being rained on, but it doesn't matter. Mileena hugs her back.

"Rocky's house?" "Rocky's house."

Chapter 19

Something New From Someone Old

As soon as the boys got the memo of what happened, Sky drove them straight to the Castillo house. Rocky looks around. He can hardly believe it. His new friends were all gathered in his bedroom. There's a bit of a mess with his clothes and various comic books scattered everywhere, but it's presentable enough. Sky and Gio sat together on Rocky's bed. Tasha and Mileena were on the floor wrapped in some of Andrea's spare towels. She graciously provided the two of them with hot tea, some clean clothes, and a bag of ice for Tasha's head. Poor girls. Thank goodness they were both still alive, but they looked worn out and scared. Tasha hisses as she removes the bag of ice from her head.

"Y'know, for a puff of smoke, Boogeyman hits *really* hard," she says. Rocky balls his fists, angry that this dumb monster has the nerve to cheapshot Tasha like that.

"I just can't believe he was apparently *waiting* on you guys. That's *insane*," says Sky. Mileena shivers, patting her hair with the towel.

"I should probably quit my job if creeps are going to keep attacking me there. But at least we know for sure Mr. Charles isn't the Boogeyman." "And you're *sure* you didn't get a good look at whoever it was after you blasted him?" asks Gio.

Mileena sadly shakes her head. Gio groans, lying flat on his back on the mattress. "Great. Once again, we've got *nothing*."

Rocky looks around. The four of them seem deflated. No way. He doesn't want this air of negativity to linger. Not in *his* room. Rocky jumps up and clears his throat.

"Uh, *hello*?! I think we're missing the point. Karma here literally called down lightning on our bad guy! If I could trade powers with anyone in this group, it'd be you."

Mileena actually seems to perk up at his statement.

"You really mean that? I honestly thought my ability was the lamest compared to everyone else." "Nah, man! You've probably done the *most* damage to Boogeyman out of any of us so far."

Tasha, Sky, and Gio all nod in agreement. Mileena smiles, giving Rocky silent thanks. A moment later, Andrea walks into the room with a stack of blankets.

"It's getting late, so I've already decided you're all staying here tonight," she tells them. Tasha chuckles, replying,

"You don't mind?" "*Mami*, it's pretty clear this evil bastard is watching you. *Hell* no, I don't mind."

Sky laughs. Kicking his feet in the air, he sings,

"Sleepoverrrrrrr!" And before Rocky can get too excited, his mother adds,

"You boys can room in here while Tasha and Mileena take the couches downstairs."

Rocky tries hiding his obvious disappointment, but Tasha puts a hand on his shoulder and smiles at him.

"I could go for some breakfast in the morning if you're up for it." "Oh! Uh, y-y-yes! Absolutely! Bright and early!"

Andrea walks over, gives Rocky a hug and kiss goodnight, then leaves. Gio leans forward and asks,

"Seriously, what're we gonna do now?" Tasha yawns, waving it off. "That's 'tomorrow' talk. For now, let's just try to enjoy the rest of the night."

Rocky grins, grabbing his remote and turning on his television. Even without the Link, he can feel everyone's need for some brevity after another near-death experience. He turns on some classic cartoons. Without a word, the five huddle together on the mattress, simply enjoying the entertainment. After a while, Rocky's eyes grow heavy and he's the first to fall asleep.

It's around 9AM when Rocky's eyes open. There's snoring from his house guests and the singing of birds outside, but otherwise, everything is fairly quiet. Rocky looks over the edge of his bed. Gio and Sky are wrapped in blankets, spooning comfortably on the carpet deep in sleep. Rocky yawns, steps up from his bed, and grabs his glasses off the nightstand. Though he normally sleeps in on Saturdays, today he's got breakfast to make. Rocky tiptoes over Sky and Gio, nearly tripping in the process. As he cracks open his door, he hears Sky's sleepy voice behind him.

"Hey, little man, how much of that conversation did you hear last night?" he asks. Rocky bites his lip. Of *course,* Sky knew he was eavesdropping. He couldn't help himself. There was no use lying, so Rocky says,

"All of it. You know I don't care about you being gay, right?" "I know. You're a good kid." Rocky stomps his foot. "I'm *not* a kid!... But thanks."

Sky grins, going back to sleep. Rocky leaves his bedroom, wondering what kind of dummy Chris Spinner was to discard someone as cool and genuine as Sky.

Downstairs, Rocky begins cooking while the girls are slumbering peacefully in the living room. He also starts up the coffee machine, knowing they're all going to need caffeine. Because he has guests, Rocky ends up making his favorite dish. *Chorizo con huevos.* Cheesy omelets, fried chorizo sausage, and a side of hash browns. The smell of sizzling food wakes up Tasha and Mileena, who zombie walk into the kitchen. Tasha thanks Rocky for the coffee and gives a kiss on the cheek, which almost makes him drop his spatula.

Just as he's finishing up, Sky and Gio come downstairs and join them. Rocky makes everyone's plates and passes them around. Tasha takes a bite first. Her eyes roll back as she practically eats her fork as well.

"Rocky, you are *seriously* talented," she compliments. "I see why this is your favorite thing to cook. This is honestly the *best* breakfast I've ever had," says Sky. Mileena and Gio both nod in agreement, their mouths too full to speak. Rocky is too flustered to say anything back, but beams with pride. Receiving praise from his friends makes him feel on top of the world.

After breakfast, Tasha makes the call that they all take the day off from any Boogeyman or Mr. Charles business. With that, Sky and Gio express interest in going on a proper date.

Mileena opts to hang out with Tasha, to which Rocky asks to go. His mother had work to do, and he didn't want to risk being attacked by the Boogeyman solo. Besides, it's more time he gets to spend with Tasha. They grab more coffee, say goodbye to the boys, and then head on their way. Before they engage in downtime, Tasha suddenly remembers needing to grab her sister Bree's food stamp card so she can restock on groceries. With that, Mileena drives the three of them to the retirement home, Pleasant Brooks.

Rocky fails at hiding his discomfort when he, Tasha, and Mileena step through the front doors. He'd never been to a nursing home before, but everything was pretty much what he expected. Dull elevator music. Senior citizens meandering about with their walkers and canes. Funky smells. Old portraits. Just a general sense of burden, aging, and...dying.

Rocky shivers. He's happy to be young and hopes to stay that way as long as possible. As the three approach the front desk, a pretty-faced black woman in her late twenties with billowing, curly hair wearing burgundy scrubs greets them.

"Tasha? What're you doing here? It's a Saturday," she asks. This must be Bree. Rocky can't help smiling. Both sisters were blessed with their looks.

"Didn't you get my text? I'm here to pick up the card so I can get food for the house." Tasha replies. Bree sighs, standing up from her chair. "No, I haven't checked my phone. I *work*, remember? Just hold on real quick so I can grab my purse from the break room." Bree grumbles while she walks away.

Tasha rolls her eyes. From what little Rocky knows, she and her sister haven't exactly been close lately. As Tasha and Mileena start talking about plans for when they leave this place, Rocky looks to the left and spots a familiar figure at the end of a hallway. With a closer look, he sees none other than Isaac Charles in the distance. He's holding a gift bag while taking a drink from the water fountain. Rocky turns around and taps Tasha's arm.

"Yo, Mr. Charles is here," he tells her. Quickly, Tasha, Mileena, and Rocky scoot to a corner away from the hall in case they'd be spotted. How crazy was this? After an entire night of spying to no avail, Rocky now sees him out of nowhere.

"Do we just wait and hope he doesn't see us?" asks Mileena. Rocky scratches his chin, an idea popping in his head.

"I can see what he's doing here," he suggests. "Are you crazy? We don't need him asking questions if you get busted," says Tasha. Rocky shakes his head.

"Hello, invisibility! Also, I don't go to the same school as you. He won't recognize me even if I get caught."

Tasha and Mileena look at each other, then back at Rocky. He clasps his hands together and adds, "Trust me."

Tasha sighs. "Fine. Just be quick about it." "He's probably just here to visit a family member or something. Are you sure this is worth it?" asks Mileena. Rocky shrugs. "I'll let you know."

With that, he turns on his heel and hides behind a rather tall potted fern. He looks around, making sure no one can see him, then wills himself invisible. Hidden from sight, Rocky goes down the hallway. He's able to see Mr. Charles turn a corner just in time. Crouching down, Rocky stays close to the wall, making sure to keep a reasonable distance while trailing his target.

Rocky Castillo in total stealth mode, baby.

The boy follows Mr. Charles around several more corridors, always at a thirty-foot distance. Eventually, Mr. Charles comes to a stop at Room 429. A CNA posted by the door tells him something Rocky can't hear before leaving. Mr. Charles enters the room, leaving the door slightly cracked open. Rocky gingerly makes his way closer and crouches right behind the door. Just in case his focus breaks and he becomes visible again. He's nervous but also weirdly excited. Hopefully, he won't waste Tasha's time with this. They needed *something* concrete to go on.

"Hello, Irene," he hears the man greet. The creaky voice of an old woman responds, "Who are you? I took my medicine already, and I don't want to take any more damn pills!"

"Irene, it's me, Isaac." "Oh! I knew that. You know I get foggy sometimes." "I know, Irene. It's been a couple of weeks since I last visited." "Oh, don't fret. You're such a sweet boy."

Rocky covers his mouth and stifles a laugh. Does someone think that Isaac Charles is a sweet boy? This Irene lady seemed too nice for her own good.

"Anyway, I came with a care package for you. Those muffins from 3rd Street you like." "Oh, thank God! You know, they don't let me have things like this here. I'm 84, not dead." "You're 87, Irene." "Don't get smart with me, Isaac! I know how damn old I am! I'm,... Oh. You're right. I *am* 87."

Rocky can hear the sadness in her voice. He feels bad. She must have some memory issues in her current age.

"Tell me, how's my grandson doing?" he hears Irene ask. Then he hears Mr. Charles sigh. "We've been over this, Irene. He's gone. He's been gone for twenty years. I tell you this almost every time I visit." "And I tell *you* every time that he isn't. He comes to me sometimes, same as you." "As a ghost, right? Come on, Irene. I really don't want to tell the nurses about these delusions again but I will." "They aren't delusions, Isaac! My grandson's ghost comes to me!" "Irene... never mind. Look, enjoy the muffins. I'll try to swing by again soon." "He's real, Isaac! He's real!"

As Mr. Charles exits the room, he goes to the opposite end of the hall to find the CNA who greeted him. While his back is turned, Rocky silently takes off back the way he came. *Like a ninja!* He thinks. Rocky makes his way back to the lobby where Tasha and Mileena are waiting. He drops his camouflage, sweating slightly after focusing on his ability for so long.

"So, any news?" asks Tasha. Rocky nods. "I think so. Let's go outside."

As the trio exits the front doors and find a place on the side of the building, Rocky shares everything he heard. Once he's finished, Mileena asks,

"Not to sound rude or anything, but how is any of that relevant?" "I have a theory," Rocky starts, "How long have there been rumors about Hillstone Park being haunted? About twenty years, right? And Mr. Charles said Irene's grandson has been gone for twenty years. We know now that The Boogeyman is the haunter of the woods *and* that Mr. Charles has some sort of history with him. Plus, Irene said the ghost comes to her. Therefore-" "Irene's grandson is possibly the Boogeyman," says Tasha.

Rocky smiles and nods. "Boogeyman is kind of a ghost when you think about it," he adds. Mileena shrugs. "Sure, whatever. But how do we find out who her grandson/ghost is?" she asks. "Let's interrogate Mr. Charles." Rocky jokes. Well, mostly. Tasha chuckles.

"That's *beyond* a bad idea. However, since Irene stays here at my sister's job, let me try to look into it tomorrow." Rocky groans. "Tomorrow? Can't we just do that while we're here? We're so close to figuring everything out *right now*." "Rocky, I already said we need to take today off before we do anything else. So yes, tomorrow." "But Tasha,-" "*Tomorrow*, Rocky!"

Tasha crosses her arms, giving him a very no-nonsense look. Rocky lowers his head, frowning deeply.

"I'm sorry. I just... I want to help. The Boogeyman almost got you guys last night." Tasha leans down and puts a hand on his shoulder.

"You did well, Rocky. I promise I'll do what I can, but you're right. The Boogeyman *did* almost get us last night. I didn't get the best sleep cuz of that, so I think we need to do something fun first before we go back to hero duty."

Rocky sniffles. He doesn't know why that got him emotional, but his heart fills with joy. Tasha was right. He did well. He got information that could potentially turn the tide of their situation.

"So uh, where are we going until then?" he asks. Mileena taps her pocket.

"I got some good tips yesterday. After grocery shopping, let's grab some ice cream." "Hell yeah!"

Chapter 20
Dates and Ghosts

Gio spends a rather blissful Saturday with Sky. After breakfast at Rocky's house, the two head out to do something Gio hasn't done in a long time: go to a roller rink. He pays for their entry fee while Sky covers snacks. Gio is severely out of practice on skates and fumbles like a baby deer. Sky is surprisingly smooth on wheels and helps Gio straighten himself out after a few harmless falls. While skating around the rink, Gio grabs Sky's hand. In public. In front of everyone. It was fairly packed there since it was a Saturday. He can tell the older boy is a bit uncomfortable with the attention, but he doesn't let go. In fact, Sky tightens his grip and pulls him forward, kissing him as they glide along. Gio is more flustered than he's ever been before. He was so used to initiating pda with girls that being the one getting wooed was a nice change of pace. Especially considering Sky's history. If he ever sees Chris Spinner, the boy is gonna catch Gio's baseball bat to the face.

After skating for a couple of hours, they leave the roller rink and go to a movie for the rest of the afternoon. Gio pays for them again, but he doesn't mind. The two watch some comedy that's been out for a month, so there's almost nobody else in the theater. Sky puts his arm around Gio, who, in return, rests his leg on Sky's lap. Their fingers intertwined throughout the entire viewing. Gio loves how easy it is being with Sky. With Tina and other past girlfriends, there was always a sort of pressure. He had to bring them somewhere extravagant and push the limit of his allowance. Always be on his ps and qs behavior-wise. Take endless selfies for their social media and just generally be the pretty boy people expected him to be. And Gio doesn't resent that at all. What he felt for all those girls was genuine. He still likes girls. He'll always like girls. However, with Sky, things were just different in the best way. Gio felt like he could be himself more. He could burp. Snort when he laughed. Order a bacon cheeseburger without judgment. Enjoy the moment without taking pictures and coming up with captions, or not worry about buying jewelry right away. He could just be Gio, and that was enough. After the movie, Gio invites Sky to come back to his place and hang out for the rest of the day. Sky seems a bit hesitant at first but accepts the offer.

As the two reach the front door of his house, Gio hesitates before putting his key in the lock.

"Sky... we're dating, right?" he asks.

Sky scratches behind his ear, not answering. Gio shakes his head. He can feel the uncertainty through the Link as well as Sky's irrepressible thoughts of doubt. Gio slaps his hands to his sides.

"Are you seriously still in disbelief about us?" he asks. Sky nervously bites down on his bottom lip. "I can't help it, Gio. I've had a great time today, but-" "But nothing, Sky."

The two stand there in silence. Gio doesn't want to push, but he can't keep repeating himself either. Eventually, Sky smirks and says,

"You're right. I'm a dummy." With a giggle, Gio replies,

"Yes, you are. And you still haven't answered my question." "Do you really want to date me? The fat, poor degenerate?" "If by that you mean the cute, funny, brave knight, then yes."

They laugh together. Gio takes Sky's hands. He can see through the self-deprecating humor. Gio leans up and kisses Sky, who kisses him back. It's electrifying how much he's enjoying himself. That is, until the front door swings open and his mother, Ava, appears.

"Giovanni!"

Gio and Sky immediately jump apart. He feels dumb for not noticing her car in the driveway.

"Where the hell have you been?! You never came home last night!" his mom demands. "Mom, relax. I forgot to tell you I was spending the night," says Gio.

His mother crosses her arms, looking Sky up and down. "Spending the night, huh?" she says suspiciously.

Sky holds his hands up.

"It's not what you think, Ms. Carano. Gio and I were with our friends and-" "That's Mrs. McFadden to you. And don't you worry about what I *think*," she says pointedly. Gio covers his eyes, racked with sheer embarrassment.

"I'll uh, I'll see you later, Gio." Sky stammers.

Before he leaves, Gio grabs his arm and kisses him one more time, right in front of his mom. Sky smiles for a second, then speed walks away. As Gio walks into the house, Ava slams the door behind them.

"You've just given up on girls now, Giovanni?" Gio angrily spins around. "No, Mom, I haven't just given up on girls. I knew I was bi before we even moved here." "And you're just telling me this now, because?" "Because I knew you'd react like this!" "Like what, Gio? What am I reacting like?" "Just forget it, Mom." "Gio, I just want you to set a better example for your sister." And with that, Gio snaps.

"Phoebe is not my sister! And besides, Sky is a really nice guy and I'm going to keep seeing him!"

Ava pinches the bridge of her nose.

"I'm sorry." "And also I-!... Wait, what?"

Ava leans against the wall with a heavy sigh.

"I'm sorry, Gio. I know you think I've been a lousy mom lately. It's probably true. I don't even know what's going on with you anymore."

Any anger Gio was holding on to dissipates entirely. He wasn't expecting this. Like, at all. Gio walks over to Ava, awkwardly patting her shoulder.

"Mom, it's just been a lot going on this past year, okay? The move, you're getting married,... I'm still processing everything, and it feels like you didn't care."

Ava opens her eyes, which glisten with potential tears.

"Of course I care, Giovanni. I just wanted to make a better life for myself since you're almost grown up. That doesn't mean I don't care about you. You're still my bambino."

Gio cringes. His mom hadn't called him bambino since he was in elementary school. Still, it's nice.

"I'm sorry too, Mom. Just don't try to force me to love Kevin or Phoebe, okay?" "That's fair." "And give Sky a chance, would ya? I really like him."

His mom is visibly uncomfortable at the mention of Sky, but she swallows her pride and nods. Gio knows she has certain feelings about the LGBTQ community, but it was a start.

The next day,...

Sunday morning, Tasha awakens with a start. In the dream she was having, but there's a vague recollection of the Boogeyman reaching out and grabbing for her. She makes a leap of faith before he can get her, and as she does, she doesn't come down. In fact, Tasha continued to rise higher and higher, the sky coming to greet her just before she opened her eyes. As her consciousness comes clearer, Tasha notices something odd. She doesn't feel her mattress or blankets under her. Just air. Almost as if she's... elevated. Literally. Looking down, Tasha realizes she's floating about two feet above her bed!

"What the-?!"

Willing herself down, she plops loudly back on the mattress. Thankfully, Bree was already gone and didn't hear the noise. Tasha sighs exasperatedly, her heart hammering in her chest. It seems she has some sort of secondary ability to... float? Not the wake-up call she would've liked. She wants to feel excited about it, but for the most part, all she feels is frustration.

Tasha had hoped her dreams about Boogeyman would've eased up after spending her Saturday eating ice cream and going shopping with her friends, but it didn't. Her sketchbook had gotten several more entries of the shadowy monster over the last few days, which was really starting to bug her. Tasha tended to draw on inspiration. Not fear. There's a text message on her phone from Jasmine asking if she can come over to help her study for an upcoming test. Tasha replies, telling her 'Maybe later'. She had something to do. After freshening up, Tasha rides her bike to the Caffeine Commute for her much-needed espresso, then makes her way to Pleasant Brooks.

It doesn't take Tasha long to find Bree when she steps into the building. She spots her sister exiting one of the rooms, wheeling out a cart full of clothing and bedsheets. When Tasha walks over to her, Bree immediately rolls her eyes.

"Tasha, what are you doing here now? Do you need the card again?" Bree asks, annoyed.

Tasha does her best to ignore the attitude. Bree wasn't always this ornery. In fact, Tasha remembers her being quite the party girl while she was in college. The girl who showed up and showed out at every social event and danced her butt off with a smile on her face.

Tasha looked up to Bree well before she was her caretaker. Their Mom and Dad's passing took its toll on her as well. Still, Tasha wishes her sister wouldn't treat her like she was some sort of burden, especially after bailing on her eighteenth birthday.

"I need your help with something. Can you spare a minute? Please?" she asks.

Bree looks left and right. There weren't many workers or residents around at the moment. Seeing this, Bree says,

"Fine. Let me just drop off this laundry real quick, and I'll be right back." "Okay."

Tasha takes a seat near the front desk and leans against the wall. She was tired. It was her senior year of high school. She should be worrying about what to wear for prom or applying for colleges. The past two weeks have been the strangest, stressful, and mind-boggling of her entire life. She's grateful for meeting her new friends. She's even enjoying having superpowers. However, she's also had several close calls with death from a malicious stranger and more questions than answers. Even if they find out who the Boogeyman is... what next? Do they go to the police? Would that even be helpful? How do you arrest a guy who can turn into smoke? Tasha twirls one of her locs between her fingers, taking deep breaths to try and calm herself. *One thing at a time, girl.*

Five minutes later, Bree returns to the front lobby, rubbing sanitizer on her hands.

"Okay. What's going on, sis?" she asks. Tasha stands up from her chair, looks Bree in the eyes, and asks,

"What can you tell me about one of the residents here named Irene?"

Bree is naturally perplexed.

"Irene? Irene, who?" "I don't know her last name. I just know my principal, Isaac Charles, comes here to see her sometimes." "Oh. That's Irene O'Hara. I don't really know that much about her. She's been here since before I started. Got some slight dementia, but she's nice for the most part." "Are she and Mr. Charles related?"

Bree shakes her head.

"No. Actually, she doesn't have any living relatives on file."

Tasha is hit with confusion. That can't be right.

"Wait, so she doesn't have any kids or grandkids?" she asks. Bree shakes her head again. "No. She talks about the ghost of her supposed 'grandson', but-" "Did she say a name?

What's the ghost's name?" "Tasha, there is *no* ghost. That's just her condition kicking in here and there."

Bree then squints her eyes. "Hold up,... why do you need to know?"

Tasha nearly tells her. She wants to tell her. However, this isn't like Andrea. Bree was her sister. Her last immediate blood relative. Things between them were already strained, and telling her about everything that's been happening might only make things worse. Tasha sighs.

"It's fine. I'm sorry I bothered you."

Bree doesn't press the issue. Instead, she says,

"Corty. Irene claims the ghost's name is Corty."

Bree pats her sister's shoulder and goes back to her duties. Tasha smacks herself on the forehead. 'Corty'. What was she supposed to do with that? She sighs. Maybe Bree and Mr. Charles were right. Just the ramblings of an old woman losing her memory. Feeling at her wits' end, Tasha leaves the building in a huff.

Outside as she mounts her bike, Tasha is suddenly hit with a peculiar sensation. She looks around. It's sunny. Mildly chilly. Quiet. There's a handful of cars in the parking lot next to the building and a wide lawn with the Illinois state flag. Everything seemed normal. And yet... she feels eyes on her. She's not sure where this feeling is coming from, and she doesn't want to find out. Tasha gets in gear and pedals away as fast as she can.

Corty laughs to himself, watching the girl ride her bike away in fear. These damn kids were getting sharper by the day, but they still knew better for now. He stays in his gray Cadillac, watching through his tinted windows as the redhead disappears into the distance. Good.

Now he could do what he needed to do. Corty coughs violently as he exits his vehicle. The lightning bolt from that mixed girl had done him good. Too good. Maintaining his shadow form was physically taxing as is, but that attack took everything in him to heal from. He was *still* healing from it. But that was okay. Once he recovered, the kid gloves were coming off. First, Corty had to relocate the Heart. Then he tried attacking the little brat's head on. And both times, they barely slipped from his grasp. Everything Corty has worked to keep under wraps was on the verge of collapsing, and he'd be damned if five random toddlers were going to ruin it.

Corty lowers his baseball cap over his eyes, shoving his rough, calloused hands in his coat pockets. He might not have had enough power for another attack, but he could do a quick in and out for Irene. Poor woman. Corty hates that he has to do it this way, but seeing his true face would only further agitate her increasing dementia. Pretty soon, he was probably going to have to stop visiting her altogether. Slinking around to the back of the facility, Corty begins to morph. For two decades he's had this ability, and the transformation was still something he never quite enjoyed. It was like the uncomfortable, pins and needles sensation of a foot falling asleep, only his entire body. From the bottom of his shoes to the brim of his hat, Corty's flesh, blood, and clothing all evaporate into swirling, black and gray smoke. He was now the Boogeyman. Fitting name the kids have for him. After all, he was a monster. Only a monster would kill their best friend,... Corty immediately shoves that thought away. It wasn't his fault. It's what he's been telling himself all this time.

In his misty state, Corty floats around to the back of the living quarters. He knows the way by heart. Luckily, it was a Sunday, so there was little to no chance of anyone spotting him. Just outside the window of Room 429, Corty easily slinks his shadowy body through the mesh screen into the bedroom. Corty collects himself in the corner, waiting for the old lady to see him.

At 87 years old, Irene O'Hara was a short, 5"2 elder with a hunched back, thinning white hair, and scarily thin arms. She was in her bed, her milky eyes glazed over as she watched football on the flatscreen across the room. With how perfectly still she was, Corty wasn't entirely sure she wasn't already dead. He was a floating black mass in the corner of her room. One would think she'd notice. This wasn't the first time he's done this. Hell, it wasn't even the hundredth. Loudly, Corty clears his "throat". In an instant, Irene's eyes seem to go back to normal. She gasps, looking back and forth.

"Who's there? I'll warn you, I'll get Buster on your ass!" she yells.

Corty feels so bad. Buster was a Rottweiler she had had a long time ago. He died right before she was committed to Pleasant Brooks. Corty doesn't say anything. Instead, he forms into his humanoid shape while still in shadow mode. Irene smiles, which is also kind of sad. Her skin was so incredibly wrinkled and worn, he was worried her smile might cause it to tear.

"Oh, my grandson! My sweet Corty! How are you?" she croaks. Corty could almost cry. He wasn't her grandson. Not by blood. But she was the only person in this world he ever cared for,... other than Brian. Corty doesn't answer her. Irene snaps her bony fingers.

"I asked you a question, young man!" she grimaces.

Corty chuckles softly to himself. Even in her final years, Irene was a short-tempered spitfire. He still doesn't speak. His altered voice in shadow form tended to spook her. Instead, Corty just looks at her. Possibly for the last time. After he deals with these kids, he might have to call it quits. For good this time. Without a word, Corty waves at her, then gently floats backwards out of her window. As he demorphs under the windowsill out of sight, Corty can faintly hear the sound of Irene softly weeping. It breaks his heart. With his visit complete, Corty goes back to his car and heads home. Once he was done resting up, he had the perfect way to shake up his targets. They were going to pay. They were all going to pay!

Chapter 21

Beat-'Em-Up Bonding

The following Tuesday,...

The past few days have been *very* stressful for Sky. After his wonderful date with Gio, Sky was stuck overtime watching his little cousins the rest of the weekend. Uncle Paxton's dealer had apparently decided to increase their operations. With this new shift in "business", Uncle Paxton had been out much longer than usual. To the point where Sky hadn't seen him all day yesterday, meaning he was stuck taking care of everything for the kids. Dinner. Cleaning. Homework. Bathtime. Piper wasn't so bad, but Parker, Pierce, and Perry were absolute madness. Every thirty seconds was filled with one or all of the triplets yelling, running around, or being difficult. It was a miracle Sky got them all up and ready for school this morning, but at the cost of him barely getting any sleep. Sky never liked his uncle's dealer, but at the very least, he had his uncle on a set schedule. This wasn't going to work anymore. Sky needs to put his foot down. It was bad enough that he and his friends had no further clues to help solve their Boogeyman crisis.

According to Tasha, all they had was a single name. Corty. Nothing helpful came up on internet searches. And apparently, the old lady Mr. Charles visits doesn't have any family. It was only a matter of time before Boogeyman struck again. Sky groans. This was so *frustrating*! He couldn't even try hanging out with Gio to make himself feel better since he didn't have the time.

After walking Piper to her bus stop, Sky decides he's had enough. He stomps to his uncle's bedroom and vibrates the doorknob loose to unlock it. As he walks into the messy room, he sees Paxton's body lying under the sheets on his mattress. Sky nearly loses it right then and there. He didn't even know he was there after being gone all day and night. Sky had gotten maybe four hours of broken sleep and had to wrangle the kids by himself! He stomps over to the bed and yanks the sheets off Paxton's body.

"Get up!" he demands. "Where the hell have you been?! I had to do everything and-!"

Sky pauses as he sees Paxton's face. He has a busted lip, a black eye, and a large welt on his forehead. Sky turns on the light, which makes Paxton groan.

"Go away," he grumbles sleepily. Instead, Sky touches Paxton's shoulder and gives him a small but effective vibration. Paxton spasms awake, sitting up with a yelp.

"Yah! What the hell was that?!" he exclaims. "What happened? You look like crap!" Sky says, concerningly.

For all the man's faults, he was still family. Paxton shakes his head.

"Look, boy, I just got into a little bit of trouble, that's all." "Dammit, Uncle, this isn't something I can ignore! *What happened?!*"

Sky restlessly taps his foot as he stands in the hallway. What happened to his uncle was heightening his already present anxiety. Not knowing what else to do, Sky decides to skip class. It would be pointless to try to pay any sort of attention. He texts Tasha, Mileena, and Gio individually, asking them to meet him by the gymnasium after class. It was empty at this time of day. Some forty-odd minutes later, the other three met him right by the gym doors as everyone else rushed to their next class. Gio gives him a hug and a kiss.

"What's going on, babe? I've been getting very stressed vibes from you." "Yeah, me too. I hope this is important. I don't wanna be late for bio," says Mileena.

Sky exhales, and he tells them,

"I need your help. My uncle, he... well, he was jumped last night."

Tasha gasps.

"Oh my God! Is he okay?" "He's pretty beaten up, but he'll live. But what happened was his dealer sent him all the way to Harbor Row in another gang's territory to sell. The other guys didn't like that."

Sky can't help feeling embarrassed. Harbor Rowe was an adjacent township infamous for its crime rate. Sky knows his friends are aware of his uncle's illegal activities, but he still doesn't like bringing it up. Sky balls his fists.

"These other guys jumped him when they saw him selling in their neighborhood and took all his money. This Boogeyman situation hasn't gotten any closer to being solved, and I'm... I'm angry! I want payback!"

Gio slides his hand up Sky's back and onto his shoulder.

"Don't feel bad, Sky. We know your situation." Mileena nervously runs her hand through her hair. "This... this is all just..."

Sky chuckles. "It's okay, your highness. I never wanted you guys to be remotely involved with this stuff. But this is my *family*. I already told my uncle he needs to quit and get an actual job. But in the meantime, we *need* that money. And I need to do something before I actually go crazy."

Tasha steps forward.

"Let's do it then. Let's get payback." Sky's eyes bulge. "You mean it?" he asks. Tasha firmly nods.

"Hell yeah, I do. This is for family."

"Rawr. I like the fierce side of you." Sky says with a purr.

The four of them chuckle. But that was only one 'yes' so far. Gio speaks up next.

"Nobody beats up my boyfriend's uncle and gets away with it. I'm in." Sky's brain practically shorts out and restarts. *Boyfriend? Did Gio Carano just call me his boyfriend?!* Sky looks into Gio's eyes. Yes. Just yes. Finally, it came to Mileena.

"Let's kick their asses."

As soon as they're done talking, Sky, Tasha, Gio, and Mileena sneak out of the back building through the gymnasium and gather in Mileena's car. It's been years since Sky had played hookie and he can't deny their excitement. He's skipping school to go kick some butt with his new friends. As Mileena drives them away from campus, Sky tells her to go to Olligrove Middle School so they can grab Rocky. If they were going to do this, it had to be the whole unit. Rocky may be the youngest, but he's Sky's friend, too. Plus, his invisibility comes in handy.

Once they reach his school, Sky and Tasha sneak inside the building and use their Link to locate Rocky. They find him in world history class, telling his teacher they need to see him. Once they get him out in the halls, all Sky has to say is,

"We're gonna go fight some bad guys. Are you in, *Luminator*?" "Just *try* to stop me!"

As they sneak him out of the building, Rocky makes sure to send a message to Andrea letting her know ahead of time that he is with the group. She won't be happy they're taking her son out of school to steal from criminals. Hopefully, once they explain the situation, she'll understand.

Before engaging in the task at hand, the gang makes a few more stops. First, Mileena's house to grab her bow. Next, go to Gio's house to get his baseball bat. Finally, the supermarket, where they grab compression sleeves for Sky. While there, Mileena also buys five oversized navy blue hoodies with matching bandanas. They change into said hoodies in the car and finally make the drive to Harbor Rowe. It's similar to the part of Olligrove that Sky lives in, only *much* sketchier. It was no wonder Uncle Paxton got robbed there. Luckily, Sky was given a description of the neighborhood where the gang ambushed him. An old warehouse near a rundown tire shop. As soon as the warehouse is spotted, Mileena parks her vehicle down the block. Sky, who was in the passenger seat, unclips his seatbelt with trembling fingers. He's equal parts nervous, angry, and excited.

"Last chance if anyone wants to back out," he warns. Tasha leans forward, placing a gentle hand on his shoulder to calm him down.

"We're not backing out. What they did to your uncle was uncalled for. However, if we're gonna do this, we need to do it right. With a *plan*," she insists. Gio nods in agreement. "Yeah. We can't just barge in through the front door," he adds.

Sky ponders what to do. They were both right. The element of surprise was on their side, but it needed to be used correctly. A lightbulb seems to go off in Rocky's brain. Grinning, he immediately concocts a strategy.

"Okay, I got it. Tasha, Sky, and I can go to the left side of the building. Sky can shatter the windows, which will catch those dummies off guard. Honestly, you're both the best at fighting, so you can hold them off. Meanwhile, Gio rushes in and uses your speed to find the money. Mileena, you provide him with support and try to cover us. I'll go invisible and stay out of sight as much as possible, but be ready just in case you need backup. Sound good?"

Everyone states their approval, each of them impressed with the plan. Rocky grins with excitement.

"Good. I just have one request." "What?" "We use our codenames."

Mileena shivers as she turns off her car.

"I'm already not thrilled about skipping school. Let's just do this before I realize how insane this is," she quips.

Sky bites his lip in anticipation. As they all bring up their hoods and tie the bandanas around their mouths as makeshift masks, Sky feels them slipping into their respective personas. Tasha becomes Angel. Gio becomes Pace. Mileena becomes Karma. Rocky becomes The Luminator. Sky tightens the knot of his bandana last, now Shakedown.

Following the plan, the group splits up to take their positions. Pace and Karma wait by the front door, bat and bow in hand. They know once the commotion starts, that will be their cue. Shakedown, Angel, and Luminator slip around to the back of the building, right below the windows. They take up almost the entirety of the wall, so Shakedown had plenty to work with. Luminator peeks his head up to get a view inside, then crouches back down.

"There are about ten guys in there. They're all just talking," he informs. "Did you see any money?" asks Shakedown. "Not really, but one of them walked upstairs with a black messenger bag. I bet that's where it is," replies Luminator. Angel puts her hands on both their shoulders.

"We may have superpowers, but these guys might have guns. If it gets too sticky in there, we get out while we can. Understand?" They both nod. "Good. Luminator, disappear, but keep your eyes peeled."

Their young friend snaps his fingers and vanishes from sight. Shakedown takes a deep breath to try to calm his nerves. He can handle himself in a brawl, but this was a whole other level. Then again, if they can fight a shadow monster, he can handle a warehouse full of uncle-beating thugs. He stands up and presses his palms against the windows. It was go-time.

"One... two... three!"

With one more deep breath, Shakedown spreads a strong wave of oscillation throughout the entire window. There's a loud rumbling sound that catches the attention of several gang members inside. As soon as they spot him, *BLAM*! A huge portion of the glass shatters outward in a devastating spray. Three of the thugs get caught in the crossfire as shards of glass cut at their arms and legs. The rest of them are in a panic, wondering what just happened. Shakedown and Angel jump through the massive hole he created and get into proper fighting stances. A particularly buff man with a scorpion tattoo on his face yells,

"Get these clowns!"

As the men start rushing towards them, the two teammates nod at each other and go to work. One man comes in screaming with a crowbar, trying to hit Angel. She expertly dodges the swing and counters with a roundhouse kick to his face. Then she grabs him by the collar of his shirt and throws him to the other side of the room like a rag doll. Another assailant runs at Shakedown. He throws a punch, but it's sloppy. Shakedown easily blocks it and places a hand on the man's chest, sending a pulsing vibration in his chest that makes him crumble to the floor. Another grunt attempts to retaliate from the side. Seeing this, Angel sticks out her right arm and plants her feet.

"GYAHK!" The man chokes on air as he gets clotheslined by her arm, stumbling backwards a step while she remains unmoved. Vulnerable and gasping for air, Angel follows up with a front kick strong enough to send him flying into a wall. *Bam*! Shakedown gives her a thumbs up for the assist, then rushes forward to take on more enemies. The buff man with the face tattoo decides he wants a turn now. He draws a gnarly-looking hunting knife out of his back pocket and swipes at Shakedown. He jumps backwards just in time, the front of his hoodie taking the brunt of the blade. Luckily, it was thick and oversized, so only a thin line of cotton spilled out rather than his blood. Tatt Face takes another swipe, but this time, Shakedown is ready for it. He ducks, cocks his fist, then leaps into an uppercut that makes direct contact with Tatt Face's chin, using his vibration power to increase the impact. He then follows it up with a high knee to the face and a strong right hook. Tatt Face goes down, but then two more thugs spring forward and grab Shakedown's arms. He laughs at their efforts and sends disarming vibrations into both of them. They let him go instantly, reeling in pain. Angel then throws one of them across the room and elbow drops the other to the ground. As Shakedown wonders whether this was a little too easy, several more thugs come running down the stairs. Each holding crowbars, tire irons, and wrenches as weapons.

“Great. They have backup," he grumbles. He's a good fighter, but he'd be lying if his stamina wasn't already taking a hit. Angel smacks him on the shoulder.

“What, you gettin’ sleepy? We got this, friend!” she encourages.

Just as she says this, the front door is kicked open. *Zoom*! In comes Pace barrelling at cheetah speed, zipping past two grunts who try and fail to swing at him. He jumps in the air with a *beautiful* corkscrew flip and kicks them simultaneously. Pace then leaps over another thug, spins around, and knocks him upside the head with his baseball bat.

Apparently not out for the count yet, Tatt Face springs from the floor and swipes at Shakedown with his knife again. Caught off guard, he receives a nasty cut to his left shoulder. Shakedown yelps, leaping away from the psycho. Tatt Face tries to go for another attack when, *thwip*! He screams in horror. Why? There's an arrow in his foot. Karma! Said Ally sticks close to the entrance, shooting non-lethal arrows into the arms and legs of several more thugs. And when she eventually runs out of arrows, Karma uses her luck powers to make her opponents fumble or completely miss their attacks. Hilariously, some of them even hit each other.

In the midst of the melee, Pace runs up the stairs while his friends take care of the rest of the crew. The rush of the fight is enough for Shakedown to ignore the bleeding gash on his arm, but he can already feel his energy waning. On top of that, several of the goons who were knocked down are starting to get back up.

Meanwhile upstairs, Pace is trying his best to finish things quickly before his adrenaline boost dies down. The messenger bag was sitting on a table, but it was surrounded by three more men.

Jeez, how many of them are there?! he thinks. Pace prepares himself. While technically not a fighter, flipping around was still effective. The three men all charge at once. Pace uses his superior reflexes to dodge every strike, then takes a swing at each of them with his bat. *Clonk! Clonk! Clonk!* One gets hit in the shin. The other two in their solar plexus. They all go down wincing and whining. Pace flourishes his bat.

“Too slow, losers," he taunts. The goon who was hit in his shin grimaces at him.

“Nah, bruh! *You* are!” he retorts.

Before Pace has time to react, the man whips out a pistol from his jeans and aims it at him. *BLAM*! Pace howls as a bullet hits his right calf. Though it only grazes him, it's enough to have Pace fall to the floor. He's never been in a fight before, let alone gotten *shot*! It stings like hell and he's definitely bleeding. The man at fault wobbles as he gets to his feet, aiming the gun at Pace's head. He scoots backwards in a panic.

"Wait! Don't do it! Wait! Wait! No!"

The man grits his teeth, prepared to fire. *Fwoosh*! A spotlight level beam of light shines directly in the man's eyes, painfully blinding him . He screams, waving his arms around at nothing until he drops the gun. Pace looks over and sees none other than Luminator at the top of the stairs. The man recovers and spots Luminator, reaching down to grab his gun off the ground.

"Ah! He sees me!"

In a panic, Luminator fires a dozen white colored orbs and goes invisible again. Though technically harmless, the orbs swarm the assailant like a pack of bees. He swats at them in frustration to no avail. Pace then takes the opportunity to attack and throws his bat like a spear. *Bonk*! It hits the man in his temple, and he goes down at last.

Luminator reappears and dismisses the orbs. Pace gives him a thumbs up, then forces himself to stand. His calf practically screams in protest from the bullet wound, but Pace pushes through. Their mission wasn't over yet.

"Thanks for the assist." "You're welcome, now *hurry up*!" Luminator insists.

Working through the pain, Pace grabs the messenger bag and limps downstairs with his friend.

Back on the lower level, Shakedown, Angel, and Karma are all standing victoriously over nearly a dozen downed men. Some of them were groaning or whimpering. Others were knocked out cold. Shakedown walks over to Tatt Face as he seems to be in charge and leans over him. The man pants heavily, giving him a death glare while trying to grasp the arrow in his foot. It's not very effective. Shakedown reaches down and snatches the man's hunting knife away.

"Let this be a lesson to not take things that don't belong to you. Got that?" he taunts. Tatt Face scowls in disgust.

"You're freaks! You're all *freaks*!" he yells. Shakedown chuckles. "Well, you're not wrong."

He then pushes two fingers against the guy's chest. Using the last of his energy, he fires a series of harsh vibrations throughout the man's body that disrupt his entire physical being. He grunts and howls, his body locked and shaking in what was essentially an induced seizure.

"Agh! I feel it in my *bones*!" "Good."

Just as Shakedown sheaths and pockets the knife, *WEEEEEEEEE-OOOOOOOOO!*

The unmistakable sound of police sirens sounds off in the distance.

"Time to go!" Angel orders. She, Karma, and Luminator run off right away. Noticing Pace's leg wound, Shakedown scoops him up bridal style.

"Babe, my legs still work." "Shut up and let me carry you!"

Holding on tight to his partner, Shakedown aka Sky Harris, exits the warehouse with his man in his arms and a bag full of money.

Chapter 22
A Wicked Ultimatum

With two members of their party injured and bleeding, the gang doesn't head back to Mileena's car yet. She doesn't want to explain the blood stains on the seats to her father. Instead, they run around the block, snatching off their bandanas and hoodies as they hear police sirens near. Quickly, they find an alley between two convenience stores and sit on the gravel. Tasha lays her head against the brick wall, finding herself shaking from the adrenaline rush. What they just did was stupid and dangerous and the most exciting thing she's ever partaken in. Mileena takes their bandanas and tightly wraps them around Sky's shoulder wound and Gio's grazed calf. Their healing factor would take care of the rest. Ever the ball of energy, Rocky jumps up and screams,

"WHOO! We did that! We totally *did* that! Holy *crap*! You guys were amazing back there! Those creeps didn't stand a chance against us!"

Tasha roughly tugs on the boy's sleeve.

"You wanna announce that to the whole neighborhood while there's police still out there?" she warns. But then she smirks.

"We *were* pretty good, huh?" Mileena smacks her on the shoulder.

"'Pretty good'? Girl, you and Sky fight like rockstars!" she compliments.

Tasha sticks out her tongue.

"That's cuz I got it like that."

The flex was well earned, Tasha feels. She is really glad she never slacked on her lessons before her father passed. It all paid off big time. Sky smiles with pride as well.

"My uncle is slightly homophobic, but in a 'supportive' way. He said, 'I'm not gonna have a queer for a nephew if he can't throw hands.' Anyway, we wouldn't have been able to get through those guys without Lady Luck and Sir Flips-A-Lot."

Mileena flips her hair and bats her eyes. "Oh, it was effortless," she says jokingly. "By the way, Sky, how'd those compression sleeves work for you?" "Like a charm. You were right. My arms feel *way* less sore."

Gio then grabs Rocky by the arm and pulls him into a friendly headlock.

"Let's not forget about our VIP here!" he says. To which Rocky seems surprised.

"Me? I was barely involved. You guys did all the work." "Little man, I was literally seconds away from becoming a hashtag before you stepped in. Seriously. Thank you."

Rocky turns red but smiles anyway. Sky then wraps an arm around him and says,

"You saved my boyfriend, so don't sell yourself short. Well, not any shorter than you already are." "Hey!"

Everyone laughs together. Tasha is particularly happy to hear Sky refer to Gio as his boyfriend. *Finally*. She was this close to knocking their heads together if they spent one more day circling around each other. After the laughs die down, Tasha grabs the messenger bag.

"Before I open this, I think it's only fair that our brave knight gets a majority of whatever's in here. Any objections?" She asks.

There are none. Tasha nods and unzips the bag. There are bags of contraband in there, which she does *not* want to touch, but there are also several rolls of cash bound in rubber bands. She practically drools seeing so much money at once.

Counting it out, the bills added up to 1,500 dollars. Tasha gives herself, Gio, Rocky, and Mileena 200 a piece. The remaining 700 go to Sky. The blond nearly cries as he pockets the cash, thanking them all hundreds more times.

"Wait a second, why *did* the cops just show up? We were only there for like, five minutes." asks Tasha. Mileena slowly raises her hand. "I may have called in via anonymous tip that there was gang activity happening at that warehouse while you guys were out back," she confesses.

Tasha shakes her head.

"Well, good thing we finished when we did. C'mon, let's get out of here."

After gathering themselves, the party sneaks around back to Mileena's car and quickly drives off before they can be spotted by the authorities. Though they do manage to see Tatt Face and several of his goons being handcuffed, which was very satisfying.

Naturally, Tasha and company head to the Castillos' house. Rocky makes a joke about his place becoming their base of operations before Andrea calls and chews him out for skipping class. Tasha apologizes for possibly getting him in trouble, but he insists it was all worth it. She hopes that's true.

For the rest of the afternoon, the group simply hung out in the living room and watched trashy reality shows. Tasha could almost laugh. Less than an hour ago, they were going head-to-head with over a dozen armed grown men. Now here they were quietly watching TV like normal teenagers. But they weren't normal. Nothing about any of them was normal anymore.

Around 4pm, Andrea finally comes home. And she does not look happy.

"I'm going to have to ask you all to leave so I can talk with Rocky about these *antics*."

The teens clear out immediately. After giving Rocky hugs, everyone else is dropped off at their respective houses. Sky is to take care of his family with the money they earn. Gio and Mileena both need to catch up on homework. Tasha herself is feeling a little sore from the fight and just wants to unwind.

Once she gets home, she hops in the shower for a good thirty minutes. Afterwards, she feels inspired to add a new piece of art to her sketchbook. Still invigorated from the memory of the warehouse fight, Tasha is burning with inspiration to draw. After some time, her creation ends up being her and her friends in their hoodies and bandanas jumping into action. Being 'Angel' was a rush unlike anything she'd ever felt before. Plus, being able to help Sky while also taking out her frustration on a bunch of dirtbags was downright therapeutic.

We oughta have a team name. I'll have to ask Rocky about that.

Sometime later, around 7pm, Tasha places an order to have wings delivered for dinner. Feeling like she's been neglecting her lately, Tasha calls Jasmine and invites her to come over to eat. With everything going on, she could use some semblance of normalcy. Jasmine accepts the invite, letting Tasha know she'll be over in thirty.

Forty-five minutes go by. Tasha thinks nothing of it. Jasmine wasn't known for being punctual. The wings are delivered. Ten more minutes go by. Nothing still. Tasha texts her asking if she's close. No response. Tasha looks down at her phone.

"Where is she?" she asks herself. She ordered extra just for her. Just as Tasha considers calling Jasmine again, her phone starts ringing. The caller ID says Tamika. Jasmine's mom. Tasha answers.

"Hey, Ms. Watson. ... Wait, *what*?! ... Oh my God, what happened?! ... I'm coming right *now*!"

Tasha books it as fast as she can on her bike all the way to the Olligrove ER. Her legs burn, but she pushes through. Her friend needs her!

As Tasha bursts through the front doors, she spots a black woman with a braided ponytail speaking to the nurse at the front desk. Tamika.

"That's my *daughter*!" she exclaims. The nurse calmly replies, "Ma'am, trust me, we're understanding, but we can't let you back there just yet. The doctor will be out shortly, so *please* remain patient."

Tasha runs over to Tamika and gives her a tight hug.

"Oh, Tasha, thank *God*." "I got here as fast as I could. What's going on with Jasmine?" "I still don't know. She was heading to your house, and the next thing I know, I get a call telling me she's *here*."

Tamika begins trembling. Tears of worry and frustration streak down her face.

"This is my fault. She said she'd be fine, but I should've given her a ride. I should've-" Tasha just hugs her tighter.

"Don't do that, Ms. Watson. *Nothing* is your fault," she reassures.

At that moment, both a doctor and a police officer enter the lobby and approach Tamika.

"How is she? Is she okay? What happened, dammit?!" she demands. The doctor pulls out his clipboard and clears his throat.

"Jasmine is stable. She's got a mild concussion and a broken left arm, but other than that, she's in relatively good condition. We have her on some medication for the pain as we speak," he informs.

Tamika breathes a sigh of relief with a hand to her chest. Tasha looks from the doctor to the officer.

"Why's *he* here then?" she asks.

The officer puts his hands on his belt and says,

"There's one more thing about this situation the doc forgot to mention; we believe your daughter was attacked. There are marks on her neck that indicate strangulation."

Tamika's breath shudders as she once again goes into a panic.

"What?! My baby was *attacked*?! Oh lord. Doc, please, can I see her? *Please*?!"

The doc nods and ushers them to follow. As Tasha falls in line behind them, a hot, sour taste fills her mouth. Strangulation. That's what the officer said. Of course, objectively speaking, there are all kinds of sickos in the world who prey on unsuspecting women. It could be any number of rotten souls that dared to assault Jasmine. But Tasha's intuition rarely steered her wrong. She has a really bad feeling that she knows who did this.

A minute later, the doctor leads them into a patient room. Tasha nearly breaks down then and there, seeing Jasmine propped up in the hospital bed. She has left her arm in a sling and gauze wrapped around her forehead. She seems a little out of it due to whatever meds the doctors have her on, but she still sits up straight at the sight of her mother and her friend. Tamika kneels down in front of the bed and grabs her daughter's free hand.

"Oh lord, Jasmine! How do you feel, baby?" she asks.

Jasmine gulps, then immediately grimaces. Just like the officer said, there were angry, purple bruises on her throat. Poor thing. It must hurt like hell to try to swallow. With a crackling rasp in her voice, Jasmine replies,

"Like I swallowed a jar of porcupine needles and washed them down with lighter fluid." "Jasmine, I'm gonna need you to answer a few questions for me if you can," says the officer, pulling out a notepad. Jasmine nods.

"Where were you when the incident occurred?" "I was on Moore Avenue at the bus stop by the beauty store." "I see. And *did* someone attack you?" "Ahem,... yes." "If you don't mind me asking, how did it occur?"

Tasha anxiously bites her nails in anticipation. *Please don't be him. Please don't be him!*

Jasmine painfully clears her throat again and then answers,

"I was just waiting on the bus when all of a sudden I... No, forget it. You're gonna think I'm crazy if I-" "Jaz, tell us!" Tasha interjects.

She, Tamika, the doctor, and the officer quietly wait for her response. Jasmine holds her mother's hand a little tighter.

"Like I said, I was waiting on the bus and I felt these arms grab me from behind. They were long. Like... freakishly long. Everything happened so fast, I can barely remember how it went down." "Any detail you can spare will help," says the officer. Jasmine swallows and continues,

"This is gonna sound insane. The arms dragged me into the alley. It was dark, so I couldn't make anything out but the guy who attacked me, he looked like... a shadow."

Tasha stands in shock, her fear confirmed. The Boogeyman hurt her friend. A deep cold floods her veins. Her situation just got much worse than she could've imagined. The officer skeptically raises his eyebrow.

"'Shadow'? You did say it was dark in the alley, and he was probably wearing all black. Are you sure there aren't any other discerning features about this creep?" he asks. Jasmine shakes her head and winces in pain.

"No. Not that I could see. I tried screaming for help, but then his fingers got all long and weird, and he was strangling me. After that, he heard someone coming and then threw me against the wall." "I'm assuming that's how you got the broken arm and head bruise?"

Jasmine nods, squeezing her eyes shut as she begins to cry. Tamika is not much better as she hears the details of her daughter's assault.

"I think that's enough for now," suggests the doctor, "We're going to need to keep her for overnight surveillance. In case any more symptoms from her injuries show up." "Well, I'm not leaving," says Tamika.

Tasha balls her fists, her nails digging into her palms. She turns on a heel and begins walking away before she causes any unintentional damage.

"Where are you going?" Jasmine asks behind her. Tasha looks back.

"To handle this." "Young lady, we're on the case!" the officer calls out, but Tasha is already halfway down the hall.

Strong emotions are bubbling inside of her like a pot of boiling water threatening to spill over. Quickly, she finds the nearest women's room and runs inside.

Luckily, it's unoccupied. Tasha runs to the sink and leans against the counter.

He hurt Jasmine! He hurt Jasmine! She thinks over and over. Hot tears leak from her eyes. *Hold it together, Tasha! I need to be strong! I need to do something! I need to-*

"AHHHHHHH!!!"

Tasha screams and punches the wall. *BAM*! Her fist sinks right through the drywall like butter. Tasha stands there panting as she looks at her hand. It's covered in plaster, but there's no pain. *I'm so strong,* she thinks, *but I can't put my fist through what I really want!* She kneads her fingers into her scalp, trying as hard as she can to focus.

Suddenly, a very familiar tingle itches at the back of her head. Tasha grips the counter even tighter. The porcelain cracks under pressure from her strength.

No. Not now. Please! Sure enough, black swirling mist begins to creep from under the door. Tasha backs into the corner, not sure whether to square up or call for help. Either way, there's not much she can do against this monster by herself. The black mist creeps into the bathroom, slowly shaping itself into a humanoid form. To Tasha's surprise, the Boogeyman doesn't make any moves. He just stands there, staring at her with no face. It's incredibly unsettling how still he is.

"Don't worry. I'm not going to attack you. Not here anyway," his raspy, distorted voice tells her.

Tasha gulps. She's pretty sure her heart is about to burst out of her chest the way it's beating.

"Why?" she manages to ask, "Why her? Your beef is with *us*!" Boogeyman chuckles long and slow.

"Consider your friend a warning. I'm through playing games. Keep snooping and next time it's someone... closer. Like your sister." "Don't you touch Bree!" Tasha snaps. Boogeyman chuckles again.

"Not only will I touch her, I'll snap her damn spine in half! And not just her. Your precious teacher. The fat one's uncle. The waitress's father. The fast one's itty bitty baby sister! Even with all your pathetic powers, you can't be everywhere at once!"

Tasha feels herself on the verge of tears again. He was serious. She knows he is. Her legs buckle, and Tasha falls to the ground on her knees. Even with all of her impressive strength, she's powerless.

"What *is* this? What are you doing?" she asks.

The Boogeyman steps away from her, turning into his cloudy form to slink back under the door.

"What I have to do. You just remember what I said. I'm closer than you think."

The cloud disappears, leaving Tasha to marinate with those ominous words. She rises from the floor and wipes her eyes. She and her team were in serious trouble, and she had no clue how to make anything better.

After gathering herself as best she could in the bathroom, Tasha exited the hospital. She looks at her bicycle and moans. She's tired, frustrated, and emotional, so the thought of biking home seems repulsive. Instead, she calls Bree who is thankfully off work by now. Within ten minutes, Bree pulls up and Tasha hops in.

"I'm so sorry I wasn't here earlier. Tamika called me, but I wasn't able to answer the phone. What happened to Jasmine?" asks Bree.

Tasha leans her head against the window.

"She got attacked by the Boogeyman," she says on autopilot.

It isn't until Tasha finishes her sentence that she realizes what she just said and immediately wants to slap herself. Bree is rightfully confused as they stop at a red light.

"'The Boogeyman'? Who the hell is the Boogeyman?" she asks.

Tasha bites her lip. There's the million-dollar question. What can she say without revealing what's really been going on for the last few weeks?

"He's... a bad man," she eventually replies. "Tasha, is something going on that I need to know about?" Bree asks her.

Tasha thinks back to what the Boogeyman said to her in the restroom.

Keep snooping around, and next time it's someone... closer like your sister. Tasha would love more than anything to confide in her Bree. The way she used to in the old days. Before they lost their parents. Before Bree had to sacrifice her fun-loving ways to be Tasha's full-time guardian. No. She can't involve Bree as well. She can't add to her stress and give her more to worry about. Tasha's lost too much already. Losing Bree as well would ruin her. Tasha swallows her words and shakes her head no. Bree looks like she wants to press, but instead just keeps driving.

Once they return home, Bree calls Tamika to get more details on Jasmine while Tasha trudges upstairs to her room. She flops face first on her bed, grips her pillow, and lets herself go. It starts off as shuddering breaths with a handful of tears. But quickly, she finds herself being completely swallowed by everything she'd been trying to hold in. Tasha sobs, and sobs hard. She isn't sure for how long. It feels like forever. She hasn't cried this much since her parents' funeral four years ago. Bree had to hold onto her as she watched their caskets descend into the ground. It's an image that's stayed with her. All Tasha wants is to make things better and to protect her friends. And so far, she's failed at both.

Chapter 23

Night School

Tasha's pillowcase is soaked with mucus and tears, but it doesn't matter. After an unknown amount of time, a knock on her bedroom door catches her attention. Tasha quickly blows her nose and wipes her eyes, then opens her door. Bree is standing there with a pack of pecan shortbread cookies. Tasha smiles weakly as she accepts the offering. These were her favorites.

"Thanks, sis," she croaks. Her voice is slightly hoarse from crying. Bree nods.

"I figured you needed these. Also, you have company."

Tasha already knows who it is. As she descends the stairs, sure enough, Sky, Gio, Mileena, Rocky, and Andrea await her in the living room. Rocky runs over and hugs Tasha's waist. She hugs him back, grateful for the affection.

"I'll uh, I'll give you some privacy," says Bree at the top of the stairs.

Tasha then leads the others to the couches and takes a seat.

"We came as soon as we could," says Gio. "Yeah, we got *major* down vibes from the Link and knew something was wrong," says Mileena. "I'm still fired up from earlier. Whose ass do we gotta kick?" asks Sky. "Everyone, give her a moment," Andrea interjects.

Tasha grins anyway. Their support means the world to her.

"It's okay. Well, actually,... something *really* bad happened."

Tasha gives the details about Jasmine's attack and Boogeyman's threat. By the time she's done, she's on the verge of crying again.

"I... I don't even... oh my god." Andrea mutters. "He's out there. Watching us and waiting for us," says Rocky with panicked eyes.

Andrea softly strokes her son's hair to try to calm him down. Gio swallows, tugging at his curls.

"This is bad, guys. This is *really* bad. If he gets his hands on my mom or, god forbid, little Phoebe..." Gio sniffles, shuddering at the thought.

Sky wraps an arm around him and kisses his cheek. "I won't let that happen. *We* won't let that happen. We'll think of something. We have to," he proclaims.

Mileena looks at Tasha and says, "You said he told you he's 'doing what he has to', right? Why do you think he's going through all this trouble?" Tasha shrugs her shoulders. "I don't know. He didn't care to elaborate when he said he'd snap my sister's spine in half." "*Exactly*! That means we're *this* close to finding out whatever Boogeyman is hiding."

Tasha slaps her hands on her legs.

"Look, I like the sentiment. Especially from you, Mil. But what're we supposed to do about this? None of our loved ones has healing like we do. Jasmine's lucky to still be alive."

Everything falls silent. Tasha hates feeling so defeated, but what else could be done? She was starting to regret ever going in that secret tunnel at all. Now, not only were they in danger, but so was everyone close to them. Andrea reaches over and grabs Tasha's hand.

"You're not defeated, Tasha. The Boogeyman is clearly doing this as a last ditch act of desperation. Do you think he'll actually leave you alone after this 'message' even if you do stop prying?"

Tasha looks at the woman. She had a point. Andrea looks from Tasha to her son to Mileena, Sky, and Gio.

"I know you're all scared. Trust me. I've been on the verge of a nervous breakdown myself just being a spectator. But the five of you *have* to see this through."

Rocky shakes his head. "You didn't see what happened the last time we fought him, Mom. We almost didn't escape." he says.

The others all murmur in agreement. Andrea scoffs.

"After everything you guys have told me, I think you might surprise yourselves come Round 2. You're all strong in your own ways. But together, you could be unstoppable."

Tasha closes her eyes, leaning her head against the back of the couch. Andrea's words are lovely. She wants to believe them. She wants to feel her motivation return. But at the moment, she's just tired. Emotionally. Mentally. Physically. Even though it's only 8pm, Tasha's ready to call it a night. As she yawns, Andrea gives her a gentle pat on the head.

"It's gonna be okay." she whispers.

Tasha lets her consciousness slip off into slumber. *I hope so.* One by one, Rocky, Sky, Gio and Mileena join her on the couch. The Link seems to be affecting them in a similar fashion. Soon enough, the five youths all fall asleep leant against one another.

Andrea Perez Carolina Castillo looks down at the group as they sleep peacefully on the couch. She shakes her head. They were good kids. None of them deserved this burden. Least of all Rocky. Andrea never pressured him about it, but she's always had concern for her only child. The poor boy was born premature with an absent father and a struggling eighteen year old for a mom. Growing up, Rocky was always reserved and shy. All he wanted to do was play video games, read his comic books, and cook. There was nothing wrong with that of course. Andrea has always encouraged Rocky's creativity, but it always made her sad she couldn't help him with everything else. Rocky was shorter than average and considerably introverted, so other kids always saw him as an easy target. Andrea has considered moving back to Florida with the rest of her family several times. She figured maybe being around his relatives and Puerto Rican roots would help bring him out of his shell. But then one fateful day, she's roped into watching a handful of detention bound students and *everything* changed. Rocky was now excited about things. Smiling. Going out. Being social. And living out his dreams of having superpowers. Something Andrea is still trying to wrap her head around. However, she was honored to be a pseudo-member of this little gang. Sweet, brave Tasha. Open, comical Sky. Cool, level-headed Gio. Pragmatic, intelligent Mileena. Andrea really couldn't have asked for a better team. Unfortunately, this entire Boogeyman situation has them all down and scared and tired. This Boogeyman, whoever he was, makes her blood boil. The sheer audacity he had to attack her baby! But Andrea doesn't have any powers. She couldn't do anything to help them.

Or can I? A potential idea comes to her head, and suddenly she can't sit still. Andrea jumps from her seat and almost says something. Then she looks down at the faces of her son and his friends. Poor things. They looked exhausted. Especially Tasha. *Best not disturb them. I can take care of this,* she thinks. Andrea grabs her purse and her car keys and makes her way to the door.

"Um, hi. Can I talk to you for a sec?" a voice asks behind her.

Andrea turns around and looks at Bree. Andrea was 32 years old. Bree seemed to only be a few years younger than her. It was interesting. Bree approaches her, nervously tugging on her sleeves.

"Listen I uh, I couldn't help but listen in while you guys were having your discussion." she says.

Andrea makes sure to keep her face as neutral as possible. It wasn't her place to divulge Tasha's business.

"And what did you hear?" she asks. Bree chuckles with a tired shrug. "I have no idea what I heard. But I do know that something out there wants to hurt my sister like it hurt Jasmine. Some... Boogeyman."

Andrea looks at the sleeping teens then back at Bree. She nods and says,

"Yes. I can't really explain right now but-" "No. It's fine. I want Tasha to tell me whenever she's ready. It's just... I haven't been the greatest sister to her. I missed her big birthday, I have no idea what she's been up to, and now *this*. Whatever you've been doing for her, thank you for stepping up where I couldn't."

Andrea shoulders her purse, sternly looking Bree in the eyes.

"Tasha is a remarkable young woman and she loves you dearly. Be present for her." she says. Bree chuckles once more.

"I see why she likes you." Andrea nods in acknowledgement and leaves. It was time to do her part.

Andrea arrives at the school parking lot making sure to stay close to the front. It was well after school hours. Any club or group activities should be over by now. There are a few cars still around, so she wonders who's still there. As Andrea walks up to the front door, an elderly security guard shines a flashlight in her face.

"Hey! Who goes there!?" he demands.

Andrea blocks the light with her hand, fishing her lanyard with her ID out of her purse.

"Relax! I'm a teacher here." she replies. The security guard lowers the flashlight once he recognizes her. "Ah. Sorry about that. Is there a reason you're here so late? Most everyone has already left." "I forgot something in my classroom is all. Figured I'd get it now while I'm still awake." "Can't fault a guy for asking. You're the second person to come here around this time."

Andrea raises an eyebrow.

"Really? Who else?" "That handyman of ours, Mr. Mays. He's been tardy a lot recently. Anyways, go right in."

Andrea purses her lips as she enters the building. That was odd. Then again, there was no shortage of things in need of fixing around the school. Maybe he was just tired. Andrea's heels seem louder than usual as she walks through the dimly lit linoleum hallways. Andrea had never been here at this time of night before. Without the constant noise of students walking and talking in every direction, everything feels eerily quiet. As she walks past the teachers' lounge, she spots Mr. Mays on a stepladder changing the light in there. She's never spoken with the man but he always seemed friendly enough. Apparently, he had a bit of a rapport with Sky every time he left detention. As the man reaches down to grab a tool, Andrea notices some scarring in zig-zag patterns on his forearms. *Huh. Never seen scars like that before,* she thinks. Mr. Mays sees her and waves. Andrea waves back then continues walking. She had a mission at hand.

After a minute, Andrea reaches the other side of the building and arrives at the principal's office. She goes to open the door but it won't budge.

"Damn. Of course it's locked." she says to herself.

She knows it'd be unlocked during day hours, but she didn't want to risk Isaac walking in on her. She considers asking the security guard or Mr. Mays if they had a spare set of keys. Suddenly, someone taps on her shoulder out of nowhere. Andrea flinches, nearly jumping out of her skin. As she turns around, she curses at herself once she sees who it is. Catherine-Bethany Charles. The last person she'd expect to see at that moment. The girl holds up, holding up a key in her hands.

"Jesus Ms. Castillo, chill. If you wanna get in there, you'll need one of these." she says with a cocky smirk.

Andrea sighs. Knowing what she does about the principal's daughter, her patience was about to be tested.

"How did you get that?" she asks. Catherine-Bethany puts the key in the lock and turns it. "I have all of Dad's important keys copied."

The door to the office opens with a loud click that makes Andrea nervous. Every sound they make feels amplified. The two stroll into the office and turn on the overhead light. As Andrea walks over to Isaac's computer, Catherine-Bethany begins opening the drawers under the desk. The teen asks,

"So Ms. Castillo, why are you snooping around in my dad's office? Not that I care."
"I'm looking for... information. Why are *you* here?" Andrea retorts. Catherine-Bethany scoffs.

"I got busted smoking cigarettes this past weekend and my parents freaked out about it like lames. Dad confiscated them and I couldn't find them anywhere in the house, so I figured they were here in his office."

Andrea scratches her head in confusion.

"You really snuck in here to find your *cigarettes?*" she asks incredulously. Catherine-Bethany rolls her eyes. "*Duh*. I'm not 21 so it's not like I can easily buy more. I thought teachers were supposed to be smart or something."

Andrea bites her lip to keep from cursing this girl out. She's well aware of Catherine-Bethany's affinity for pushing buttons. Swallowing her pride, Andrea uses her administrative ID to login to Isaac's computer. If there was anything he had that would help solve this Boogeyman mystery, it might be somewhere in his personal archives. She clicks through various files and folders, looking for anything out of the ordinary. So far, all she finds are meeting dates and scheduling info. Andrea tries checking out his saved media and scrolls through that. There's countless pictures of Isaac doing menial things around the school or shaking hands with board members. Nothing terribly interesting. That is until she remembers something the group told her. The picture they found at the old ranger station was from twenty years ago at least. Andrea types in the date from two decades ago and is brought to the collection of Isaac's photos from that era. *Bingo.* It doesn't take long for her to eventually find a picture similar to the one they described. Young Isaac. A black man with braids, a blond woman, and a second guy with a wild mane of hair. Below her, Catherine-Bethany eventually finds what she's scrimmaging for and pulls out a pack of cigarettes out of an old cassette box.

"*Ha*! I knew he'd hide it in something old and dumb." she says.

Andrea takes personal offense to that. She remembers a time when cassette players were all the rage. Before the girl leaves, Andrea taps her on her shoulder.

"Hold on a sec. I need to ask you something." "No, I won't tell my dad you were going through his computer. As long as you don't tell him about the cigarettes." "That's not what I meant."

Andrea points to the photo on the screen.

"Do you know who these people are?" she asks. Catherine-Bethany snorts. "No. My dad's past is too boring for me to care about. There *is* a picture just like that in the front drawer though."

Andrea opens said drawer. Lo and behold, the very same picture is on a printed polaroid among a pile of paperclips and pens. She turns it around and sees there's writing on the back. *-Bff's, Alex, Brian, Isaac, and Corty.-*

Andrea scoffs at the sentimentality. Isaac was so clearly a dork even back then. But now she knows for sure that this Corty individual is someone from Isaac's past. She looks back at the picture, trying to guess which one was Corty. If she figures this out, this could change *everything* for Rocky and his friends. As Catherine turned to leave once again, Andrea needed to get something off her chest while she was there.

"Do you feel bad at all?"

Catherine puts her hands on her hips. "Feel bad for *what*?"

Andrea stands up from her chair. "Talking to people the way you do. *Treating* people the way you do. Especially Tasha Simone. Remember her?" she asks with repressed anger. Catherine rolls her eyes. "Look, she got *herself* in detention when she pushed me. It's not my fault she can't control her emotions." "Don't give me that crap, Catherine. I understand your dad spoils you and lets you get away with everything, but that's no excuse to provoke people."

The young girl seemed genuinely perplexed at someone trying to hold her accountable.

"Look, I was just saying my opinion. *She* took it personally." "Oh, you mean when you made those racial comments and brought up her deceased parents? Let me tell you something, young lady; that stank attitude of yours needs a *serious* adjustment." "You can't talk to me like that!" "Or what? You gonna make comments about me too? I'm Hispanic *and* a single mother so you've got plenty of ammo. Go ahead!"

Catherine stands there for a moment, huffing angrily. Andrea simply stares her down, *daring* her to say something smart.

"Okay. Fine. Maybe, *maybe* I took it too far. But whatever." Catherine says at last. Andrea shakes her head. "I've gotten to know Tasha a lot recently. She's a great person. I suggest you apologize the next time you see her." the woman suggests.

Catherine huffs in annoyance then finally takes her leave. With that out of the way, Andrea sits back down to take a closer look at the polaroid. *C'mon. Which one are you, Corty*? She types in the name "Corty" into the computer to see if the name matched anyone in the old database. There's no initial results, so she comes to the conclusion Corty must be a nickname. Instead, she types in Brian and tries to match it to any number of students named "Brian" from twenty plus years ago. After seeing four other Brian's from that year, she finally sees one who's photo matches the one on the Polaroid. Brian Ashmore. The young black man with braids. From there, Andrea clicks on his graduating class that year to see if she can make another match. Keeping her eyes peeled, she eventually finds a matching Alex. The blond woman in Brian's arms was Alex Moon. She scans the picture of the graduating class Brian and Alex were in. No sign of the young man with wild black hair with them, so whoever that was must be Corty. Andrea looks from the computer back to the picture in her hand. She glances closely at him, willing something, *anything* to help her out. All of a sudden, a random factoid flows through her brain. Mileena mentioned hitting the Boogeyman with a particularly strong bolt of lightning so hard that he had to retreat. Survivors of lightning strikes tended to have a skin reaction called Lichtenberg figures, which were scars in the shape of... zig zags. Fear clutches Andrea's chest.

No. That's crazy talk, Andrea. It doesn't make any sense. There's no way. Before she confirms anything to herself just yet, Andrea takes one more inspection at the picture.

The young man with wild hair who had to be Corty. *What would he look like two decades later?* she wonders.

Suddenly, *CHYURRRRR.* The computer shuts off with a loud whirring noise. *CHYURRRRR.* The office lights click off as well. *Oh no.* Andrea quickly jumps up from her chair and runs out into the hallway. *Tak. Tak. Tak. Tak.* One by one, the already dim lights of the hallways cease to illuminate all around the school. Out of nowhere, Andrea hears the squeaking of tennis shoes coming her way. She nearly has a heart attack upon seeing Catherine-Bethany running towards her, eyes wide with fear.

"Ms. Castillo, what's going on? I was on my way out of here when the power went out!"

Before Andrea can answer her, the last overhead light above their heads flickers out, leaving them in near complete darkness. Catherine reaches out and grabs Andrea's hand, nearly hyperventilating with panic. Andrea tries her best to keep her composure, but she already knows. She's in danger. Quickly, she takes her phone out of her pocket with shaky fingers. Her hands won't stay still enough to text, so she taps on her contacts and starts a voice message.

"Rocky, listen to me very carefully. I'm at the school, but I think I might be in trouble. Look up Brian Ashmore and Alex Moon. I went through Isaac's computer, and they're in that picture with him. Also, I'm pretty sure Corty is-" "Ms. Castillo, *what* is happening?!" Catherine-Bethany interrupts.

Andrea shushes her as something at the end of the hall catches her attention. A beam from a flashlight comes into view as the old security guard strolls in from outside.

"Hello?! Is anyone still-?"

THWACK! A harsh impact echoes and the guard is knocked limp on the ground by an unseen force. Andrea and Catherine take two steps back, both petrified of whatever is in the vicinity.

"I'm *really* scared, Ms. Castillo. What do we do?" Catherine whispers.

Andrea protectively grabs hold of her arm. Pain in the neck or not, she was still an innocent. A dusty boot steps into the beam of the flashlight on the ground, illuminating the outline of a familiar figure.

"*It sucks that I have to do this. I always liked you, Andrea.*" a warbly voice croons.

Andrea yanks Catherine with her.

"It's him! *Run*!"

The two make a break for it as fast as they can. Their pursuer morphs and gives chase.

Chapter 24

Desperate Times Call for Bad Ideas

It's roughly 7am when Rocky awakens. He sits up straight, his sleepy brain not registering where he was until he looks to his right. Sky is holding Gio. Mileena is curled in a fetal position. Tasha is in the middle, using Gio's shoulder as a pillow. His friends were all snoring and sleeping peacefully. Rocky rubs his eyes as he stands up from the couch. Right. They came to Tasha's house after they felt her in emotional distress. Rocky thinks about how he had one of the most exciting days of his life, fighting actual criminals, just to be brought down to harsh reality a few hours later. He wonders where his mom is and why she hasn't woken them up. It was a school day after all. He figured he wouldn't be lucky enough that she'd call him out again.

"Mom?" he calls in a croaky voice. There's no answer. Rocky scratches his hair. He walks around the living room, checks the kitchen, and even goes upstairs. No sign of her. Rocky pulls out his cellphone to call her, then slaps himself on the forehead. His phone was dead. He'd forgotten to charge it last night before they came over. Rocky goes back to the living room couch and gently nudges Tasha's arm. He hates to wake her out of the sleep she so clearly needs, but he's starting to get a feeling that something wasn't right. Tasha's eyes slowly open.

"Oh, man. Did we really sleep all night like that?" she asks quietly. Rocky nods. "Yeah. Also, can I borrow your charger? My mom's not here and my phone's dead."

Tasha wipes a line of drool from the side of her mouth and stands up with a stretch. Once she sees the time from the clock on the wall, she groans in annoyance.

"Jesus, we're gonna be late for school," she says. One by one, she nudges Sky, Gio, and Mileena awake. They all grumble and complain as they stir to consciousness. Tasha hands Rocky her phone charger and goes to the kitchen to start the coffee machine. As Gio checks his cell, his brows rise with curiosity.

"Yo, check this out. I just got a text from my mom. She says the school notified her that classes are canceled today," he announces. Mileena checks her phone next. "My dad's saying the same thing to me," she says. "Me, too. From my uncle," adds Sky. "Really? Why?" asks Rocky. Gio replies,

"According to her, they're saying issues with power."

Sky sits back down on the couch with a grin. "That's fine with me," he says. "That means we can just chill."

While the others start discussing what their next move for the day should be, Rocky's phone finally blinks to life. Immediately, he sees a notification from Andrea. It's a voice message from last night. Rocky's brows furrow, wondering what his mom got up to while they were asleep. He presses play and holds the phone to his ear. There's some heavy breathing at the start.

"Rocky, listen to me very carefully. I'm at the school, but I think I might be in trouble. Look up Brian Ashmore and Alex Moon. I went through Isaac's computer, and they're in that picture with him. Also, I'm pretty sure Corty is-" "Ms. Castillo, what is happening?!" "Shhh!" There's a brief pause and the sound of footsteps. *"I'm really scared, Ms. Castillo. What do we do?" .... "It's him! Run!"*

The voice message comes to an end. Rocky's entire body goes rigid. His mouth dries up. His chest tightens. He can hear his heart banging in his ears like a marching band drum. He tries to speak, but his breath comes out in stutters.

"She- she- she...!"

The more Rocky tries to talk, the worse everything gets. His skin feels too hot. His hands are shaking uncontrollably. His chest tightens even more, as though a pair of invisible hands were squeezing his lungs. This was bad. This was so incredibly, unbelievably *bad*!

Rocky reaches out for help and falls on all fours. Tasha, Sky, Gio, and Mileena run over to him, their faces wrought with worry.

"Bro, what's wrong?" "Rocky, are you okay?" "Speak to me, little man!" "Rocky, talk to us!"

Rocky hears all their voices, but they're dulled out and distant with his heartbeat and short breaths taking over his hearing. Rocky tries talking again, but all that comes from his mouth is harsh gasping. Since he suddenly doesn't know how to verbalize, Rocky uses his last resort and physically broadcasts through the Link, *Air! I need air! I'm dying! I'M DYING!*

Mileena is smacked in the face with realization.

"Oh my God, he's having a panic attack!" "Rocky! Look at us! You're going to be okay!"

Sky tries, but everyone's words still feel so distant. He's in the middle of an ocean, miles away from shore, being dragged away by the current. Drowning. Drowning. Forever. Tasha covers her mouth, on the verge of tears herself. Suddenly, Gio kneels down to Rocky's level and wraps his arms around the boy. Rocky grasps onto Gio's shirt for dear life, trying his damnedest to *just breathe!* Gio rests his chin on Rocky's shoulder, strokes his back gently, and sings.

"*~Did you eat today? Have you yet put something in your stomach? Did you eat today? You gotta be good to your tummy. Red beans and rice. Or a hot, sweet apple pie. C'mon, baby, tell me what you like.~*"

Rocky's frowns against Gio's shoulders. "What the-?" "Shhh. Just breathe. I'll sing it again. *~Did you eat today? Have you yet put something in your stomach? Did you eat today? You gotta be good to your tummy. Red beans and rice. Or a hot, sweet apple pie. C'mon, baby, tell me what you like.~*"

Rocky squeezes his eyes closed, manually willing himself to inhale, hold, then exhale. Inhale, hold, exhale. He's still adrift at sea, but he doesn't feel like he's drowning anymore. Hesitantly, he asks,

"One more time? Please?" Gio obliges. "*~Did you eat today? Have you yet put something in your stomach? Did you eat today? You gotta be good to your tummy. Red beans and rice. Or a hot, sweet apple pie. C'mon, baby, tell me what you like.~*"

Rocky loosens his grip on Gio's shirt. He can feel the peak of his attack descending. Oh, so slowly, but it is descending. After about a minute of getting his breath back, Rocky finally lets go. Gio smiles at him softly.

"What- what *was* that?" asks Tasha. Gio replies, "I used to write these silly songs when I was little and learning how to play guitar. The night my dad broke up with my mom and left her high and dry, she... she had a panic attack. All I wanted was to help her feel better, so I hugged her and sang that song. It seemed to help back then, so I did it again now."

Sky wipes a tear from his eye.

"That was probably the cutest thing I've ever heard," he says with an exaggerated manner. Rocky chuckles for a millisecond, but then he remembers why he just panicked. He holds up his phone and replays the message for all to hear. Once it's over, Mileena balls up her fists.

"Dammit!" Green energy sparks from her and cracks the glass casing of the clock on the wall.

"Mr. Charles' computer, of *course*! We're so stupid! We could've thought about this days ago and been there to protect her!" "Don't do that to yourself, Mil," Tasha interjects, "We've had a lot on our plates." "Also, am I crazy, or was that Catherine-Bethany's voice with Andrea?" asks Sky. Tasha rolls her eyes.

"That was *definitely* her." "Mom said look up 'Brian Ashmore' and 'Alex Moon' and that they were in the picture with Mr. Charles. Maybe we can figure out who Corty is. It sounded like she figured it out when,..."

Rocky's eyes close. He doesn't want to say it out loud. The Boogeyman got his mother. At best, she's injured like Tasha's friend Jasmine. At worst... Sensing his thoughts, Tasha puts her hand on Rocky's back. He looks at her with tears in his eyes.

"That's my *mom*, Tasha."

She pats his back. "I know. Trust me. I know." Tasha then looks to the rest of the group.

"First Jasmine, now Andrea? Nuh uh. We're ending this. *Today*!" she says with determination. "Not to be 'that guy' but... how?" asks Gio. "First, we look up these names and see what we can gather." "Then what?" "We'll figure it out!"

Tasha points at Mileena.

"You got access to the car today?" she asks. Mileena shakes her head. "No, sorry. My dad said I've been 'hogging it' recently." "Take my car then," says a new voice.

Everyone turns and sees Bree standing at the living room entrance. She takes her keys out of her pocket.

"I don't know what's going on, but I know this Andrea woman means a lot to you. I also know that something is after you. You say you're gonna end this today? Then end it."

Tasha is flabbergasted as her sister hands her the car keys.

"What about you? Don't you need to go to work?" "I called off."

Tasha embraces her sister.

"I *promise* I'll explain everything. I put that on Mom and Dad." "You'd damn well better or I'm gonna whoop your behind for keeping secrets from me." "As *if* you could."

Tasha gives Bree one more hug, then beckons the others to follow her out the door like the leader she is.

"Let's go!" she commands. Sky, Mileena, and Gio follow suit. Before Rocky does the same, Bree says to him,

"I only met her for a second, but I can tell your mom is a special woman." Rocky pauses. Then he grins and says, "So is your sister."

With a fire under his butt like never before, Rocky runs after his friends and joins them in Bree's SUV.

Sky gets behind the wheel and drives them to Olligrove High first. Once they reach the parking lot of the school, Sky parks the SUV right next to Andrea's car, which is still there. Other than a few electrician vans and a moped, there seems to be no sign of anyone else around. Rocky tries calling Andrea's phone just to see what would happen. It goes straight to voicemail. Rocky curses to himself. He's holding on to any shred of hope that she's still alive. He can't imagine his world without her, so he won't. In the front seat, Tasha is on her phone searching for the names his mom gave them.

"Anything yet?" asks Mileena. "Yeah. These pictures are definitely a match. Listen to this: Brian Ashmore, missing person's case right here in Olligrove." "Wait, what?" "It says right here that he was reported missing at the age of 19 and hasn't been found since-" "Let me guess; twenty years ago." "Bingo." "What else is there?" asks Gio.

"According to the police report, he has a criminal history with his best friend, Samuel Alencort." Rocky's eyes widen.

"'Alencort'? That's gotta be Corty!" he says. "You're right. Check this out."

Tasha turns and holds her phone for the others to see. On the screen are two old mugshots. One of Brian, the man with the braids, and the other guy with the long back hair. "What's it say about him?" asks Rocky. Tasha reads on,

"After the two reportedly had a falling out, Samuel was viewed as a possible suspect. However, due to insufficient evidence and a lack of leads after several weeks of investigation, the case was dropped and Samuel left town to unknown whereabouts." Gio scoffs.

"But he *didn't* leave. He's been right here in Olligrove this whole time, haunting Hillstone Park. The question is, why?" "It's obvious," Sky replies, "He was probably responsible for Brian's 'disappearance' after all. And we were getting too close to the truth. There are still a few puzzle pieces we're missing, though." "Before we go any further with that, what's Alex Moon got to do with all this? She's gotta be the woman in the picture. Maybe we should try to find her and ask." Mileena adds. Tasha looks her up and shakes her head.

"No can do. She's currently in Albuquerque, New Mexico. Mother of three. Enlisted in the armed forces."

Gio grumbles,

"Great. *Another* dead end." "Just hold on. The day's not over yet," says Sky.

Rocky rubs his temples. So much new information and yet it *still* wasn't enough. His brain hurts. With a sigh, Mileena says,

"So Corty, aka Boogeyman, is definitely responsible for Brian going missing and has been hiding out in Olligrove for the last two decades. Brian's girlfriend gets out of dodge. We know that Irene O'Hara and Mr. Charles are connected to them and that Corty is now lashing out at us for discovering something we weren't supposed to."

"And now he also has Andrea and Catherine-Bethany," Tasha adds, "They're both alive, I can feel it... But they're in trouble." Mileena slumps in her seat.

"Well, we still can't do anything yet. There are gaps in our intel that need filling." "How are we supposed to do that if Alex is across the country?" asks Gio.

Rocky looks out of the car window at the high school. There was one other way they could get what they needed. It was risky and could severely backfire. But he doesn't care. His mother's life was on the line. He *cannot* lose her! Rocky looks at the group, clears his throat, and speaks.

"My mom found out what she did by going through Mr. Charles' computer, right? Well, I've got an idea. A *really* bad idea."

Isaac Charles has had a very stressful morning. He wakes up at his usual time of 5am to arrive at the school to find that not only is Ernie the security guard unconscious, but someone severely tampered with the wiring and shut off power to the majority of the campus. Damn these kids. It was probably one of them. Ernie is sent to the hospital. City workers are called to try and fix the power. By the time the maintenance people were done repairing the damage, school hours would be halfway over, so he went through the annoying process of canceling classes for the day and getting the word out. To make matters worse, he hasn't seen Catherine-Bethany since last night. Ever since he and his wife Theresa discovered her smoking habit and confiscated her cigarettes, she'd been more ornery than usual. Poor thing. His precious baby was always a headstrong girl. Isaac hates telling her no. Usually, he doesn't, but this was one line he had to draw. While handling the school cancellation, Isaac went to his office and found that Catherine-Bethany had apparently caught on to his hiding place and stolen them from his drawer. Isaac pinches his nose. She must've gotten his keys copied again. Now he has to get another set. He was going to have to have a serious talk with her... once he finds out where she is.

Catherine-Bethany's moped was still in the parking lot when he left the building. But she wasn't home. Isaac goes back to the house and tries calling her. No dice. It seems strange that she wasn't there when her transportation was still at the school.

Sometime later, Isaac gets a message from Theresa asking him to pick up some more flea shampoo for their golden retriever, Milo. He begrudgingly agrees. Dog stuff is more of a Theresa thing. He personally can't stand the mutt. But of course, she's already at work, and his schedule is now wide open. Isaac grumbles as he exits the front door and hops in his black Chevy Suburban. He was hoping to stay in and kick his feet up while waiting for his baby girl to come home.

"I'd better not have any more problems today," he says to himself. Isaac pulls out of his driveway and heads to the nearest dollar store. If he's grabbing anything for Milo, it's going to be the cheap stuff. About a mile down the road, Isaac is humming along to one of his old-timey jazz records when *POP*! There's a shockingly loud popping noise, and the entire right side of his vehicle leans heavily to the right.

"Jeez!" Isaac yells as his car begins to lurch concerningly. The road he was driving on was well-paved with no debris or potholes of any kind. What could possibly have flattened his tire? He smacks his dashboard as he pulls over.

"Great. This is what I needed. This is *exactly* what I needed!" Isaac brings the car to a stop and steps out. He's on a stretch of road between his neighborhood and the shopping center a few miles away. Hopefully, it wouldn't take too long to call someone to come and change his tire. It's something he's never had to do before, and he's damn sure not doing it today. Isaac walks around to the other side of his car and is struck with a bizarre sigh. Rather than a piece of glass or a sharp rock, there's an arrow embedded in his tire. An *arrow*! He crouches down, gently touching the feathers at the end of the shaft. Someone just shot this at his car,... but why?

"Car trouble, sir?" someone asks behind him. Isaac's peripheral vision catches a flash of blond hair. Before he can turn his head to see who it was, a hand grabs his shoulder, and whomp! Every muscle in his body locks up with painful contractions as a series of rough vibrations gets fired into him. Isaac falls to the ground on his back, his body involuntarily shuddering against the asphalt. All he can do is groan in pain as a familiar-looking, heavyset young man stands over him with his arms crossed.

"Hey, Mr. Charles. We're gonna need you to come with us," he says. Through his teeth, Isaac asks, "What- nygh!- is going on?!"

Instead of answering him, the young man grabs onto Isaac's shirt and roughly hoists him up. He tries fighting against it, but he's hit with another pulse of body-wrecking vibration that makes him go limp. What *was* that?! He attempts to open his mouth and scream for help. Someone sticks a line of duct tape to his mouth from behind, then places a pillowcase over his head. His world goes dark as he feels himself being manhandled into a car. He stays quiet, knowing there's nothing he can do against his captors. *I should've had the shampoo delivered*!

Chapter 25

Friendship Can Be Fatal

He isn't sure how long the drive was, but Isaac can tell he's nowhere near his neighborhood. Blinded and muted, he is helplessly yanked out of the backseat of whatever vehicle he was in and forced to walk forward on what feels like concrete and dust.

"Move your butt, old man!" "We'll take the pillowcase off in just a minute." "Are you guys sure about this?" "Darn right I'm sure. He's our last resort." "Here. Pull up a chair. And grab me some more duct tape."

Isaac can just make out all of the voices through the fabric of the pillowcase. A mix of male and female, but they're all young. Like the snot-nosed punks he oversees on a daily basis. Had he been kidnapped by a gang of his own students? Also, 'last resort'? *Him*? Isaac has absolutely no idea what knowledge he possesses could be so pertinent that it warrants this action. Every layer of his clothing dampens with fear-induced sweat. A moment later, a pair of hands roughly sit him down on a wooden chair. Then someone begins taping his hands behind his back and his legs to the chair. Isaac's nerves are shot, wondering just what the *hell* was going on. A female voice slinks behind him and says,

"Listen, I'm going to remove the pillowcase and the duct tape from your mouth, but that's it. You got that?"

Isaac nods. The cloth is removed. He can see again. Standing in front of him is... Tasha Simone? The big blond boy Isaac finally recognizes is Sky Harris, the longest-running detentionee in Olligrove history. Then there's a tall boy with brown hair, a short, racially ambiguous girl he faintly recognizes, and an even shorter kid with glasses, no older than twelve or thirteen. Isaac looks all around him. They seem to be in some dusty, abandoned building in the middle of a giant empty parking lot. As he looks up and sees an old sign, he remembers what this place used to be. The Superstar Megamart. Isaac huffs angrily through the tape on his mouth. Why would several of his own students dare to drag him here?! Tasha snatches off the duct tape, which stings his lips.

"We're gonna ask you some questions, Mr. Charles. And you're *going* to answer them."

Isaac wriggles his arms and legs to no avail. They're secured to the chair. He practically spits at the girl as he replies,

"How *dare* you?! You wreck my tire and kidnap me for some *questions?!* I am a man of reverence! Your *principal,* for God's sake! I should press charges against you! As a matter of fact, I will!"

Tasha crosses her arms.

"No, you're not. Not if you want to see your daughter again," she tells him. Isaac wriggles helplessly in the chair.

"Wait, you have my *daughter?!* Now I'm *definitely* pressing charges! I don't know what kind of sick game this is, but-" "*We* don't have her, you idiot," Tasha interrupts, "But we know who does."

Sky walks forward.

"Does the name Samuel Alencort ring a bell? Or should I say Corty?" he asks. Isaac freezes. It was a name he hadn't heard from anyone other than Irene for a *very* long time. But that doesn't make any sense.

"You have to be mistaken. Corty is.... Corty is gone. He hasn't been around since-" "Since your old pal Brian Ashmore 'disappeared', right?" Tasha finishes.

Isaac begins to sweat. How do these kids know about Brian? Or Corty? *Oh no. Do they know about-?... No. They can't. They can't!* His mind races at a million miles per hour. His entire presence reeks of guilt and fear. The young boy with glasses steps up and glares at Isaac with pure rage. He's short. Skinny. Harmless. Isaac almost laughs. What was this little punk doing here among these riffraff?

"My mom is Andrea Castillo. She and Catherine-Bethany are in danger because of Corty, so tell us what we need to know or else."

Isaac's face twists in confusion. What the hell does Ms. Castillo have to do with anything? The man scoffs at the child.

"I've had enough of this! Release me at once and tell me where my daughter is right now! *Now!"* he demands.

In retaliation, the boy angrily raises his fist when something impossible happens. *Shing!* A ray of blinding white light shines from the boy's palms directly into Isaac's face. He wails as the beam painfully berates his corneas, burning his eyes. Isaac screams, involuntarily rocking his chair, which makes him fall backwards. The moment he makes contact with the ground, his toupee embarrassingly falls off, leaving his balding head naked for the world to see. Isaac thrashes his head side to side as dots blur his vision.

"What the *hell* was that?!" he cries out. Sky and the taller young man walk over and push him back upright in his chair. Isaac's vision comes back, but he's left shaken from the experience. The young lady behind Tasha finally speaks up.

"Mr. Charles... Isaac,... we *really* don't have time for this. Stop being a stubborn prick for once, and we'll let you go after." Then the tall boy pats him on the shoulder and adds, "Rocky here is gonna permanently blind you if you don't cooperate."

He points to the boy whose hand was still inexplicably glowing. Isaac sits there, gasping as he tries to make sense of his current circumstances. These kids were... oh. Oh no.

"You've all been touched by that heart," he whispers. The five raise their brows.

"So you know then," says Sky. Isaac's head hangs heavy. All these years, he thought that particular secret was behind him. Something he'd almost forgotten about. His bottom lip quivers. If what they're saying is true, and Corty was still around after all,... it was going to be over for him. The older man looks at Tasha in particular with pleading eyes.

"There are consequences if I tell you."

Rocky goes to raise his hand again, which makes Isaac flinch. Tasha lowers Rocky's arm and slowly makes her way to Isaac. She leans down, staring at him head-on. There's resolve and fire in her brown eyes. The corners of her mouth are tight with repressed fury.

"You wanna talk about 'consequences'?" Tasha asks quietly, "My friend Jasmine Watson was attacked by Corty, who broke her arm. He's tried to kill me and my friends here several times. This man has injured one of your students, stalked five others, and now he has *your* daughter and one of *your* teachers captive. There's *already* been consequences!"

Tasha then shakes her head as she bends over to untie his ropes. They fall slack to the floor, but Isaac makes no attempt to escape. Even if he wanted to, there wouldn't be much he could do. Instead, he sits there, on the verge of tears. He knows they're right. This all *had* to be true. Alex was across the country. And Brian... was dead.

"A-a-and my Catherine-Bethany? H-how do you know he has her?"

Tasha takes Rocky's phone and plays him the voice message Andrea sent last night. When he hears Catherine-Bethany's scared voice on the recording, he nearly breaks down crying. Tasha, Rocky, Sky, and the other two (who reintroduce themselves as Gio and Mileena) stand in a semi-circle around him. Isaac closes his eyes and sighs.

"Where do you want me to start?" he asks, dejected. Any gusto or authority he tried to previously convey is all gone.

"Who exactly are Corty, Brian, and Alex, and how do you know them?"

"Well, Corty and Brian grew up together. They were both orphans who spent a lot of time in and out of foster care. I didn't meet them until they were a little older, but from what I remember, Brian and Alex met during their junior year and started dating. Corty couldn't really hack it and dropped out of high school before senior year began. But he and Brian were still pretty inseparable. Everyone knew Brian and Corty were the rebellious type, and Alex already had a rep as a party girl. Together, the three of them got into all sorts of fun. And trouble."

"Right. And how do *you* fit into this exactly?" asks Gio. Isaac bites down on his lip.

"Look, it's no secret I'm not a 'popular' guy. It's always been that way since I was young. By the time I was a senior in high school, I'd made no impression other than being a teacher's pet and having thinning hair at a young age. I'd always seen Corty, Brian, and Alex here and there, and how people thought they were cool. But I never talked to them until graduation day. I overheard Brian talking about throwing a rager and that he needed to score some alcohol. I looked older for my age, and I wanted to find an 'in' for myself, so I uh... offered to get the drinks for him."

Mileena shakes her head.

"I had a feeling you were *that* guy." "Hey, do you want me to finish the story or not?!"

Mileena silences herself but continues to sneer at him. They all do. Just like everyone else does. It's nothing he isn't used to.

"*Anyway,* after graduation, they started letting me hang out with them. I knew it was mostly because I could score beer for them, but I didn't care. We were our own little gang, and I was happy to finally have friends."

Isaac can't help but smile to himself as he recounts those days. As short-lived as they were, they were the best times of his life.

"I'm assuming that old shack in Hillstone Park was your guys' getaway or something?" asks Gio. Isaac nods.

"Yes. It's an old ranger station from *years* ago. From what I remember, the city decided to build a newer facility closer to the entrance instead of renovating the old one, so they took it off the map and left it to collect dust. Corty found it when he was younger after running away from one of his million foster families and used it as his own hideaway for years. After a while, it's where he, Brian, Alex, and I would occasionally hang out when we wanted to get away from all the bs."

"What about Irene O'Hara? Who is she?" asks Rocky. "Her? Oh, Irene was Corty's next-door neighbor for the majority of his teens. She was a lonely old lady. Corty would go to her whenever he was hungry or didn't feel like going all the way to Hillstone. . He'd fix up anything she needed around the house and in return, she'd cook for him. He claimed it was because she always had extra food and a comfy couch, but I knew he cared for her. She cared for him, too. Over time, she started referring to him as her grandson. Irene was the only constant in Corty's life other than Brian. Sadly, after a while, she started losing her memory and couldn't live by herself anymore."

The five teens all look at each other, then back at Isaac. The easy questions were out of the way. Now comes the hard part.

"What do you know about the Heart?" asks Sky. Isaac shrugs.

"That's *still* a mystery. And before you ask, no, I don't have any powers." "Then what *do* you know about it?"

Isaac sighs.

"It came that summer after we graduated on the fourth of July. I was wrapped up running errands most of the day, so Corty, Brian, and Alex started their party early. According to them, they were smoking at the shack in the woods and it just... came to them." "'Came to them?' What, like it fell out of the sky or something?" "Yes, actually. While the fireworks were going off, it fell out of the sky right in front of them. We still have no idea where it came from. They said it called to them, and they touched it. By the time I finally got there, they were all freaked out and woozy. Corty decided to stash the Heart away, but he never told me where. The next day, they all found out that they had these... abilities. Brian could generate electricity from his hands. Alex could move things with her mind. Corty... well, I'm sure you're familiar." "Shadow monster. Yeah, we know." Rocky finishes.

Tasha pushes some of her hair behind her ears and crosses her arms.

"Okay. Now tell us about what happened to Brian," she says. Isaac squeezes his eyes shut. It's such an awful memory. He's worked so hard to repress it and leave it behind for the sake of... well, himself. Tasha loudly stomps her foot.

"We don't have time for this, *Isaac*! Do you care about your daughter or not?!" "Of *course* I do!" "Then *TALK!"*

As Tasha's demand echoes throughout the rickety old building, she reaches down with one arm and lifts the chair holding Isaac off the ground like he weighed nothing! Isaac whimpers in horror as he's held aloft against his will. Helpless. Tasha locks eyes with Isaac and lets go. Both he and the chair plummet to the floor, knocking him over in the process. He's left breathless as he falls into his back, letting out an embarrassing wheeze. Sky helps him back up.

"You heard the boss," he says quietly before rejoining his friends. At risk of being lifted or blinded again, Isaac quickly recounts everything he can from that era.

"You've got to understand something! After they got their powers, *everything* changed. They were always the rowdy type. But with their abilities, they upped their antics. Breaking and entering. Burglaries. Destruction of property. It was a *lot* going on, especially with Corty. He was kind of our ringleader, so he *really* enjoyed pushing things to the next level. I wasn't really involved with anything they did. But I never spoke up about it either. It started off as mostly harmless fun and underage drinking, but then... I was just scared of them. There were a couple of times where Brian and Corty actually got arrested, but they always slipped right back into old habits.

Eventually, as summer came to an end, I stepped back from the group almost entirely since I was going off to college. Not that they cared, of course. But surprisingly, Brian still stayed in touch with me. He and Alex were going through a bit of a rough patch since he was getting bored with all the criminal stuff. On weekends, I would come back and still hang out with him. I could tell he was feeling aimless, but Corty was his lifelong friend, and Alex was the love of his life. I had no idea what to do for him. I just tried to hold on to nostalgia, but things only got worse from there. Not only was Corty getting too gung-ho about using his powers whenever and however he wanted, but I also found out that he and Alex started having an affair behind Brian's back."

"How did you know?" asks Sky. "Brian asked me to do his laundry one day, and he told me to grab a jacket he left at Alex's. When I pulled up to her place, I heard moaning and other noises from the front door. Corty's car was in the driveway. It was easy enough to figure out what was going on, so I told Brian about it. He was *not* happy. Friendship; over. Relationship; over."

"That must've been the falling out that the article mentioned. Is that what made Brian disappear?" asks Mileena. Isaac shakes his head.

"No. *Corty* made Brian disappear... because of what happened *after* the breakup. After the split, none of us spoke to each other until early fall. Alex called everyone and said she had something to tell us, so we all met at the old shack in Hillstone." "Why you?"

"She thought I could be a mediator between Brian and Corty. Also, she said I needed to be present since I 'snitched'. Turns out, Alex's news was that she was possibly pregnant." "Let me guess, Brian threw a fit," says Sky. Isaac scoffs.

"That he did. Brian starts swearing a storm and calling Corty every epithet in the dictionary. Corty's always been a hothead, so he wasn't taking those insults lightly. He's accusing Brian of stepping out on their friendship and not pleasing his girl enough. Brian yells at *him* for taking things too far and never taking responsibility. Alex and I tried to calm things down, but nothing we said worked. Next thing we know, the two of them start taking swings at each other. And that's when things *really* got ugly."

Hillstone Park, twenty years ago,...

Poor young Isaac Charles. He and Alex Moon can't help but look on in terror as their former friends start going at it as if they weren't lifelong partners in crime. Brian stands there, raw electricity pulsing between his fingers. He has a bloody lip, a bruised cheek, and a look of pure rage. Corty stands across from Brian with a black eye and a busted nose. His skin and denim jacket still smoke from Brian's lightning. His black, rockstar hair is frazzled, sticking out like a lion's mane. It would be kind of funny if Corty weren't so scary. While Brian is (justifiably) angry and defiant, Corty brushes off his shirt with a soft, twisted laugh.

"You guys are best friends!" Isaac yells. "Seriously, cut it out! If you two want to be mad at someone, be mad at *me*!" Alex pleads.

The young woman touches her temples, trying her best to telekinetically push the two of them away from each other. Brian is moved back about five feet, but Corty stubbornly stays planted right where he is.

"You've done it now, Brian! You *abandoned* me! After everything we've been through! This is *your* fault!" he spits out. Brian balls his fists, his eyes and fingers sparking with blue crackling energy.

"I tell you, I don't wanna hurt people anymore, and your solution was to sleep with my girlfriend!" Brian laughs sarcastically as he spits out a bloody loogie.

"What else do I expect, right, *Samuel*? Nothing's *ever* your fault. You're *never* the problem. But we both know if it wasn't for those powers, I'd beat you senseless! Just like when we were kids."

"You guys, enough! I brought us out here so we could try to actually talk this out! I don't even know if I *am* pregnant!" says Alex. Isaac looks at her. Alex. Poor, beautiful, feisty Alex. She's usually a super bubbly free spirit. He's never seen her so full of fear and guilt. Then he looks over at Corty. Wild, bold, fearless, Corty. Isaac was always scared of him, even during their good days. The man shoots out his arm, which turns into a long, shadowy tendril. It whips and strikes Alex in the chest. She screams as she and Isaac are both knocked to the ground.

"You stay out of this! Baby or no baby, that's *your* problem!" Corty then turns his attention to Brian, who's stunned, speechless, seeing him strike down their former third musketeer. "As for *you*! You think you're big and bad just cuz you can make sparks! Let me show you what *real* power is!"

Corty then fully morphs into his shadow form and immediately flies at Brian. His opponent fires a bolt of electric energy but misses entirely as he gets engulfed in darkness and dragged downhill into the woods. Isaac is borderline hyperventilating as he and Alex scramble up from the dirt. The blond looks at him with pure spite.

"You just *had* to open your mouth, huh? You were always a weasel, but I never took you for a snitch, too!" "I'm sorry! I'm sorry! I'm sorry!" "Damn right you're sorry. Come on!"

Alex grabs Isaac by the collar and yanks him along down the hill. The two hear the sounds of grunting and fighting not too far ahead. But the piles and piles of fallen autumn leaves and branches make it hard to keep their footing. By the time they make it to the bottom of the hill, it's too late.

Alex and Isaac stare incredulously at the thick elm tree in front of them. Brian is hanging two feet above the ground with a sharp wooden stick sticking out of his chest. Blood trickling to the ground. His head hangs. Lifeless. Alex covers her mouth, muffled screaming being all that's heard as Isaac crumbles to the ground and retches. Brian was dead. *Brian was dead!* They were only about a minute behind! How could this happen?!

"I didn't mean to do it! He pushed me!"

Isaac looks up and sees Corty back in human form, walking from behind the tree Brian was pinned on.

"He's dead! He's freaking *dead*, Corty!" Isaac yells. He jumps to his feet, hiding behind Alex. Alex uses her telekinesis to slowly pull Brian's body off the trunk and lay it gently on the ground. Her body trembles as several rocks, branches, and bushels begin to float between her and Corty.

"Murderer," she whispers. The word hangs in the chilly autumn air. Corty points at her, his eyes wide and manic.

"Brian was like a brother to me! I'm not a murderer! I'M NOT A MURDERER!"

He stomps forward, knocking the floating twigs and rocks away. Isaac waits on bated breath as Corty gets in Alex's face.

"This... this is *your* fault!" he accuses. Alex angrily shoves him away..

"He was your 'brother', but you had *no* problem sleeping with me just because he upset you? Don't you *dare* blame me!"

Corty then turns his arms into shadow tentacles that wrap around her and Isaac's necks. They both struggle as they gasp for air, their throats being constricted by an inky mass.

"Listen to me *very* carefully; if either of you tells a soul about this, I will *kill* you. I'll kill you, and I'll kill your families. And if you think about telling the cops, just remember how *easily* I can escape any cell they put me in. None of this will *ever* be outed, or I will *snap your necks!"*

The shadow tentacles then violently smash Alex and Isaac's heads together. The impact is ungodly painful, but it's only felt for a second as Isaac slips into unconsciousness.

The older man slumps in the chair, his eyes streaming with tears after recounting the worst day of his life.

"By the time we came to, Brian's body was already gone. He was reported missing not too long after that day when he didn't show up for a court date. The police questioned us but... I just couldn't say anything. I knew Corty meant business. Alex had enough to deal with being pregnant. Once the case was dropped, Corty vanished off the face of the earth, and Alex joined the military. That's all I know, I *swear.*"

Tasha, Sky, Gio, Mileena, and Rocky all stare at Isaac with pure, unfiltered disgust.

"Corty killed Brian... and you just got to go on with your life like nothing happened!" says Tasha.

"What was I supposed to do?! His shadow form can't be contained behind bars, and he's already crazy! Corty was going to kill me, too, if I said anything!"

There's a moment of silence. Isaac continues to softly weep. He knew how this must look for him, but what other choice did he have at the time? He was a dweeb. A loser. The butt of the joke. He never stood a chance against Corty, even before he had powers.

"So is that why you visit Irene? To try and ease your crappy conscience?" asks Gio. Isaac nods. Tasha exhales. "After we handle Corty, you need to come clean to the authorities."

Isaac immediately panics, jumping off the chair and onto his knees.

"*No!* I can't do that! I'm a principal and a family man! Don't you realize that would jeopardize *everything*? My job! My livelihood! My-" "SHUT UP!" Tasha screams.

He shuts up. "Corty never left, you idiot!" says Mileena, "Where do you think those rumors about Hillstone being haunted came from? Or Irene claiming to see his ghost? He's been here the entire time right under your nose." "But-but how?" "We're still trying to figure that out."

Rocky approaches Isaac, his fists glowing with angry red light.

"You let a murderer get away with killing your so-called friend. He's hurt more people now because of *you*! My *mom*!"

Tasha gently pulls Rocky back and looks down at Isaac with a fierce look of determination.

"We're going to get Andrea and Catherine-Bethany back, but just know your family is already in danger the longer Corty's around. You are *going* to come forward once this is all over. Do you understand me?" "Please, just-" "NO!" Tasha angrily interrupts,

"As of today, keeping this secret is a privilege you do *not* have! Do you understand me?!" she reiterates. The sheer power and authority in her voice render Isaac speechless, especially from someone so young. He nods. She was right. They were all right.

"I just want my baby girl back. *Please*!" he pleads. Tasha turns her nose up. "We'll get her. You find your own way home, *Isaac*."

The young woman walks away. The others follow her, all giving Isaac one last dirty look before exiting the building. As they leave the premises, Isaac curls into a fetal position on the dusty floor and cries.

Chapter 26

Battle Plan for Breakfast

After the capture/interrogation of their school principal, Sky drives the group back to the Castillo house. Because where else would they naturally go? They know they have to deal with Corty ASAP, but after what they just learned, they needed to stop and process things first. Not one word is said during the drive. Once they reach the house, the group gathers at the kitchen table. Gio sits on Sky's lap, who absentmindedly strokes his hair. Mileena and Tasha sit next to one another and simultaneously lay their heads on the table. Rocky, too antsy to sit still, busies himself by doing what he does best. Cooking. He grabs a box of pancake mix and goes to work making breakfast. Other than the sounds of dishes clanking and food sizzling, everything is uncomfortably quiet. After about ten minutes, Rocky presents everyone with plates of pancakes, scrambled eggs, and mixed fruit. It looks good. Smells even better. Yet still, none of them have much of an appetite. After taking a small bite of food out of pity, Sky finally speaks up.

"It's funny. I figured Mr. Charles had some sort of history being that much of a prick, but I never imagined *anything* like this." "Our principal isn't the Boogeyman. Just an accessory to the cover-up of the Boogeyman's first victim," says Gio.

Tasha shakes her head.

"No. We call that murdering creep by his name. *Corty*. The Boogeyman is the name of a monster. Corty is a man. A low-down, trifling man." "I just can't get over the fact that he killed his best friend. I mean, how could a person *do* something like that?" asks Gio. Mileena lifts her head up from the table.

"You heard the story. Corty doesn't seem like the guy who'd own up to his messes. Why *else* would he stick around under the radar for twenty years?"

Rocky aggressively stabs his pancake with his fork.

"Don't know, don't care. We need to find out how to take him down so I can get my mom back." "Even if we manage that, what then? Do you really think Mr. Char- I mean Isaac is gonna tell the authorities the truth?" asks Mileena. Tasha takes her phone out of her pocket and sets it on the table.

"I was recording our conversation the entire time. It's plan B in case he doesn't keep his end of the deal," she informs them all.

"You realize that would mean we'd probably have to tell the police about *us,* too, right? Maybe even show them our abilities. Expose *everything*." Gio points out. Tasha shrugs. "It's not ideal, but it's the best leverage we've got. If we go down, we take Isaac and Corty with us."

The other four slowly murmur in agreement. Tasha rubs her left temple. This was all so unbelievably stressful. She has no idea if the choice she made was the right one, but she isn't going back on her word. Rocky clears his throat as he sets down his fork.

"So what do we do right *now*? We're losing time," he says. "I know, little man. Trust me, we all want Andrea back," says Sky. Mileena drums her fingers on the table while she tries to think.

"Let's go over what we know about Corty. There's something about him and his powers we still haven't figured out yet." "What?" asks Tasha. "His limits," Mileena answers, "We all have limits and drawbacks to what we can do, but we don't know Corty's. As far as we know, he's pretty much unstoppable."

Suddenly, Rocky perks up.

"Yes, we do! The answer's been there this whole time!" "What do you mean?" "Think about it, why hasn't Corty tried to attack us *every* single day? And when he does, it's always short. My guess? His shadow form takes a lot of energy."

All of their eyes widen.

"You're right, *R*ocky!" says Tasha, "It's been almost two and a half weeks since we found that Heart, and he's only attacked us like three times."

Gio stands up from Sky's lap.

"Maybe it's like my adrenaline boost. He can only do his shadow thing for a short amount of time before he needs to recover."

Rocky slams his fist on the table.

"Then that settles it. We wear him down until he can't hold his shadow mode anymore and knock him the hell out!"

Sky throws up his hands.

"Hold on just a second. How are we supposed to tire Corty out before he kills us first?"

Tasha walks over and lays a hand on Sky's shoulder.

"We do what Andrea says and work together. I've been thinking about this. That first fight, he snuck up on us and had us cornered. We were just defending ourselves long enough to try to escape. But when we were taking on those thugs yesterday, we were working in tandem." "And we kicked their butts," Mileena adds with a devilish smirk. Sky's bright smile returns.

"Careful. You're starting to actually give me hope that we can win," he jokes. Tasha chuckles.

"I'm just saying that if we manage to hit him where it counts all at once, we can bring Corty down. After that, we'll just have to figure it out as we go."

Rocky stands up from the table.

"Teamwork. Simple as that. Now let's get my mom back!... Oh, and Catherine-Bethany too, I guess."

"Rescue mission on a Wednesday morning. I suppose now all we gotta do is figure out where they are," says Mileena.

Gio twirls his fork around in his hand, looking out the kitchen window at the sunny suburban neighborhood. What a juxtaposition to their situation. He sets his fork down and, with a deep sigh, says,

"We know *exactly* where they are."

Andrea's eyes slowly blink open as she comes to consciousness. Her head is killing her. There's an uncomfortable feeling of wood and dust underneath her. *Where am I?* she wonders. As the blurriness of her vision clears up, she sees a young girl with brown hair lying right next to her, still knocked out. Catherine-Bethany. That's right! The two of them were... Oh no. Andrea goes to reach for her, but she can't. She looks down and sees that her hands have been bound with zip ties. So have Catherine's. Andrea slowly raises her head. The last thing she can remember is her and Catherine-Bethany running for their lives down the dark hallway. The two of them barely got more than a hundred yards before what looked like black tentacles whipped around their ankles and dragged them towards an inky black mass.

Andrea gets a look at her surroundings. They were both in the corner of the living room of some old wooden house. The place was a mess. There's a broken window near the front door. A metallic desk, a few knocked-over chairs, a table, a map on the wall, and what looks to be a broken half of an old sofa.

This must be the abandoned ranger station the kids told me about. If that's true, then we are in deep- Andrea's thoughts are interrupted by the sound of heavy footsteps coming from the kitchen. Quickly, she scoots backwards up against the wall behind Catherine-Bethany. Andrea is scared. Incredibly scared. After everything she'd heard from her son and his friends, she's surprised she isn't dead already. She can only hope that the voice message she sent put them in the right direction. The footsteps get louder, and her captor comes into view. A pot-bellied, middle-aged bald man with countless dark circles under his eyes, rough, unshaven stubble, and zigzag scarring on his forearms. Funny enough, he was still in his worker uniform and overalls. He stands there in the middle of the living room with a bottle of whiskey in one hand and a rusty pipe wrench in the other. He looks at Andrea while taking a swig of whiskey. From the looks of it, he's been nursing the bottle for some time already. Summoning all the bravery she can muster, Andrea sighs.

"So, should I call you Corty or just stick with Mr. Mays?" she asks. Corty half laughs, half coughs as he gulps down more whiskey. He places the cap on the bottle then slams it on the table.

"Doesn't really matter to me. It's not gonna change anything about your situation," he replies. Andrea looks down at Catherine-Bethany, then back at Corty. It's so odd seeing him like this. He looks like a completely different person from the handsome young man she saw in that photo. The man standing in front of her now seems jagged. Callous. Devoid of any joy or virility he may have possessed.

"They're on their way, y'know. Those punks have been a real pain in my ass lately. I know they are," says Corty. "Yeah. And guess what? They're coming for *you*." Andrea retorts. Corty wheezes an overly enthusiastic laugh before doubling over into a coughing fit. Andrea stands up, getting ready to try to rush him.. Corty points his wrench towards her.

"Don't get any bright ideas, lady. I may not be at a hundred percent, but I've still got a lot of strength in my arm. *Sit*!" he demands.

Andrea sits. Her hands were tied anyway.

"You think I'm scared of those kids? Please. Their powers ain't *nothing* compared to me. Especially the little one with his light show. What a joke. Oh wait, that one's yours, ain't it?"

Corty laughs even more. Andrea isn't even offended. Instead, she chuckles as well, which makes Corty frown.

"If his abilities are 'nothing', why was he able to get the drop on you *twice* already? As a matter of fact, why go through all this trouble in the first place? This couldn't have been a part of your clearly well-thought-out plan."

Corty angrily throws the wrench at her. It sails past Andrea's head and crashes into the wall directly next to her. She sits there shaking. She isn't sure if he missed on purpose or not. "It's easier to use you two as leverage if you're still alive. But I can still change that, so *don't* mock me again!"

In that moment, Catherine-Bethany begins to moan as she finally wakes up. The second she spots Corty, she screams and crawls over next to Andrea. The older woman can't help but feel bad. Catherine is a spoiled brat with a bad attitude, but she's still just a teenage girl. She trembles like a baby deer while holding on to Andrea's sleeves.

"Where are we? Who is that? Where's my dad?!" she asks. Andrea wraps her arms around Catherine-Bethany, gently shushing her. Corty shakes his head and picks the bottle back up.

"I don't enjoy this, y'know," he says after a harsh swig. "I don't *enjoy* hurting anybody! I just do what I have to."

Andrea points at herself and Catherine-Bethany.

"And that involves kidnapping and assault?!" "*YES!*" his voice booms.

The two women flinch as Corty violently throws the whiskey on the floor. The glass shatters, splashing them with liquor and pieces of broken glass. Catherine begins snotting and crying against Andrea's arm. Andrea glares defiantly at Corty, but she knows she has to be careful. These were all the actions of a desperate man. And a desperate man is a scary man. Sometimes fatally so. Softly, she says to him,

"This won't end the way you think it will, Corty. You don't *have* to do any of this. Please, just let us go and leave my son and his friends alone." Corty sneers at her and growls, "Andrea, I am *far* too deep into this. So is your baby boy. And *you*."

Andrea gulps nervously. Catherine-Bethany continues crying into her arms. This was awful. Andrea has no idea whether or not she's going to live to see tomorrow. Much less her precious Rocky. Just thinking about him makes Andrea start to cry as well. What was she supposed to do? Corty wipes some booze off the corner of his mouth and sweeps the broken bottle pieces under the couch with his boot.

"If you're lucky, no one else has to die today," he states. Catherine-Bethany looks up, Andrea's sleeves completely drenched with her snot and tears.

"'No one else'? What do you mean, no one *else*?" she asks.

Just as Corty is about to answer her, a familiar female voice from outside yells,

"SAMUEL ALENCORT!"

Andrea perks up. Tasha! She's here! No doubt with the others! Corty smirks. "Took them long enough. You two, let's go!"

His right arm shifts from flesh and bone to a dark, shadowy substance. Seeing it happen before her very eyes in broad daylight makes Andrea incredibly uneasy. The shadow arm stretches out and splits off into several tendrils, which wrap around Andrea and Catherine-Bethany's arms, waists, and mouths. They both try to swat them away to no avail. He chuckles and walks towards the front door, dragging the two young women behind him with his tendrils.

"This ends today. One way or another, this ends *today*!"

Chapter 27

A Confrontation in Hillstone

This is it, Tasha thinks. She's standing at the base of the front porch of the old ranger shack. The same shack she declared to never return to, and the very last place on earth she wants to be. But this isn't about what she wants. It's about facing the individual responsible for so much mayhem. It helps that she isn't alone. To her left, Sky cracks his knuckles and slips on his compression sleeves. Next to him, Gio stands prepared with his trusty baseball bat. To Tasha's right is Mileena. Bow in hand and quiver of arrows at the ready. Their fifth member was on standby waiting for his signal. Some small part of Tasha's brain is begging her to turn tail and run back home. They were coming face-to-face with an actual killer with a highly formidable superpower. Literally nothing about this situation seems in their favor. Through the Link, she can feel everyone else's fear and doubt. It's pungent like the smell of a sick dog on a pile of raw shrimp. Tasha literally has to swallow her oncoming nausea. As they hear footsteps coming to the front door, Tasha shakes her shoulders to get rid of her nerves. Now was not the time to back down. Not after everything. Tasha and her crew. Jazmine. Andrea. The late Brian Ashmore. Even Catherine-Bethany. All victims of the same vile human being who doesn't deserve the gift granted to him by the Heart. Tasha balls her fists and steels her nerves. No. Now was the time for action. She said they were ending this today, and she meant it.

On my momma and daddy, I mean it. She looks back and forth between her companions. Sky, Gio, and Mileena all look at her and project a single thought: *We're with you.* From his hiding spot, Rocky projects, *Me too!* Tasha takes a deep breath. The front door was opening. Corty was about to finally be revealed to them and... Wow. Holy being of all that is decent, *wow*! Sky's jaw in particular drops. "Mr. Mays?! *YOU'RE* CORTY?!?!?!"

The man chuckles as he steps into the daylight on the front porch.

"Hey, smartass," he greets. Gio looks over to Tasha.

"Jeez. He wasn't kidding when he said he's closer than we'd think." Tasha puts her hands on her hips. This was almost comical. The school handyman was their bad guy all along. She supposes it's a good cover. Never in a million years would she have guessed Mr. Mays was actually Corty.

"Where's Andrea and Catherine-Bethany?" she asks. "Oh. They're right here," he replies.

As Corty steps further out on the front porch, Tasha and the gang see that his right arm is in shadow mode as several of his writhing tendrils drag Andrea and Catherine-Bethany outside, both of them gagged and restrained by the shadowy material. It's a relief to see they're both still alive, but the group still can't make their move yet. One step could lead to Corty easily snapped their necks. Tasha locks eyes with Andrea, doing her best to assure they'll get her out of this. They just need the right moment before they can strike.

"Tell me something," Tasha begins, "Why the 'Mr. Mays' cover? The police had nothing on you, but here you are." Corty shakes his head condescendingly.

"I see you've done your research. Well, since we're all here, I might as well tell ya. I actually *did* leave Olligrove. For a little while, anyway. Technically, I was in the clear, but Isaac's a worm. He's always been a worm. To make sure he stayed good on my threat, I came back. I knew I couldn't continue my sorry excuse of a life as 'Corty' like nothing happened, so I made a decision: leave Samuel Alencort behind and forge a new identity for myself as Howard Mays. I shaved my glorious hair, put on a few pounds, and *bam*!

Brand new person. You wouldn't believe how easy it is to be unrecognizable once you take away your defining features." "But *why* though?" asks Mileena.

Corty clears his throat, obnoxiously coughing up a ball of phlegm and spitting it right in front of her shoes. She backs away in disgust.

"'Why'? Because in my mind, it was easier to hide in plain sight instead of starting everything over in a new place like Alex did. I've always been good at fixing things, so I took the job as the nighttime handyman to keep my eye on Isaac. He stuck around the place like the loser he was, where he eventually worked his way up to being the principal we all know and love."

Corty laughs at the end of his sentence, but it's filled with wheezing and heavy breathing. Tasha takes a mental note of this. He's still a hazardous man, but he's clearly not at his full strength. Rocky's theory about his shadow form needing recovery time was looking more and more sound. Corty continues.

"As time went on, I also figured I needed to keep my eyes on this place. Make sure nobody comes within distance and discovers something they shouldn't." "So you became the 'ghost of Hillstone Park' to make sure everyone stayed on trail," says Gio.

"Bingo, kid! And it worked *gloriously*! It wasn't that hard either. After I spooked a few campers who decided to set up a little too close to my hideout, word of mouth did the rest of the work for me. Of course, once I realized that hovering around this dungheap for two decades just *might* be a bit crazy and I finally let my guard down, *BAM*! Here come you *rats* with more curiosity than common sense to mess *everything* up! Now, any more questions before we get down to business?"

As Corty asks this, his tendrils tighten further around his hostages, making them both wince and cry out muffled, pained noises. Tasha takes an angry step forward but is stopped by Sky. She curses to herself and takes a step back. This was infuriating, but they have to be smart.

"Three," says Sky. Corty rolls his eyes. "Make it quick." "One, did you ever keep tabs on Alex or the baby?"

Corty scrunches his nose in disgust. "Are you kidding me? First of all, Alex and I only slept together once. She left while she was still pregnant anyway, so no, I don't know if that bastard is mine. Either way, not my problem. Next?"

Tasha makes another mental note to look into this at another time. Her social media bio said she was a mother of three after all.

"Two; where is Brian's body? The police never found him," asks Sky. Surprisingly, Corty's face shifts from an evil sneer to forlorn and sorrowful.

"Oh, that's easy. He's right where he died. There are a billion trees out here. Not like they put much effort into searching anyway." "What's that mean?" asks Gio. Mileena scoffs. "Brian was a black man with a criminal record. How much effort do you think the police put in? *Actually,* put into looking for him?" she counters.

Everyone goes quiet. It was a harsh but accurate reality. If Brian hadn't missed his court date around the time he died, his disappearance probably would've been looked over entirely.

"Okay. Last question. Why take them?" asks Tasha, pointing at Andrea and Catherine-Bethany. Corty's eyes crack back open with malicious energy.

"Ah! Back to what's *really* important here! Well, Mommy Dearest was going through school records last night, digging for more info about me after I paid a visit to your friend. Isaac's crotch spawn just happened to be at the wrong place at the wrong time. I took them cuz I knew you'd come here. You see, I thought Jasmine was enough of a warning for you, but now I think I need to apply a little more pressure to get my point across."

With his tendrils, Corty suddenly lifts Andrea and Catherine-Bethany a good twenty feet or so off the ground, where their legs kick helplessly. On instinct, the four teens try to rush forward, but then Corty's other arm transforms into a massive clawed hand that stops them in their tracks.

"Now *this* is what it's gonna be! It's obvious you've got me at the end of my rope, but I will *not* go down for this! I'll disappear for good this time, and you all can go on with your worthless lives, but *only* if you swear you'll forget everything! Otherwise, you all die. Simple as that. Them. You. Your families. Isaac. *Everyone*! Make your choice! RIGHT NOW!"

Tasha's entire body runs cold. The man means business. Corty eyes them all with a murderous glare. They've got maybe five seconds to answer him. They're aware of every ugly detail of this messed-up history. They could take his offer. Go home. Forget everything. Let him disappear,... Let him get away. Even after his repeated attempts to kill them. Even after he's stalked and threatened them. Even after he assaulted Jasmine. Kidnapped Andrea. Murdered his best friend and coerced Isaac and Alex into lying about it. They could let him go. Key word being *could.* Tasha's eyes dart between her friends. Gio white knuckle grips his bat. Sky's hands are vibrating. Mileena has one hand behind her back, ready to grab an arrow. Tasha's body tenses as her strength intensifies. They've made their decision. Tasha yells,

"Rocky, go-time!"

Their young friend shimmers into view directly in front of Corty. The man jumps back in shock.

"What the-?" "Flash grenade!"

Rocky puts his hands in Corty's face and releases the biggest burst of light he can muster. Corty screams as a 2000-watt wave of illumination on par with stadium lights barrages his face. Distracted and blinded, the shadow tendrils holding up Andrea and Catherine loosen at last. As the two scream and fall, Tasha and Sky run forward. Tasha catches Andrea while Sky catches Catherine. It's awkward and a little sloppy, but they're both caught uninjured. The two then jump up and run to the side of the house out of sight. As Corty continues to recover from the blinding light, Rocky runs over to the group, blowing on his red-hot burning hands. Mileena notches an arrow, imbues it with her green spark, and lets it fly. *Thwack*! Corty gets hit in his shoulder with the arrow and stumbles backward into the door. Gio takes the opportunity to run forward, duck down, and *whap!* Delivers an upward swing with his bat to Corty's chin, then follows it up with a hard kick to the chest that knocks the man *through* the door. *Bam*! The front door is knocked off its hinges and sends the man to his back. Gio jumps and swings the bat downward towards the man's head. This time, Corty catches the bat in his hands and kicks Gio away from him. As Corty jumps up from the floor, he spits out a tooth. His mouth is covered in blood, and the arrow in his shoulder caused some significant bleeding, but Corty was still standing. And now, he was peeved.

"Playtime's over, kiddies!" he yells. Corty's body begins to melt and reform into the black and gray smoky being known as The Boogeyman. Gio quickly dashes back outside just as Boogeyman takes a swipe at him. He runs over to his friends and flourishes his bat like a rapier sword.

"What's the plan, boss?" he asks. Tasha plants her feet and squares her fists. "Give him hell and try not to die," she instructs.

Boogeyman flies from the house like a bat out of hell and goes straight for Mileena.

"Miss!" she yells. Her green spark hits Boogeyman, and his arm goes right over her head. Jumping into action, Sky leaps forward and grabs the arm, sending vibrations through his body. Boogeyman's smoky form freezes, rippling and shaking as Sky continuously stuns him. Rocky flicks his wrist, igniting his hands and shining a ray of light into Boogeyman's face. Though the ray doesn't cause any direct damage, the light definitely seems to bother him as it begins to cut through the solid darkness and illuminates his entire body.

"Hurry up! I can't hold him for long!" Sky shouts. He's already sweating profusely, using all of his strength to hold Boogeyman in place. Tasha looks over to her right and sees a rather large rock the size of a watermelon close by. She concentrates on said rock, summons her strength, and grips it in her hands. She lifts it above her head, runs up to the Boogeyman, and swings it downward. *Wham!* The rock smacks Boogeyman's head with a devastating blow. He roars in pain, flailing his freakishly long arms in every direction. Gio and Rocky dodge a few of the hits. Unfortunately, one of the arms reaches back and smacks Sky away. Boogeyman shakes his head, panting heavily.

"*Okay. That one hurt. My turn!*"

With an ear-piercing howl, a dozen slim tendrils erupt from Boogeyman's chest and back, giving him the appearance of a black, incorporeal kraken.

"Duck and cover!" Tasha yells. The tendrils fire out in every direction as everyone tries to gain some distance. Tasha and Rocky manage to run just outside the radius of the tendrils. Sadly, the boy's glasses get snatched off his face and snapped in half. *Whip*! Mileena's bow is snatched out of her hands, and she becomes entangled in his grip. Gio and Sky are both assaulted with multiple whipping tendrils. The two of them are only able to embrace each other as they're assaulted with painful strikes. With a roar of pain and frustration, Sky manages to snatch one of the many whips in his hand. *Bwom!* Another series of intense vibrations stops Boogyman in his tracks, stunning the monster. Mileena takes the opportunity to wring herself free of his grasp and falls to the ground on her rear. Tasha takes in their current situation.

All we have to do is make sure he tires out before we do. Easy.

Tasha takes a deep breath, squats down, and summons every drop of raw power she can muster. Her fists tighten to the point where her fingernails dig into her palms. Her body quivers, ready for her to unleash. She runs straight at her opponent.

"RAHHHH!!!!" Tasha lets loose a primal scream as she swings into a haymaker with everything she's got.

THWACK! Thanks to Boogeyman being stunned, Tasha's fist makes full contact. There's an intense rush of air that nearly knocks the group off their feet as Boogeyman is sent flying full force into the top of the shack. *KRRRRRUNCH!* The sound of snapping wood and nails crack through the air as a massive hole in the roof caves in from the impact. The extreme display of power fills Tasha with pride, but also sheer exhaustion and a killer migraine.Hissing through her teeth, she sinks to her knees. Her right hand feels slightly numb after that hit as well. Her head throbs like an elephant just stomped on her skull. Rocky and Mileena run over and help her get back on her feet. Tasha pants as though she's run a marathon, but otherwise, she's still okay. A little dizzy, but okay. Sky and Gio join them, their poor faces covered with angry red welts and whip marks. The five of them stand there, looking at the house. Dust rises from the opening in the roof. It's quiet. Unsettlingly so.

"Remind me never to tick you off," says Sky with a tired smile.

"Is it over?" Rocky asks naively. Answering his question, the Boogeyman in his humanoid but still shadowed form steps out from the now doorless front entrance. Splintered wood and glass fall off of him as he rolls his shoulders.

"Is that the best you can do?" he taunts, *"That punch was cute. Kind of ticklish."*

But Tasha hears the labored breathing in that distorted voice of his. He's not as well off as he's presenting. Sky slaps his hands at his sides.

"You've *got* to be kidding me!" he huffs. Tasha wipes the sweat off her forehead. She feels like she could nap for a week, but their work isn't over yet. She drops back into her fighting stance and grins.

"C'mon, y'all! Don't start getting tired on me just yet!" she encourages. Mileena cocks her head. "And let *you* have all the fun? Yeah, right."

With a wave of her fingers, Mileena wills, *Collapse!* Suddenly, the section of the roof above where Boogeyman stood cracks and begins to implode further. *Bonk! Bonk! Bonk!* He gets showered with various tiles, roofing, and other debris. Most of it phases through, but some seem to actually make contact with his head and knock him forward.

"Ow ow ow!" he whines. He then shifts from humanoid back to full cloud mode, floating up and expanding like a dark cumulus. As more tendrils begin to wriggle out of him, Rocky snaps his fingers.

"Everyone, split up! Divide his attention!" he suggests. Rocky then waves his arms and summons as many light orbs as he can. Dozens of tiny, multicolored lights fill the immediate area in a blinding, dazzling display. They do their job of obscuring the group as they all run in different directions. Boogeyman's vision is filled with nothing but dizzying colors, making him borderline nauseous. He groans, waving and swatting the lights like they were gnats. Once the lights finally clear, the only person Boogeyman can see is Gio. He's standing there smirking arrogantly.

"What was that you said about killing us again? You're kinda bad at it," the boy teases. Boogeyman growls, sharpening the tips of his hands into claws. *"Stay still and I'll show you just how good at it I am!"* Gio scratches his chin. "Hmmm,... nah."

Pew! He takes off like a bullet into the trees. Blinded by rage and vexation, Boogeyman flies after him. This boy was fast, yes, but Olympic fast. Not The Flash.

Gio keeps his eyes forward, not daring to look back as he can feel the Boogeyman on his tail. He stumbles a few times over various roots and bushes, but he doesn't *dare* stop. The adrenaline pumping through his body is all that's keeping him moving. *Thwack*! A single tendril whips out and slashes at a tree right by his head. Gio pivots and runs left. Boogeyman was trying to throw him off and make him fall. He can't let that happen! *Thwack!* Another tendril hits him right in the middle of his back. Gio hisses, but he continues dashing forward. It's sharp and icy, but he cannot stop! He *will* not stop! As Gio approaches a pile of boulders, he uses his momentum to jump and execute a perfect front flip over them and continue running. He's covered head to toe in perspiration. His leg muscles are on fire, but getting caught was not an option. *Run, Gio! Run!* There's a massive tree directly in front of him with tall bushes on both sides. Boogeyman was right behind him! Putting as much energy as he could into his legs, Gio makes a jump for it. Breaking his previous record of seven feet, Gio makes a miraculous *ten-foot* vertical leap! Letting his years of training take over, Gio grabs on to the nearest branch and begins jumping and flipping his way upwards like a spider monkey. The grazed gunshot wound in his calf from yesterday is screaming at him, but Gio can't care about that. Boogeyman continues clawing and breaking every branch as soon as he leaps from one to the other. As Gio nears the top of the tree, he makes a sudden realization: he's high up. He's *way* high up! However, his fear of heights is all but secondary at the moment. Gio steps onto the final branch, a good fifty feet or so above the forest floor. A fall from this height would turn him into paste if he wasn't careful. He looks down and sees nothing but the black cloud right below him.

"You done running, kid?!" asks the Boogeyman. Gio shrugs. "I don't know. Is your mouth?!" *"You little-!"*

As a stretched-out claw reaches out to grab him, Gio presses his shoes into the trunk of the tree and makes a mirthful leap backwards. Everything blurs past him as he descends through the air, praying his reflexes do what they need to do. The moment he sees a solid enough branch ten feet above the ground, Gio reaches out and grabs it. His arms nearly pop out of their sockets, and the skin of his palms gets severely scratched from the bark, but Gio successfully swings off the branch and safely lands on the ground with a good tuck and roll. *God bless you, Coach Johnson!* he thinks. Still not done, Gio runs full speed back the way he came. The Boogeyman continues to pursue, but he is slowing down a bit. Before he knows it, Gio is back in the small clearing in front of the old house. Boogeyman bursts from the treeline behind him, huffing and puffing. Just as he's about to attack Gio again, the Boogeyman stops. He notices a closer target hiding behind a bush.

"*Aha!*" He reaches out with a tendril and snatches little Rocky in his grasp.

"Ahhh! Let go! Let *go*!" he cries out. His hands light up, but then Boogeyman squeezes him, making him lose focus as he squirms in pain.

"Guys, he's got Rocky!" Gio calls out.

Tasha, Sky, Mileena, Andrea and even Catherine-Bethany all come out of hiding and gather around Gio. Boogeyman covers Rocky's mouth and says to them,

"*This is it, you little bastards! You should've taken my offer!*" After which, he swiftly takes to the sky with Rocky firmly in his grasp.

"NOOOO!!!!!!! ROCKYYY!!!!!" Andrea wails. She falls to her knees, her eyes wide with panic. Tasha attempts to will herself off the ground like when she slept last weekend.

C'mon! Up! UP! she tries. Nothing. She's still spent from that super punch. However, Mileena's hands crackle with green energy.

"This isn't over! *FALL!*"

Pshow! A bolt of chaos energy fires from her fingers and up into the sky, where Boogeyman was trying to fly away. The energy bolt hits him, and he quickly sinks down somewhere in the distance.

"Don't worry, Andrea! We're gonna get him!" Tasha promises. The four take off into the woods.

After what feels like forever, the team find themselves back in the clover field where they first found the secret hatch. The limp figures of the Boogeyman and Rocky are sprawled out in the grass. Mileena drops down and checks Rocky's pulse.

"He's breathing! Oh, thank God!" "Here, give him to me," Gio suggests. He bends down and scoops Rocky's body into his arms. They look over to the Boogeyman, who, infuriatingly, is *still* moving. Though now he's at least back in humanoid shape as he slowly wobbles to his feet.

"DAMMIT!!!!" Sky roars out in fury and tackles him back to the ground, putting everything he's got into his power. *Womwomwomwomwom!* There's a loud pulsating reverb as Sky screams and pours every bit of vibrational force into the Boogeyman. It's powerful. Far more than anything Sky had displayed before. The vibrations pound Boogeyman so harshly that the very ground beneath him begins to shake. Pebbles and small clumps of dirt bounce around them as he continues getting bombarded. With one last angry growl, Sky gives a concentrated blast that makes the dirt around them explode. Sky reels back in severe discomfort, his arms red and veiny. The Boogeyman begins twitching on the ground, shifting between his shadow and human form every half-second. His eyes fixate on the group, vengeful and determined.

"What does it take to get rid of you?!" yells Tasha. She gently moves Sky out of the way, grabs Boogeyman by the collar of his shirt, and lifts him off the ground with one arm. "*Break!"* Mileena wills. Her green energy flows into him. When Tasha uses the last of her strength to bodyslam him to the ground, he lands hard with a sickening, wet crunch. His shadow form melts away, revealing the raggedy man underneath. Now Corty once more, he glares at the group with his spine at an unnatural angle.

"You... haven't... won this!"

In a last-ditch effort, Corty manages to instantaneously morph back into Boogeyman. He ejects several tentacles that punch the teens back several feet. As Gio in particular falls flat on his rear, his arms start to feel warm for some reason. A little *too* warm. He looks down and gasps in awe. Rocky was coming back to consciousness. Only this time, he was glowing. Not just his hands either. From the top of his hair to the tips of his shoes, Rocky's entire body was *glowing*! He shimmers in all different, ever-shifting colors. An aurora borealis in human form. And like the sun, it hurts to look directly at him. Slowly, Rocky slinks out of Gio's arms and walks towards Boogeyman. As soon as a tendril tries to hit him, Rocky raises his hand. *BZZZZZZZZ!* A wide cone of golden energy casts onto Boogeyman's body. *FWOOSH!* He's on fire! The shadow form dissipates entirely, leaving only a burning, flesh and blood Corty. He wails at the top of his lungs, rolling around in the grass trying to put out the flames. Just as soon as it happened, Rocky's body dims back to normal, and he falls to his knees. Gio picks him up again and puts him on his back.

"Are you okay, Rocky? What *was* that?" asks Tasha. Rocky shrugs.

"No clue. It kinda just happened," he replies almost absentmindedly. He, Tasha, Gio, Sky, and Mileena all look back down at Corty. He's face down in the grass. Burnt, broken, and beaten. His body is smoking and charred in several places. Though the stench of burnt flesh fills their nostrils, the five all let out a collective sigh of relief. They did it. They actually did it.

"What do we do with him now?" asks Sky. "Let's get back to the shack and see if we can find something to restrain him," Tasha suggests.

"Yeah. Plus, I think Andrea's freaking out right now. We should show her that Rocky is okay," adds Gio.

"Good call," says Mileena. As they turn around, Tasha looks back at Corty's still body. "We'll be back for you."

Chapter 28

We Fought a Supervillain

The trek back to the old house is a long and arduous one, but it's all worth it the second they get there. Rocky immediately jumps down off of Gio's back and runs right into his mother's arms. Andrea cries tears of joy, peppering his forehead with a million kisses.

"Oh, *mijo!* You're okay! You're actually okay! Oh my *GOD*, I was so worried you were-!" "Yeah, me, too! I'm good, Mom, I promise. He broke my glasses, though." "That's okay, baby. I've got a spare set for you in my room."

Tasha smiles at the reunion, then looks over to Catherine-Bethany, who was pacing back and forth nervously.

"So uh... did you get him?" she asks awkwardly. Tasha rolls her eyes. Who would've thought the girl who got her in detention not too long ago would need rescuing from her? Tasha crosses her arms.

"Yeah. I think we did," she replies. The other girl sighs.

"I have *no* idea what's going on or, more importantly, why. But you saved my life, so thank you. And Tasha... I'm sorry. For the things I said to you before."

Tasha is genuinely taken aback. Did Catherine-Bethany Charles just express gratitude *and* apologize all on the same day?! Andrea throws a knowing smirk her way. Immediately, Tasha catches that she had something to do with it.

"You're welcome. But uh, do you think you could-?" "Not tell anyone you guys have superpowers? Like anyone would believe that anyway." "*Catherine*!" "Okay, *fine*! I won't tell."

Sky taps Tasha's shoulder, then gestures back to the woods.

"Oh. Right. Andrea, you two stay here and hold tight a little longer. We're just here to grab something to hold Corty."

Andrea nods with understanding. Tasha feels her cheeks burn with embarrassment as they walk into the house. Or rather what was left of it. There's debris scattered all over the floor and broken glass at every turn. Tasha uses her strength to clear as many obstructions out of their way as she can. Technically, this was government property they just wrecked, so all they can do is hope no one continues to come close to this area. Eventually, Sky finds a set of chains in the closet just above the crawlspace to the basement.

"Let's hurry up. I gotta admit, Corty sure had a lot of tenacity during that fight," says Mileena. Sky shudders.

"Bro, no kidding! He already wasn't looking good, and it *still* took everything we had to beat him. If he were healthy,..." "Don't think like that. We won. He lost." Gio encourages. He gives his boyfriend a small kiss on the cheek. It stings a little due to the scratches, but their healing would take care of that as the day went on.

"We'll be right back, Mom," Rocky assures. Andrea nods. The boy hops on Sky's back this time as the group returns to their target.

During their grueling trek back to the clover field, Sky asks Rocky,

"So, you got lasers, huh?" Rocky yawns. "Don't get used to that. I basically released all the energy inside me at once, but now I'm drained." "I getcha. Still, it was amazing seeing you all glowy and colorful like that," says Mileena. Rocky smiles.

"Thanks. I think I'm gonna call it 'Lantern Mode'."

As soon as they reach the clover field, all of their mouths drop. Corty was gone from the crater they left him in. There's a trail of dark, dried blood staining the grass leading up the hill towards-

"Oh no! The bridge!" Tasha realizes. She runs forward. The others follow.

He can't get away! Not after all of that!

A minute later, the group reaches the edge of the gorge. Corty is already a third of the way across the bridge, army crawling on his belly.

"*Hey!*" Tasha calls out.

Corty stops crawling and looks back. Though he's about sixty feet ahead at this point, the damage everyone dealt to him is extremely noticeable. Corty is covered head to toe in burns and bruises. Sections of flesh on his hands and face have been seared away, revealing muscle and even some bone. He's *horribly* disfigured and on his last leg. There's silence among everyone, with nothing but the sound of the roaring river down below. The tension in the air is palpable. Corty stays perfectly still. Then, after noticing the chains in Sky's hands, the man chuckles weakly. Corty closes his eyes and heaves himself over the side.

"NO!" Tasha yells, but it's too late. All they can do is watch as Corty's mangled body plummets over 100 feet down the gorge. *SPLASH!* The five gather around and look over the rope. All they can see is the murky water continuously crashing over jagged rocks. They wait and see if Corty pops up to the surface. He doesn't. There's no sign of him. It's as though the river simply swallowed him up. Rocky swears to himself.

"We had him. We *had* him!" he grumbles. Mileena sighs.

"I know, Rocky. I know. But we did all we could." "Do you think he'll come back?" asks Gio. Sky shakes his head.

"Not if he knows what's good for him," he replies.

Tasha backs away from the edge of the bridge and looks up at the sky. It was a clear and sunny late morning with no dark clouds in sight. She laughs internally at the irony.

"If he does, we'll be ready."

Everyone's feet are positively sore as they finally leave Hillstone Park. To give them a break, Andrea offers to drive. The first thing they had to do was stop by the Charles residence.

While on their way, the group takes the time to explain to Catherine-Bethany the context of what just happened. She takes the details about the Heart and the abilities it gave them surprisingly well. It's when they get to Isaac's involvement that she gets understandably distraught.

"So, you guys are going to make him confess, and he, what, goes to jail? He gets taken away from me and my mom?" she asks. "Catherine,... what Isaac did was wrong. And guess what? You ended up almost dying," says Tasha. Catherine-Bethany rolls her eyes.

"You realize we're going to have to give our statements too, right? But according to you, we have to leave out your superpowers and *how* you fought Corty. My dad goes to jail, and your secret stays safe. Am I getting that right?"

"Yes!" Tasha replies harshly. Catherine-Bethany sinks in her seat, her face beet red.

"The only reason I'm agreeing is because you saved my life. After we do this, I *never* want to speak to any of you *ever* again!"

Tasha says nothing further. She gets Catherine-Bethany's anger. Unfortunately, that's just the way it is. Isaac Charles was partially responsible for everything Corty had done since the murder of Brian Ashmore. Technically, so was Alex, but there wasn't anything they could do about her. Rocky, who was in the passenger seat, leans his head against the window.

"I just don't get it. How could anybody kill their best friend?" he asks. Gio points out, "According to Isaac, Corty killed Brian by accident. Everything else he did, like sleeping with his girlfriend and picking fights, was already pretty messed up, but I don't think he meant to do *that*." "Oh, so second-degree murder instead of first? That makes it *so* much better." Mileena sarcastically retorts.

"Hey, I'm not excusing anything Corty did. I'm just saying, maybe killing Brian is the reason why he became The Boogeyman," says Gio. Sky hums in agreement.

"Those two have been friends since childhood, right? I bet the fact that Corty was personally responsible screwed him up in the head."

"Exactly," Andrea adds from the driver's seat, "Just because Corty was a criminal doesn't mean he was a heartless mastermind. Did you see him when he had us? He was sloppy. Manic. Desperate. Everything he'd tried to keep under wraps all these years took a *major* toll on him. Mind, body, and spirit."

Rocky tiredly wipes his hand over his face.

"I guess," he says quietly, though he doesn't sound completely convinced. Tasha reaches from the backseat and pats Rocky on the shoulder.

"You know what I think?" she asks, "Corty said he stayed in town and disguised himself cuz he thought it would be easier than starting life over. But that's stupid. Everything he did was actually *more* complicated. I think the real reason Corty stayed was because of guilt. He held onto that negative energy just to do whatever it took." "To what?" "To deal."

To everyone's surprise, Mileena puts her head in her hands and giggles. It starts off low at first, then quickly elevates into full-on laughter.

"What's so funny, your highness?" asks Sky. Mileena looks at her friends with a genuine smile as she says,

"We fought a supervillain."

Sky starts to laugh with her. Then Gio. Then Rocky. Then Andrea. Finally, Tasha. Everyone but Catherine-Bethany fills the vehicle with loud, gut-busting laughter that brings tears to their eyes. Their lives as of late have become something straight out of Rocky's comics. Was it stressful? Yes. But it was also hilarious.

A short while later, the SUV comes to a stop in front of Charles' house. The second Andrea parks, Isaac comes running out the front door. It seemed he found a way back home while they were gone. Catherine-Bethany jumps out of the car and runs into her father's arms. Tasha and the gang stand by the car. Despite being a pain in the neck and a weasel, it's still rather sweet watching Isaac bear hug his daughter and kiss her on the forehead.

"Thank God you're okay! I was literally worried sick!" "I'm good, daddy, I'm good. But... is it true?" she asks. Isaac looks at her, then at the group who saved her. Standing there, dirty and battleworn. He gulps, hangs his head in shame, and says,

"Yes, baby."

Catherine-Bethany bites on her lip, trying not to cry again.

"So that means...?" "Yes, sweetheart. They kept their end of the deal. It's time for me to do the same."

Isaac walks hand in hand with his daughter over to the SUV. Andrea crosses her arms.

"I think I'm going to take some time off," she says. Isaac nervously rubs the top of his head.

"Yeah. I'll go ahead and put in your paid time off before I uh... well, I'm sure you know what's about to happen." "You're damn right."

Andrea looks like she's trying to hold herself back from hitting him. Isaac holds out his hand to Tasha.

"Thank you," he expresses. Tasha shakes his hand but doesn't say anything back. Her anger towards him was still pretty fresh. It's a tight squeeze when everyone piles back in the car. Isaac closes his eyes. He's grateful for the return of his baby girl, and fearful for his immediate future. Andrea drives them to the police station. It was time to face the music.

Chapter 29
Forever, ...

Friday, two days later...

Tasha and Jasmine look around, surrounded by every other senior in their section of the school auditorium. Sky was a few seats down, half asleep and not paying attention. It was packed. Every student from all four grades and most of the faculty were in attendance as well. Gio and Mileena were somewhere on the other side of the room with the rest of the juniors. Tasha looks at Jasmine with a forlorn expression. She'd had a smooth recovery so far, but she was probably going to have to stay in her cast until graduation. Tasha still hadn't told Jasmine the truth about what happened yet. Maybe she will one day.

After bringing Isaac to the station where he officially gave his confession, Tasha and the others all had to explain about Mr. Mays, aka Corty, and the death of Brian Ashmore. Barring the details about the Heart and their abilities, everything they say is true. They came upon the old ranger station by chance. Got attacked several times by an unknown stranger. Investigated what they knew. Questioned Isaac about his past. And eventually, fought off Corty after he kidnapped Andrea and Catherine-Bethany. As expected, Isaac was taken into custody and booked for obstruction of justice and lying to law enforcement. It's unknown how long he'll be in for pending his charges and jurisdiction, but either way, life as he knew it was over. Catherine-Bethany and her mother spent a *lot* of time crying. Despite Isaac's less-than-admirable behavior, seeing his family take the hit still wasn't pretty. The police are put on alert to search for Corty, but it's not likely he'd ever be found. If the rocks hadn't shredded him to pieces, he would probably bleed out or succumb to his injuries getting washed down the river. Justice was served as best as it could, but it's still bittersweet. At least Tasha finally went to sleep with no nightmares of the Boogeyman. Just an uncertainty about the future.

Jasmine nudges Tasha in the arm as Vice Principal Rita Freeman takes the mic at the podium and addresses the school.

"Everyone, settle down. I'm sure by now many of you have already heard the news, but Mr. Charles has officially been freed of his position as your school principal. We are disheartened to see him exit after his many years of service, but we will move forward amicably as I humbly take his place for the time being. Classes will resume as scheduled, but I urge everyone to remain open-minded as we proceed with this transition."

As Ms. Freeman continues to prattle on, Jasmine pokes Tasha's shoulder and points a few rows down. She looks and sees several girls whispering and snickering directly at Catherine-Bethany. The brunette tries her best to ignore the comments, but she inevitably starts trembling with tears. Tasha sighs. This was probably only going to get worse for her as the former principal's daughter.

"How annoying is it?" asks Jasmine. "What?" "That you feel bad for her?"

Tasha can't help but chuckle. Always with the jokes, Jasmine was. And Tasha wouldn't have her any other way. With a smirk, she replies, "Very."

Once school is over, this time everyone meets at Tasha's house. After coming home from the police station on Wednesday, Tasha sat down with Bree and gave her the full blow-by-blow on everything that had happened since her day in detention. Bree was a little freaked out when Tasha demonstrated her powers by lifting the couch with one arm, but eventually she got herself settled. When it was over, Bree cried. She was distraught that she wasn't available to help her through it all. Tasha comforts her, letting her know that all she wanted was to keep Bree safe so she could do what she needed without added stress. But she's glad she can confide in her now going forward. To help Tasha celebrate their well-earned victory, Bree offers to take the day off work and barbecue for the group.

Sky, Gio, Mileena, and Rocky arrive one after the other. Andrea was spending the night at a hotel to pamper herself. Good. She deserves it. The friends gathered in the living room while Bree was preparing to go to the store.

"So, do you think Ms. Freeman will be a better principal than Isaac?" asks Gio. He sits down next to Sky and snuggles against his side. Sky smooches him, hugging him closer. The two were so cute together, it was disgusting sometimes. And Tasha is so glad that they are.

"She'll definitely be more likable," says Mileena, "Maybe now the honor society will be able to use the break room in peace." "I'm just glad we're done with the Boogeyman stuff. Unless Corty wants an instant replay on his butt kicking," says Sky. Gio raises an eyebrow.

"If you jinx his return, I'm breaking up with you."

Everyone laughs at Gio's obvious joke. Everyone except Rocky, who awkwardly raises his hand.

"I hate to be a party pooper, but what are we gonna do now?" "About what, little man?" asks Sky. "Well... everything, I guess. The police raided Corty's apartment, but there was no sign of the Heart. We still don't know where he rehid it *or* where it even came from."

Tasha ruffles the top of his hair. With a smile, she says,

"We just keep doing our own thing. Everything's gonna be different now, but we'll figure it out." Mileena cracks her knuckles. "I kinda hope we get to fight some more bad guys. It felt good taking on that gang," she says. Sky laughs.

"You know that was only because I needed to get the money back for my family, right? You're starting to scare me a little bit, your highness."

Mileena winks in retort. With her being the most reluctant at first, it was both shocking and delightful seeing her this way. Rocky finally perks up and smiles.

"By the way, I totally thought of our team name; The Grovers!" Gio snorts. "I'm sorry, *what?*" "The Grovers. Cuz we're from Olligrove. Angel, Shakedown, Pace, Karma, and the Luminator; the most powerful of all the Grovers." "No way! That's obviously *me*!" Mileena jests.

"You're a nerd, Rocky. I hope you know that." Tasha says with a sly grin. Rocky grins back. "I sure am. *And* the best name giver."

Tasha leans down and gives Rocky a small kiss on his cheek. The boy blushes intensely.

"I'll be right back," she says to everyone.

As her friends get into a friendly argument over who's the strongest in their group, Tasha gets up from the sofa and heads to the backyard. She looks left and right. Nothing but wooden fences surrounded the area, so no one would see what she was about to do. Tasha closes her eyes, spreads her arms, and concentrates. She takes a deep breath and thinks, *Up!* There's an odd sensation as she feels her body become as light as a feather. A moment passes. Then, to her surprise, she begins to actually levitate off the ground! She opens her eyes and begins laughing with glee, feeling nothing but bliss as she hovers mid-air.

I did it! I actually did it! Tasha smiles peacefully. Why was she doing this? Because she could.

"Uh, sis?" she hears. Her concentration broken, Tasha lands a little ungracefully. She turns around to see Bree gawking at her. "You didn't tell me you could fly, too. Are you okay?" she asks. Tasha smiles proudly as she regains her footing. "Oh, I'm *great*!"

Albuquerque, New Mexico,...

Alex Reneé Moon-Sandoval sighs as she ties her hair into a ponytail. It was almost time to head to the martial arts tournament the twins were participating in. Her husband Glenn was already there. She's excited, of course. Cody and Madison were highly talented. She just wishes they would stop using their skills on everyone who irked their nerves. The twins were temperamental, just like their father. Luckily, they haven't used their powers on anyone in a while. As far as she knows, anyway. While Alex ties her shoes, there's a knock on her bedroom door. She opens the door and is greeted by her youngest child, who is fourteen. With his dark brown hair, tan complexion, and silver eyes, Brian Alejandro Moon was starkly different from his blond-haired, blue-eyed siblings. Though his spirit was just as potent.

"Mom, can I *please* just stay home? I really don't feel like sitting through another one of these," he says. Alex shakes her head.

"No, Brian. Your brother and sister have worked hard to get this far, and we need to support them," she retorts. Brian smacks his lips in annoyance. "Fine. But I'm not wearing my necklace." "*Yes,* you are. The last thing we need is another public incident." The young boy whines in objection.

"God, I can't *wait* until we move again. Hopefully somewhere that doesn't have another dojo for them to take over."

Brian stomps away to go get ready. Alex sighs. Teenagers. Always with the attitude. She was the same at that age. If not worse.

A few moments later, as Alex heads to the kitchen to grab her car keys, the house phone rings. Already nearby, Brian answers it. Alex notices him frowning and asks,

"Who is it, honey?" "Uhh, it's saying an inmate from the Olligrove County Jail is trying to contact you."

Alex's heart stops beating for a moment. Olligrove, Illinois. Her hometown. Her roots. She's practically bursting with curiosity (and fear), wondering who this inmate could be. She takes the phone from Brian and accepts the charges. Brian shrugs, slips on a pair of black Kevlar gloves, and goes to wait in the car.

"Hey, Alex," says a familiar voice. Alex smirks as the recognition hits her. "If it isn't Isaac freaking Charles. How did you get this number?" she asks.

"I asked my lawyer to do me a favor and look you up. I hope you're not mad." "I'm not mad. More shocked, honestly. I don't think I've heard from you since-"

"Yeah, I know. Listen, it's obvious where I am now. Long story short, the truth got out. But don't worry. I left you out of it. As far as the police know, only *I* witnessed what happened and lied about it. You're in the clear."

Alex pinches the bridge of her nose.

"Jesus. Talk about a bombshell." "I'm sorry. They don't give us a lot of time for the phone, and there's a line behind me." "Just what the *hell* happened down there?" "It's an *extremely* long story. I'll have to write about it and mail it to you. But listen, there's something you should know before I have to hang up." Alex leans against the counter.

"Okay. What is it?" "Brian's remains were found. He was under the tree. You know the one."

Alex covers her mouth in shock. Tears well up and spill from her eyes. Brian Ashmore. Her old flame. Her first love. And her biggest regret. Whatever just happened back in Olligrove must've been pretty extreme. Alex sniffles, trying to keep her composure.

"So uh, ahem, what happens now with that?" she asks hoarsely.

"I think they're going to cremate him. Someone might contact you to see if you want the ashes sent out." Isaac replies. Alex shakes her head even though he can't see her.

"No. He should stay there. I already live with reminders of Brian every single day. *And* Corty." "About Corty,-... Damn. Time's up. Look, Alex, I'm sorry about everything. I really am." "Me too, Isaac. I'll be looking forward to that letter."

Alex hangs up the phone, her mind reeling with all sorts of conflicting feelings. She thinks back to that Fourth of July over twenty years ago. The night her life changed forever. She thinks of Brian and Corty and all the trouble they used to get in together. And the fun. She sheds a few more tears, internally apologizing to the spirit of Brian Ashmore for what she did. It was a remorse branded on her heart for life. All she can hope is that Corty, wherever he was, got what came to him. A car honk from outside shocks Alex out of her reminiscing. "Mom! Are we going or not?!" Brian calls out. Alex wipes away her tears. To this day, she still hasn't told him where he got his namesake from. It's just too sad to talk about. But life goes on. So must she. Alex grabs her keys and leaves the house. As she starts her car and begins to drive, her mind wanders to one of the last times that she and her crew were still happy together,...

20 years ago,...

Pow! The can of soda explodes in a frizzy drizzle as Brian zaps it mid-air. Some of it splashes right on Alex's bare feet, but she doesn't care much. She, Brian, and the doofus Isaac were all currently in Isaac's backyard, experimenting with their powers. She'd gotten better at keeping this afloat with her telekinesis rather than just moving around, so she decided to use a six-pack of soda and target practice for Brian. He points his finger and lets another stream of lightning loose. *ZAP*! Another can explodes, this time all over Isaac's turtleneck. Why he was wearing one in the middle of summer was a mystery. Alex giggles as Isaac whines like a child, futilely trying to wipe the stickiness away.

"My bad, dude." Brian apologizes. Isaac shakes his head.

"No, no, no, you're fine. It's just... this was my grandpa's sweater before he died." Alex rolls her eyes.

"Yeah, well, he should've been buried with that thing, so I'm pretty sure we're just doing you a favor. Why don't you go ahead and change out of that and grab us something stronger than soda while you're at it?" "Oh. Sure. You guys want beer?" "Whiskey. Hurry up."

Isaac nods and scurries into the house like the little weasel he is. Brian comes over and kisses Alex on the forehead.

"You don't have to be so mean to him, sugah. He already worships the ground we walk on." Alex rolls her eyes but kisses him back anyway. Brian was hotter than hell, but sometimes he could be too nice for his own good.

"Oh, please, like you don't love it," she says. Brian chuckles. "Sometimes, you sound like Corty."

Right on cue, the couple turn their heads and see a familiar plume of black and gray smoke fall from the sky into the backyard. Corty regains his shape a moment after, back to his normal handsome self, carrying several bags.

"What's good, blockheads! I come bearing gifts!" he announces. Brian smiles, giving his best friend a fist bump in greeting.

"It's about time you got here. What was the hold up?" he asks.

Corty digs into one of the bags and presents a round dish covered in foil.

"Irene asked me to help fix her cabinets. You know I can't say no to the old broad. She'll trap me with that classic Catholic guilt. Anyway, she made me a pie as a thank you, so knock yourselves out."

Brian smirks as he immediately shoves a piece in his mouth.

"You act all tough, but I know you love helping her out. You're certainly over there enough even without pie as gifts."

Corty scoffs.

"Shut up. It's not *my* fault I'm her only neighbor worth a damn with a hammer. And since you wanna call me out for 'acting tough', check what's in the other bag."

Alex opens the bag and gasps. She reaches in and pulls out a rather large stack of cash. "You pulled a job without us? You spoil sport." "Eh, it was on the way and I couldn't help myself." "Where's this from, Corty?" asks Brian.

Corty shrugs. "That Haitian restaurant on 5th Ave. The workers were in the middle of inventory or something, and I saw an opportunity."

Brian instantly frowns.

"Wait, what? Corty, that's a local business! Plus, they're immigrants!" "So?" "'*So?!*' We usually only rob corporate stores! Not people who *need* that money!"

Corty holds his hands up in mock surrender.

"Easy there, Robin Hood. When did we ever decide *that* rule? Relax. That's what insurance is for or whatever."

Brian crosses his arms.

"I'm just saying, man, we've already got plenty of cash on hand. Plus, you're obviously handy. Why don't you go to trade school or something, and we can stop doing this crap before it goes too far? We've already got parole and everything to deal with."

Corty puts both arms around Brian and Alex and laughs.

"First of all, there's *never* such a thing as too much cash. Two, I didn't even cut it with high school. What makes you think I'd *ever* do something as lame as trade school?" "Yeah, hun, lighten up," Alex adds. At that moment, Isaac finally returns outside with two bottles of Wild Turkey.

"Found it. I had to go through my old man's private stash and-" Yeah, whatever, just bring it over." Corty commands.

Isaac quickly hands him both bottles. Corty opens one and starts chugging right away. Alex opens the other, only drinking a shot's worth before presenting it to Brian. He takes it hesitantly but drinks just as much as Corty does.

"How about I throw one of those frozen pizzas in the oven for you guys? That way you have something to eat with your drinks and you won't get tummy aches." Isaac offers. Alex laughs. Goodness, he was desperate. She loved it.

"Yeah, you go do that," she orders. Isaac smiles that goofy smile of his and runs back into the house. After swallowing a significant amount of whiskey, Brian slips from Corty's embrace and follows Isaac inside without a word. Alex stands there confused, Corty's arm still around her. She looks up at him. He looks back at her. Alex bites her lip. She loves Brian. He was a perfect gentleman to her and more than satisfactory in bed. But she'd be lying to herself if she said Corty wasn't easy on the eyes. With his wild rockstar hair, dark eyes, devil may cry attitude, and constantly open shirts displaying his sweaty rock-hard abs, he was certainly a sight to behold. Alex shakes her head. *I shouldn't be thinking like that.* Corty pouts as he swishes the bottle in his hand.

"Huh. That was weird. He *actually* seems upset." he mutters. "Do you think everything is going to be okay?" asks Alex. Corty pulls her closer. "Ah, he'll get over it. He always does. We're boys. We're all gonna keep having fun forever."

Alex looks up at the sky and takes another shot of whiskey. *Yeah,* she thinks. *Forever.*

END OF VOL. 1

Acknowledgements

I dedicate this work to my Sugars, (Qush, Cane, Cookie, Biscuit, Pixie, Woods, & Pie) my Nuggets (Jazzi, Arya, Rufus & Michaela) my Arizona fam (Durtady, Kamara, BJ, Avion & Perione) my Trio (Maliya & Brysha) my Ohio fam (William, Kalihma, DeeDee, JR, Erika, Tom, & NayNay); my circle of online friends (Skye, Percy, Sam, Alan, Patrick, Lydia, Eno, Rav, Allie, Emily, Colin, Corey & Sterling) my late Auntie Angel and grandma Deola and FAR too many more to name. Without the love and support from each and every one of you, I wouldn't have the confidence or motivation to type a single word. Last but certainly not least, I'd also like to acknowledge my wonderful publishers, Tawn & Pat. Thank you both for taking a chance on a guy in a silly duct taped costume.

About the author

Jay Jesse Edwards has had the creative bug his entire life. Splitting his time between Arizona and Ohio growing up, Jay spent countless hours reading, drawing, and even acting out stories with his siblings. He wrote his first short story at ten and developed a habit for writing fiction throughout his teens into adulthood. Outside of writing, he enjoys superhero content, sci-fi & fantasy, animals, dinosaurs, and Dungeons & Dragons. Jay currently resides in his hometown of Phoenix, Arizona with aspirations of sharing his creations with the public.

The story continues...

The Grovers Vol. 2: The Young and the Reckless

It's a typical weekday morning at the Caffeine Commute, Olligrove's most popular local cafe. Near the front window, Giovanni Emilio Carano waits patiently for his friend group to arrive. Ever since he got his abilities, Gio finds himself waking up earlier than he used to and full of energy. To help exert that excess energy, he's started going on morning jogs. But Gio has to be careful and take the backroads. That way nobody catches him going the same speed as a race horse. Also, it was the first day of the last week of school, so he was already excited. His boyfriend was graduating at the end of the week and summer vacation was right after.

"Order for... Pace?" the nice barista lady calls out. Gio quickly approaches the counter and grabs the drink carrier. He smirks to himself, knowing his codename meant nothing to anyone outside of his group. Right on cue, Tasha, Mileena, and Sky all enter the cafe as Gio brings their drinks to the booth he saved for them.

"Morning, everyone." he greets with a smile. Sky gives him a hug and kiss then loudly yawns.

"I will never understand the concept of morning people." he says. "Blame the Heart. Before then, I was a regular morning hater." Gio replies. "Mmm. Less jokey, more coffee." Mileena groans. Gio happily passes around everyone's order. Iced caramel shaken espresso for Tasha. Brown sugar latte for Mileena. Hazelnut and vanilla cold brew for Sky. And a mocha iced coffee for Gio. Decaf of course. Any extra caffeine would have him a little too wired.

"Has anybody heard from little man after yesterday?" Gio asks after taking his first sip.

Tasha shakes her head. “No. I think he feels like we’re leaving him behind.” Mileena clasps her fingers together and sighs. “I hate to say it but maybe we are. Just not intentionally.” “Didn’t you guys just spend the whole day with him for his birthday?” Gio points out, “Plus, we meet up whenever we can for hanging out and practice sessions. I love the dude. I really do. But he's being a little dramatic if you ask me.”

Sky arches a brow at Gio.

“Babe, do I need to remind you of how you were at 13? I remember a certain someone telling me how he read a poem he wrote for his 8th grade crush in front of his entire English class.”

Gio nearly chokes on his drink as Tasha and Mileena both stare at him perplexed.

“I told you that in confidence!” he berates upon recovery. Sky and the girls immediately start laughing. Gio sits there with a childish pout until they stop. Once he's done, Sky gives Gio a nudge in the shoulder.

“Oh lighten up, GiGi. I'm just saying, we were all his age. He's gonna be a little dramatic. Maybe we could try to find the Heart again and give one of his classmates superpowers.”

Tasha shudders at the very idea of endowing anyone else with the Heart’s special “side effects”.

“I know you're joking, but keeping our secret is hard enough as it is. We're just lucky Rocky is still anonymous after that stunt of his.” she says. “Speaking of which,” Mileena starts, “I've been checking the views of those videos. The highest one is currently at ten thousand.” “Ten *thousand*?!” “Yup.”

Tasha starts pushing her locs behind her ears the way she does when she's stressed out.

“Relax, fearless leader. That's not exactly viral.” says Gio. Tasha looks him directly in the eye.

“Ten thousand views in just two days, Gio. You know people on the internet are sleuths when they want to be. What happens if this *does* get viral status?”

Gio doesn't have a proper response. He can understand her point of view. They all had enough to worry about in general, let alone the thought of exposure. As Gio, Sky, and Tasha continue finishing their drinks, something seems to catch Mileena's attention outside the restaurant. Pulling up next to the building was a shiny silver and black Mercedes-Benz. The driver of said vehicle is someone who makes Mileena gasp as they step out of the vehicle. Gio and the others all look out the window to see what caused her reaction.

And when they do, Gio's jaw drops. Walking towards the shop was a devilishly handsome Asian-American man in his mid-twenties with coiffed jet black hair, dark brown eyes, a trimmed goatee, and a jawline straight from heaven. Sky raises his eyebrows.

"Yo, who is *that*?" he asks. "And is he single?" Tasha adds. Mileena rolls her eyes.

"That's my cousin Clay. From my mom's side, obviously." "That doesn't answer the 'single' question." "*Please* don't start."

As Clay walks in through the front doors, he immediately spots Mileena and heads over to their table. With a warm grin and an outstretched hand he greets,

"I thought I saw you when I pulled up. What's up, cousin? I think you were still in junior high last time I saw you."

Mileena fights not to roll her eyes.

"Hi, Clay. And yeah, I was."

Clay smiles warmly.

"Dang. Time sure flies, doesn't it? Who are your friends?" "Oh. This is Tasha, Sky, and Gio."

The three quietly wave and nod. Clay reciprocates.

"If you don't mind me asking, what're you doing here? I thought you lived near Springville now." asks Mileena.

Clay chuckles, sniffing the air with a content sigh. "What, I can't come visit my hometown? Besides, I heard there was a family barbecue yesterday."

Mileena squints her eyes. "Yeah. For my *dad's* side. You remember my parents are divorced now, right? The Yoshidas don't have to pretend to put up with us anymore." "Hey, not *all* of the Yoshidas are stuck up. And you know I could never resist Granny Lisa's fried catfish."

Mileena crosses her arms. Something wasn't quite right.

"So you're here out of nowhere after three or four years for some catfish?" she asks. Clay bites his lip and chuckles once more.

"You were always pretty sharp, huh? Well if you must know, I'm here in Olligrove on an assignment." "An assignment?" "Yup. I don't know if you heard, but I finally became a bona fide officer of the law."

Though Gio keeps his face neutral, his heart plummets into the pit of his stomach. He isn't sure why, but he can't help feeling like he and his friends might be involved with Clay's 'assignment'. Whatever that was. Mileena clears her throat.

"Oh. I mean, that's neat."

Clay proudly flashes the badge clipped to his belt loops.

"It sure is. I'm actually on the verge of becoming a detective. Y'know, we should catch up while I'm in town. I hear you had an interesting experience yourself a few months ago."

Mileena slowly blinks.

"Oh. You heard about that? I mean, it's not really that big of a deal." "Nonsense. I'd love to hear about it if you're up for it sometime. I'll be down here for a while."

Mileena crosses her arms, leaning back in her chair with a casual shrug. Gio is rather impressed with her poker face.

"Uhhh, maybe. I mean, you're busy. I'm busy. We're both busy."

Clay simply winks. "I can make time for my favorite cousin. Anyway, I'm gonna get myself some coffee. I have a long day ahead of me. See you soon."

As Clay walks away to the front register, Gio, Tasha, Sky, and Mileena all share concerned expressions.

"Is Cousin Hottie about to be an issue?" Sky whispers. Gio elbows him hard in the ribs. Mileena sighs, annoyed. "Maybe. There's obviously a reason he just talked to me like that. We were civil growing up, but Clay and I weren't close. Like, at all."

Gio drums his finger on the lid of his coffee cup, contemplating what to think. The excitement and optimism he'd felt since he woke up had quickly devolved into worry. The four teens all keep their eyes on Clay. The young man grabs two coffees, winks at Mileena one last time, then exits the premises. Gio squints as they watch Clay enter his vehicle and drive off.

"He knows something," says Gio, "But what?" "Let's hold on a second before we jump to conclusions," Tasha starts, "There's no possible way he knows about anything Grover or Heart related,... right?"

It's uncomfortably quiet. Gio wants to believe they're all simply overreacting to the minor interaction. But their collective intuition is screaming something else. Gio looks at the time on his phone. It was time for them to head to school.

"We can talk about this later. I'd rather not worry about a problem we're not having yet." says Tasha.

Gio nods as they all gather their things and head out together. All he can do is pray that it's nothing. He'd rather spend time with his boyfriend and plan their summer together. Hopefully they'll still be able to do so without any interruptions.

Once he reaches the next red light, Clay Yoshida hands over the caramel macchiato to his partner. A stern faced, middle aged black woman with tawny brown hair down to her shoulders, Detective Yvette Allman was Clay's mentor as of late.

"I didn't take you for the macchiato type, Allman." he says. Yvette doesn't smile. She rarely does. She does let out the faintest huff of a chuckle.

"You watch too many TV shows. Not every law enforcement worker with a few years under their belt takes their coffee black. I still enjoy flavor." "Well what about the whole 'donuts' thing?" he asks. Yvette shakes her head.

"Another rookie mistake. Most of the job is paperwork and waiting for results. Caffeine is still needed, but if you just have coffee and donuts the whole time, all that sugar is just going to make you crash early." "So what's the secret then?"

Allman pauses, taking a sip of her drink before answering him.

"Personally, I like eating spicy food to keep me going. It helps to have an iron stomach."

Clay makes a mental note to find somewhere they can get spicy food for lunch. They had a long day of tailing and watching ahead, so he wants to learn all he can. Once the light turns green and Clay drives off, Yvette asks,

"So, did you do what I told you to?"

Clay hums, replying,

"I did. They were right there in the coffee shop just like your intel said. Save the little one." "And how did your cousin react to seeing you?" "Mostly confused. Mileena and I never really hung out growing up, so I could tell she was definitely suspicious."

Yvette happily sips her coffee, her hard pressed lips almost forming some semblance of a smirk.

"Good. Just as I anticipated." she says. Clay almost raises his hand as if he were still in training. Technically he was, but he was in the field now.

"If I may ask, why did you want me to alert her and her friends to my presence like that? Isn't the point of this operation to be, I don't know, a little more incognito?"

Rather than answering him right away, Yvette pulls out her tablet and begins scrolling through her latest files.

"Tell me Yoshida, what *exactly* do you know about the incident your cousin experienced?" she questions. Clay shrugs. "Just what I've read from your report. Why?" he asks.

"Recent events are leading me to believe there's *much* more to the story than those kids are letting on." Yvette replies, "The local law enforcement might be fine with Isaac Charles in custody and Sam Alencort on the run again, but there's a lot more to this case than people realize. And now that those kids are aware that you know *something*, whatever they do next will likely reveal themselves. They're young. And more importantly, unaware of me."

Clay chuckles as he continues to drive.

"They warned me that you were dedicated to something odd. I assume these 'recent events' are connected to that?" "All the more reason I requested you. Here. Take a look at these."

Clay takes the tablet at their next stoplight. On screen are two different folders. One marked as "Alex Moon-Sandoval". The other, "Olligrove Activities".

Clay sighs. He's got a lot of reading to do.

THE GROVERS VOL 2: THE YOUNG & THE RECKLESS COMING IN 2026!

www.ingramcontent.com/pod-product-compliance
Lightning Source LLC
LaVergne TN
LVHW010900110826
845149LV00005B/1427

* 9 7 8 1 9 6 7 2 3 2 2 3 9 *